Note for Librarians: A cataloguing record for this book is available from Library and Archives
Canada at www.collectionscanada.ca/amicus/index-e.html
ISBN 1-4251-0105-4

PUBLISHING™
Offices in Canada, USA, Ireland and UK

Book sales for North America and international:
Trafford Publishing, 6E–2333 Government St.,
Victoria, BC V8T 4P4 CANADA
phone 250 383 6864 (toll-free 1 888 232 4444)
fax 250 383 6804; email to orders@trafford.com
Book sales in Europe:
Trafford Publishing (UK) Limited, 9 Park End Street, 2nd Floor
Oxford, UK OX1 1HH UNITED KINGDOM
phone +44 (0)1865 722 113 (local rate 0845 230 9601)
facsimile +44 (0)1865 722 868; info.uk@trafford.com
Order online at:
trafford.com/06-1862

10 9 8 7 6 5 4 3 2

A HOLE IN THE OCEAN

By

Ron Palmer

In the folk law of the boating community
a boat is said to be a hole in the ocean into which
one forever throws money.

<u>Books by the Author.</u>

Building a Foam Core Boat.

Travels With Himself.

Sharks That Walk on Land.

I dedicate this book to my very good friends:
Jim and Margo Brady, Debbie Gibson, Judy Hardy
and Norman Scholes.

When you have problems it is then that you
know who your friends are.

Now, land and life, finale, and farewell!
Now Voyager departs! (Much, much for the is yet in store ;)
Often enough hast thou adventur'd o'er the seas,
Cautiously cruising, studying the charts,
Duly again in port, and hawser's tie, returning:
-But now obey, thy cherished secret wish,
Embrace thy friends-leave all in order;
To port, and hawser's tie, no more returning,
Depart upon the endless cruise, old sailor!

"Now Finale to the Shore,"
from Walt Whitman's Leaves of Grass, 1871/1891

CHAPTER ONE

PREPARATION

......, chance favours only the prepared mind.

Louis Pasteur

"I don't want you to go."

The intensity of the statement made me look at her with surprise. It had never occurred to me that anyone cared enough to worry about my taking this trip. But then for the last several months I had been totally absorbed in the planning and the purchasing of the extra equipment needed for a single handed round the world voyage to consider much else.

With as much re-assurance that I could muster I reached out and grasped her arm, and smiled. "I'll be alright, don't worry."

If anything the concern deepened. "It's dangerous, and I don't want you to go."

"Life is dangerous, and there have been many that have done this single handed thing before." I looked at her, willing an understanding. Then with a touch of asperity, I said, "You forget I've spent my whole working life at sea."

Her look didn't change any. And it made me feel uncomfortable. To give me time to think I looked away and scanned the Marina, resting my gaze on my boat at the far end of the dock. 'Ron's Endeavour', a forty foot sloop of van de Statd design. This boat was built with a foam core hull, a strong construction and was a fine sea boat. And I had no qualms about taking off in such a vessel.

The boat was so named by my wife. Endeavour was Captain Cook's ship on his first voyage of discovery to the Pacific, and as I have an abiding interest in all things Cook, what better name?

This diversion gave me time to reflect on a previous conversation with a neighbour who was also concerned about me going of into the wild blue ocean. This lady believed that sea creatures had human qualities. In this particular instance a memory of hurt and revenge being the topic. She was convinced of this to the point of being concerned that I could be attacked by a whale that had suffered injury by some other person. A Moby Dick situation one would assume no doubt. When a person has such convictions, and although one doesn't necessarily agree, one can only respect the concern. And I don't mind saying this premise stuck in my mind.

'Good heavens,' I thought. 'If there is this much concern from both these friends, it is just as well there isn't someone with a deeper and more personal relationship in my life.'

Turning again and thinking a note of humour might ease the situation, "Come on now, lighten up," I said, breezily. "You know how it is when you are young? You feel that you can do anything and will live forever."

At least the look of concern went, only to be replaced by exasperation, then a pitying shake of the head. "For goodness sake, Ron, you are seventy-one." At this she couldn't help but laugh. A short derisive laugh maybe, but at least it eased the situation.

"I still don't like the idea of you going."

I nodded trying, to understand her concern. "You know my situation. There is nothing here for me now." If I stayed I would have to put up with people gossiping about my wife and I having split up. Already there was a cock-eyed rumour going around about our finances, as if that was any concern to anyone but us. That's the Island for you. A small community thrives on gossip. They do say that if you haven't heard a rumour by 10 o'clock in the morning, then start one.

There was a time during the past few months when I questioned the wisdom of what I was planning. But that was purely financial. Having purchased high priced items necessary for an off shore venture, I baulked at having to spend even more. By then the money had been spent and the equipment would have been of no use had I not gone deep sea. After all, a life-raft may be of some use, should the expedition be abandoned but, certainly not necessary in close waters when equipped with an inflatable dinghy. A Hydrovane self steering system? A sea-anchor with six hundred feet of one inch nylon line? Certainly these would not be necessary in the enclosed waters of British Columbia either. And a Satellite telephone would have been a luxury on this coast. However, I consoled myself by the conviction that the expenditure was one off and before the voyage was over my financial state would be less parlous. Ah! Yes. 'The best laid schemes, o' mice and men gang aft agley', to quote Robbie Burns. But then one cannot foretell the future.

Insurance for the boat was not forth-coming as no company would insure unless there were at least four people on board. Which begs the question: How can one sail single-handed with four people on board? Once the word was out that I was setting out around the world via all the exotic places there were many people wanting to come along but all were politely turned down. In my present frame of mind I didn't want to be bothered with people. In one case a female acquaintance became quite insistent on coming along and was only dissuaded by a mutual friend who made it quite clear that it wasn't all cocktails in the cockpit. When told of this, I couldn't help remarking that sometimes one had to go below for cocktails if the weather was bad. Fortunately the issue was dropped without me having to become rude. Medical insurance was not forth-coming either. Yes, this was possible, but the premiums would have been prohibitive. And let's face it. Would a doctor come out to the middle of the Pacific should I need medical assistance? In cases like these one must weigh the risks and make a decision. A recent kidney infection got me thinking on medical lines but, as they say lightning doesn't strike in the same place twice. One concession I did make was to get a prescription for pain killers, just in case I was hurt badly.

It was my intention to set off the middle of April, after the Spring Equinox and the expected gales which are prevalent at this time of year. This plan fell through almost immediately as I was laid up with the aforementioned kidney infection. As this was accompanied with a fever of 103, this delay was most fortuitous. Then there came the business with the lawyers dealing with a legal separation. This became a most trying and frustrating time, which delayed departure until early May.

So here we were, we two, one convinced I was nuts, the other believing it was probably true but going on this adventure anyway.

"You'll see me off on Saturday, won't you?"

"Yes, of course." Not too happily, I surmised.

*

Planning a blue water cruise is no small task. There are so many things to think of, and so many pieces of equipment to check. When there is only one brain dealing with these problems then it is no surprise that something will get left out and especially when there is a desire to get the show on the road, so to speak.

Purchasing and fitting the big, expensive items took priority in the early stages, particularly the Hydrovane steering system as this required hauling the boat. Fitting the brackets to carry this equipment could be done in the water, but is not advisable, for the obvious reasons that something may be dropped in the water and possibly lost. After hauling the boat, cleaning and painting the bottom with anti-fouling paint can be carried out to deter marine growth becoming attached to the hull and creating a drag. A topside coat of paint also gives a well maintained look to the boat. Checking the cooling water and service intakes for blockage and, if necessary, clearing; checking the propeller; securing nuts for tightness, and the rudder for slackness in the seals; are small but important jobs that can only be done at this time.

There are quite a few self steering systems on the market, and no doubt they all have their good points. I chose Hydrovane particularly for the fact that there are no lines leading into and cluttering the cockpit. In fact it steers the boat quite independently of the boat's integral steering capabilities. When the boat is put on the required course and the vane positioned to the wind for steering, it is only required for the boats rudder to be set to counter the pressure on the boat's bow. If the boat tends to go off course the wind on the vane alters, causing it to compensate the self steering rudder, so bringing the boat back on course. It is almost like having the three extra people on board that the insurance company required. The message being: If a long sea passage is planned then don't leave home without one. In life not everything is perfect, and in this, even this wonderful device needs to be watched, as I later found out. That, however, does not detract from the Hydrovane's efficiency.

The rigging of the Satellite phone antennae, fixing the life-raft and arranging the sea-anchor parachute and rode was just a matter of course and proceeded without any problems. It must be said though that a bulky life-raft and a sea-anchor with six hundred feet of rode hanging off the cockpit rails caused a bit of a clutter, albeit arranged on the port side only. But then, safety at sea is paramount and some clutter would be willingly tolerated during this adventure.

In the event of a storm, a set of fibreglass shutters were fabricated and bolted to the forward facing windows. The design of the boat called for windows on three sides of the cabin and made allowance for the fact that should a storm develop the boat would be heading into the wind and therefore only the forward facing windows would bear the brunt of the weather. Although I had been assured that the glass was guaranteed to withstand a solid object being hurled against it with a hurricane force wind, I felt compelled to take out this extra insurance. The shutters could easily be removed for maintenance if required, or to enjoy sunnier climes.

It was during this preparation time that I had to engage a lawyer to represent my case regarding a separation agreement with my wife. It was the start of April, and as I was nearly ready to leave this became a source of irritation. However, this delay as it turned out, was a blessing in disguise, a double whammy even. Quite by surprise I was taken with the aforementioned kidney infection and laid low with a fever. Even taking a pee was a slow, uncomfortable process. During this enforced stay a violent storm passed through our area. My boat was determined to leave the dock without me by parting its mooring lines. Fortunately, a group of fellow boat owners came to the rescue and put out extra lines, securing the boat safely to the dock.

The local marina is usually sheltered, with the prevailing winds being from the SW and giving shelter on all sides but one. On this occasion the wind from the NW exposed the marina to the elements, and as my boat was on the last finger it took the brunt of the wind and the seas that surged around the breakwater.

April rolled by with the interminable delays with the lawyers doing their thing. The good side was, with the help of antibiotics my infection had cleared up. Waiting is always frustrating when on the threshold of something eagerly anticipated and, in this case, there was the added concern of getting to Panama and through the Canal in time to cross the Caribbean and the Atlantic before the hurricane season. 'If you can wait, and not be tired by waiting', to quote Kipling. That is a comfort of sorts I suppose and as there was no alternative then one must put up with a little frustration. All things come to an end sometime and by the beginning of May I had the clearance to leave. All that remained to do was the storing of provisions. This was the first occasion when the gremlins struck.

On this Saturday morning, the planned day of departure, my friend was helping bring on board the frozen provisions, and much to my relief no mention of her not wanting me to go came up in the conversation. She had probably accepted the inevitable. Most of these items were meats accumulated over the past few months won at the Legion meat draw, and also the frozen vegetables purchased for the trip. It was now that the deep freezer refused to operate. On checking the compressor I found that the fuse had blown. This prompted a dash to the service centre for replacement fuses. As it turned out this was not the problem. The freezer still didn't work. As it was a weekend there was no chance of getting a fridge technician to check it out. Besides, all the people who were coming down to see me off at the allotted time would start to show within the hour. To send them away was not a consideration, and I wasn't prepared to have another delay. On discussing the problem we decided to get blocks of ice and hope the products would last for a few days and delay the inevitable spoiling. Some small items would go into the fridge freezer section and keep frozen that way. After a trip to the grocery store for tinned meat, I felt life wouldn't be too hard. A food freezer was a luxury anyway and I resolved to carry on without it.

So it was then that the trip would start without a freezer.

At ten o'clock quite a crowd of friends and well-wishers had gathered on the dock. I'm not considered to be an emotional sort, but I was quite flattered by this gathering and some people that I would never have thought would be present turned up, and it was quite touching. After hugs with the ladies and handshakes with the men I went on board with the many gifts from these good people. The muffins, the wine, and the single malt scotch more than made up for the loss of frozen meat, as these were given out of friendship.

The lines were cast off and putting the engine on slow ahead I eased the boat around the end of the dock. With many waves of farewell I was off on the odyssey of my life.

CHAPTER TWO

BRITISH COLUMBIA to PANAMA

Now voyager, sail thou forth, to seek and find.

Walt Whitman

The first part of this momentous adventure was from my home base to Oak Bay Marina, on Vancouver Island, a matter of only four, maybe five hours motoring. There I took on fuel and water, and spent the night in the last but one time I would use the bunk before Panama.

Maybe I shouldn't refer to a home base, as on the expiry of the yearly contract I had given up the right to the berth my boat had occupied. This relinquishment had caused some discussion as I could have kept the rights to the berth by continuing the payments, and been assured of a place when I returned. The Marina was part of the housing sub-division and as such was private to those who owned property and lived there full time. The fees were nominal; other boat owners would use my slip while I was away, and I would be assured of a berth on my return. I gave this some consideration, but rejected it on the grounds of the length of time I anticipated being away, and the possibility that I might not return. This thought could be called a premonition, although a possibility would be a better description. Besides, due to the terms of the separation agreement I didn't own any property anyway, which made the whole exercise academic.

When some distance away into Swanson Channel I turned and took one last look at the Island that had been my home for the last eighteen years, it must be said that there was no deep emotion attached to this. Just a look, as one does on these occasions. I'd had a good life there, but it was time for the next part of my life, and to find out what that would hold. The weather was fine, with hardly any wind and the waters calm, glassy almost. The clear skies and warming sun cheered me on my way. So it was goodbye Pender for a while.

Life was good; contentment was creeping in, as it always did when I was at sea. I had travelled these waters many times over the past few years and they were familiar enough to have no special interest apart from which route to take amongst the many islands that dotted this part of the world. As it was to be some time before I sailed these waters again, and as the tides were favourable, I decided on transiting John Channel and pass close by the town of Sidney, and then James Channel to transit Merry Channel into Oak Bay and the marina there. This route would be close enough to the shore to have one last look at this wonderful part of the B.C. coast and to store in the memory bouquet. Could I be inadvertently storing nostalgia I wondered? Time to put on the autopilot and make a cup of tea.

By early afternoon I was passing through Merry Channel, and today the usual turbulence from the tide rips wasn't too bad. The steering, had to be constantly corrected as the up-welling eddies pushed the bow one way then the other. It is a short passage into the Bay so we were soon through and heading towards the marina. The Bay is dotted with several small islands, most of which are not much bigger than rocks which must be avoided, or one could, embarrassingly, come to grief. Although I had been through here on several occasions I still felt the need, and the mental security, of steering with my eyes on the chart and directing my course accordingly. Occasionally an open boat propelled by a roaring outboard motor would hurtle by at high speed, leaving me rocking in its wake. No doubt they knew where they were going. Oh! For such familiar optimism.

Before long I was tied up to the fuel dock and attended to by a pleasant fellow of middle age. This I found interesting. Usually the dock-jocks are much younger. I don't suppose it matters one way or the other in this modern day of political correctness. There wouldn't be any discrimination here in a marina than anywhere else I suppose. But then it is noticeable when faced with the unfamiliar. He was very pleasant, helpful and chatty.

"Nice boat," he said, with a look of wistful envy. "Where are you going?"

"Panama, first. Then hopefully around the world."

"I'm going to do that one day." Then as an afterthought. "I guess I'll have to get a boat though."

This statement gave me cause for reflection.

"You could always crew for someone," I said, trying to be helpful.

"Yeah, that's true. Maybe I should take sailing lessons, though."

I looked at him for a moment as he gazed into the distance. He was thinking no doubt of sailing away to tropical climes.

"Yes, that might help." I offered.

The conversation threatened to become ridiculous at this point, and as the fuelling was completed I busied myself with handing the hose back to him and securing the filling cap.

The fuel tank arrangement consisted of a 50 gallon main, and a 25 gallon secondary. Over the past year or so, long before this planned voyage, the secondary tank had been used for the warm air cabin heating system and the diesel fuel content had been gradually diluted with kerosene. Kerosene is a much better fuel for the heater as the summer diesel available in BC is likely to gum up the works. However, with kerosene being mixed in with diesel this tank now contained fuel that was not recommended for the engine, and as I would be operating in warmer climes this tank became extra to requirements. All the effort to convert to the heating system did seem like a good idea at the time.

"I need a berth for the night," I remarked to the dock jock.

"Sure. I'll just check with the office." With this he pulled out his walkie-talkie and made the arrangements.

The berth that I was assigned was a bit of a squeeze with forty feet of boat to manoeuvre around a tight turn, and the wind picking up didn't help any. After a couple of tries at getting in bow first and not doing much good a stern first finagling did the trick with helping hands taking the mooring lines.

Securely moored it was time to take on water. There were two tanks on board, one on each side of the fuel tank compartment, interconnected, and both holding a hundred gallons. I had been assured by experienced deep water sailors that water was never a problem, but then, I had the capacity. So why not use it?

So, by early evening the boat was fuelled and watered. Being well aware of my cooking skills I considered taking a walk and one last meal ashore. However, on reflection it would be sensible to cook at least one piece of meat before it went off, and there were frozen vegetables that would soon become inedible. There was still time to go and pay the Marina dues before the office closed, and then stretch the legs before making a decision about the evening meal.

*

Being a morning person it was no problem to wake up as soon as it started to get light, have the usual cups of tea, breakfast and potty time and be ready to leave. Having stayed in this Marina on previous occasions I took the precaution of not accepting a key for the gate as this was on deposit and the office didn't open until seven o'clock. To hang about so the key could be returned was not an option.

The wind had died over night and the morning air was still with not a soul moving about. When I started the engine I was concerned whether nearby boaters would be startled from their bunks this peaceful Sunday morning. To avoid the engine alarms doing their irritating thing it is necessary to first put the disengaged throttle on full power before switching on. The initial roar is a unique feature of the Volvo Penta. It likes a boost of revolutions when first starting to reset the alarms. Immediately on firing I returned the throttle to neutral and the engine was set for operation. No irate bodies appeared demanding to know what the racket was all about, so, it was just a case of slipping the moorings and moving out of the berth and onto the next stage of the adventure.

The air was cool as I moved out into the channel and I put on a warm jacket. The sun was coming up though, so it promised to be a warm day.

It was just a short run out of Oak Bay and to the Trial Islands. The tides were once again favourable. To take the shorter route between these islands and the near shore would save the best part of an hour on the passage to Port Renfrew some sixty miles away.

As the early morning had promised, it was turning out to be a lovely day. A little cool out on the water but out of the breeze the sun was warming and pleasant. Apart from the occasional recreational fishermen there was not much to take note of and I was absorbed by the scenic shores of lower Vancouver Island. Coffee time came around ten o'clock, and having restrained my desires up until now, I could sample one of those wonderful muffins Bertie and Pammy had given me. And what a delight they were. I was hard pressed to restrict myself to only one. It would be a long trip and only right that the pleasures should be prolonged as long as possible. High fibre they were too, so it made sense to spread the load as one might say. No pun intended.

The morning passed quickly. Then lunch came with a cold meat and salad. Afternoon progressed with nothing to mar the pleasure of being out on the boat enjoying the solitude. The constant noise of the engine was a distraction of sorts, but then the batteries needed a good run up while there was still a chance of topping up with fuel.

By mid-afternoon I was entering the indentation of the coastline that was Port San Juan. It was so named by the Spanish when they explored this coast in the mid 1700's. These days this part of the coast is generally referred to as Port Renfrew, named after the small town that lies some 3 mile towards the head of this indentation.

The marina, such as it was, lay behind the protection of the Government jetty. While rounding the end of the jetty to locate a berth, I was puzzled to find that there was just one float, and that secured in a temporary manner to the side of the jetty. In fact the marina didn't exist. The last time I came here, and the first, it was on my circumnavigation of Vancouver Island and it was in thick fog. Then I made no attempt to approach the marina but rather chose to anchor off for the night. When the fog had lifted a little it was possible to make out the masts of numerous boats. So it was that I deduced that a marina of sorts actually existed.

Shortly after mooring to the float and viewing the situation with some dismay, I realised that, as it was low water, the jetty top was some considerable height above, and I had no means of getting ashore. While I pondered this problem a man appeared and looked down.

"Afternoon!" I called. "There doesn't seem to be a ladder here so I can get ashore."

At this obvious statement he shook his head. "We had a storm come through here a couple of weeks ago and took out the floats. They will be replacing them later this year when they've completed the work on the jetty."

I looked around at the jetty. It seemed to be complete to me but then I couldn't see it from the top. I did notice though, and then I wasn't surprised that the floats had been taken out by a storm. Probably it was the same storm that came through while I was laid up with the kidney infection. Although the marina was on the landward side of the jetty, supposedly to give protection from the elements, the view through the pilings was unrestricted as far as the eye could see, as far as the Pacific Ocean. The jetty pilings would have given no protection at all and the wind and waves would probably have roared right through and carried away the floats. The simple answer to this would be a breakwater on the seaward side of this jetty. Maybe this would be included in the new plans.

While pondering the problem of marina protection I was distracted by a rattling noise. I turned around towards this disturbance and a ladder appeared over the edge of the jetty and was lowered down onto the float. The gentleman who greeted me earlier popped his head over the edge.

"I brought this along. Don't take it away with you," he said, grinning.

"I won't," I said with a derisory laugh. The thought of carrying away an article of this size was being farcical to the extreme. "Thank you."

With a grin and a friendly wave he disappeared leaving me to put out extra mooring lines and shut down the engine. As a reserve I carry a five gallon container of diesel and this I added to the main tank. This was in the scheme of things as I could refill the container here at Port Renfrew. Or so I thought. Fish boats came in here so it followed there would be a refuelling facility. But apparently not. Oh well, the lack of five gallons of extra diesel wasn't the end of the world as I didn't anticipate motoring. The engine would be used only to charge the batteries should the solar panel not keep them topped up.

As a security measure I tied the bottom of the ladder to the float leaving it free to move up and down against the jetty with the movement of the tide.

So it was then that I was settled down for the last night in Canada before taking off into the broad Pacific Ocean. Surprising though it may seem, the enormity of this didn't particularly provoke any emotional response. Not that I didn't wonder why. I supposed that if this is what I'd planned to do, therefore would get done. Feeling no vacillation makes for a much simpler life.

After dinner I climbed ashore to take a walk and make a phone call. I could see then, when reaching the jetty deck, what had been meant by other work being carried out first before tackling the marina. The jetty deck had been concreted with a thick slab which must have taken some planning and effort, not to mention vast amounts of concrete. There was probably no money left in the budget to attend to floats.

While on shore I soon found that most places were closed, not that there was much in the way of facilities anyway. Port Renfrew is a small community, a pub, and a hotel and not much else. But there was a call box so it was possible to phone to base and give a progress report. No doubt my need to make contact was more to do with easing the transition from those that I've known to the prospect of spending some weeks without the social contact of other human beings. It had been my decision to take on this adventure, and my resolve to see it through, so the separation was totally acceptable. The revelation that my dog just lay on the front step apparently waiting for me to come home was hard to take, and gave me some remorse. Consoling myself that she was well looked after and would no doubt have plenty of people to take her for walks, all I could do was harden my heart.

Boarding the boat was made a little easier by the fact that the tide had come in sufficiently to make the descent shorter. It was with some apprehension that the weather report for the morrow gave 40 knot winds from the southwest. This was troubling; to set out with such winds right on the nose was discouraging to say the least. To stay here on this float after the marina had been wiped out gave cause for even more apprehension. The latter though, would be the lesser of the two evils. Deciding to wait and see, which the best therapy often is, I settled down to make the first of many daily entries into the journal. This was a duty that would become an evening ritual, and would be something in my old age to read and relive. Maybe, even something to write about on my return.

*

My first task upon waking this Monday morning was not to prepare tea as usual, but rather to switch on the VHF for the weather. It was with some relief that the high winds reported the previous evening had passed over central Vancouver Island to give a gentler weather pattern.

With an easier mind I turned my attention to making tea. There is only one thing better than a cup of tea in the morning and that is two cups. I never have been able to adopt the North American habit of drinking copious cups of coffee first thing in the morning and throughout the day. It strikes me as being more of a drug than a pleasure. Having one cup of coffee for elevenses with a muffin is, however, civilised. Although I must admit to elevenses being at ten o'clock which can be construed as a habit of sorts I suppose?

The morning formality of tea and a breakfast of cereals, dried fruit, nuts and banana took a little over half an hour. This conglomerate of good things to eat would keep me healthy and, I hoped regular. As there was little chance of exercise to ward off constipation, what better way was there than eating a high fibre breakfast? This I could do while the supplies lasted, which from the amount that I laid in, would be for quite some time.

The morning was bright and clear, a perfect day for a sail. The tide had risen high enough to just push the ladder onto the jetty deck. There was no one about this early in the morning so it was fortunate that the tide had come in and I needed no assistance.

Letting go of the mooring lines and backing off the pontoon I gave myself clearance to turn into the channel and head for the open sea. Up went the mainsail as soon as it was prudent to do so. Having to clamber out of the cockpit to perform this task I found it better to do so in still waters rather than be bouncing about in a swell. At the same time the fenders and mooring lines were collected and taken back into the cockpit for stowage. It would be quite some time before these items would be used again. There is a saying that any task performed at sea should be with one hand for the boat and one hand for oneself. A steady platform to work on is a bonus too. With-in half an hour the buoy at the entrance to Port San Juan was abeam and I set a course to cross the Juan de Fuca Strait for Cape Flattery and away into the Pacific Ocean. The intention was to first make for the outer edge of the Continental Shelf before heading south, some 200 hundred miles off shore. This is to avoid considerable discomfort from standing seas should the weather deteriorate, bringing high winds. It is when the sea bed becomes shallower that waves drag on the bottom causing them to become steep and dangerous to small vessels. I don't suppose that big ships care too much for them either. However as long as the weather remained clement there would be no reason for concern.

Now that the die was cast, there was no turning back; I had a chance to look around at my new environment. The coastline of Vancouver Island was becoming blurred and the features which were earlier pronounced had become indistinct, while Cape Flattery as yet seemed so far away. I must admit at this point I had a vague feeling of sadness at leaving all this behind.

A large container ship on my port side was heading out to sea, its size making me feel insignificant and vulnerable. There was no danger from him though as ocean going ships stay within the traffic separation zone and he would be long gone before I needed to cross. This thought prompted me to take another look around for any other vessel that wanted to share this part of the world.

Away from the shelter of Port Renfrew the boat, starting to feel the swell lifting the bow, rolled easily as the waves passed underneath. The breeze was proving to be quite cool so abandoning the course to the autopilot I went below to put on a survival suit. These I consider to be misnamed in the present circumstances: rather a 'warm and cosy' suit would be more appropriate, as having donned this item of clothing I was immediately insulated from the chill.

It was now mid-morning and time for elevenses. After taking another look around the horizon to check on any shipping and finding that I was alone in the world I busied myself with the kettle and preparing a filter of coffee. The distance to Cape Flattery was fifteen miles which gave me plenty of time to enjoy the coffee and the muffin before stopping the engine and giving over the voyage to sail. At this early stage I felt I needed time to become acclimatised and comfortable with my surroundings. There was no need to rush. There was a long time ahead before arriving in Panama. The wind was out of the northwest at five knots, not a great velocity to propel the boat forward at speed, and as it would be advisable to round Flattery before dark, I kept the motor running.

Cape Flattery was so named by Captain James Cook in 1778 while on his third and last epic voyage to the Pacific, claiming that he was 'flattered' into thinking there would be a safe harbour beyond this point of land. Alas! He was not to find out as he was soon driven off shore by a gale and would not make landfall again until Nootka Sound.

Cape Flattery is the north-west extremity of what is now Washington State, between the continental mainland and the coastline of Vancouver Island lays a stretch of waterway called the Strait of Juan de Fuca.

Juan de Fuca, an old Greek pilot in the employ of Spain alleged discovery of the Strait in 1592. Alleged, because these claims to his discoveries were treated with scepticism by his employers. And, in the light of subsequent proof to the contrary, his claims really were far fetched.

According to the story, Juan de Fuca was sent by the Viceroy of Mexico in search of the Strait of Anian, the fabled passage which would enable a more direct and quicker route to the Orient from Europe. The Northwest Passage if you will.

And I quote: In 1592, beyond California, between latitudes 47 degrees and 48 degrees, he found a broad inlet, into which he entered, sailing for more than twenty days, passing by islands and landing at divers places, seeing people clad in beasts' skins. A fruitful place it was, rich in gold, silver, pearl and other things. In due course he arrived at the Atlantic Ocean, and sailing back through his passage to Acapulco.

He received neither reward nor gratitude from his masters. This in the light of things is not surprising, as we now know, in this modern day that this is blatant fantasy. But even at the time in history the Spanish knew that such a passage to the Atlantic could not be true, because the English had given all their voyages over to the search for the Northwest Passage, and as the Hudson Bay was so well charted, and the only ice free possibility, there could be no easy passage from the Atlantic to the Pacific.

Juan de Fuca was dismissed, his services no longer required.

How different history would have been if Cook had entered the Strait of Juan de Fuca and charted the coastline to disprove once and for all the claims of this eccentric pilot. It remained for Captain Barkley, a fur trader, in his ship the 'Imperial Eagle' in July 1787 to honour Juan de Fuca. Captain Barkley immediately recognised the strait as the one discovered by de Fuca and so named it after him.

Shortly after noon Cape Flattery was safely rounded, the engine was now shut down, the foresail run out, and I was on our way. With several hundred miles of ocean to traverse I must admit to feeling somewhat cut off from the world. Oddly though, now the earlier feeling of sadness had passed, a sense of elation that I had undertaken this venture became dominant. To sail around the world in a small boat was something that I had denied ever wanting to do, my argument being that I had stared at enough seawater during my years in a seagoing career to ever want to do so again. But now to be on my own was infinitely more desirable than to be amongst people: It's a funny old world.

During the afternoon the wind increased to fifteen knots and right on the starboard beam. This was a most favourable point of sail for making a course for the deep water off the Continental Shelf. If the weather held, then tomorrow evening we would be cruising on a southerly course in the deeper waters of the Pacific.

After a sandwich and a cup of tea (Ah! that so delightful nectar.) for lunch the afternoon progressed easily until dinner time. When I opened the freezer the euphoria built up during the day suddenly dissipated at the sight before my eyes. It hadn't taken long for the ice blocks to melt, partially granted, but sufficient, for what should have been individually wrapped meat and packets of frozen vegetables in an unmoving block were items swilling back and forth with each roll of the boat. With dismay I selected a piece of pork, surmising that this selection of meat would last the least length of time before spoiling. I also rescued a soggy bag of peas I might as well make the most of the vegetables as well while the going was good as I didn't hold out much hope for the contents of the freezer to last for many more days. So it was then that I ate dinner with a slight feeling of dejection, only to be lifted a little by a glass of wine.

Twilight is a time of day when it is the most difficult to see ships. It is not dark enough to see their navigation lights and losing the brightness of the day it is difficult to make out their shape. It was a placid evening with the clouds clearing to let out the stars, and the pleasure of keeping watch for shipping in the cockpit made the chagrin of the freezer problem soon evaporate. One cannot dwell too long on the inevitable, so it is best to put it out of one's mind. What supplies could be saved by using the small freezer in the fridge, little as it was, was already dealt with. The enormity of the clear night sky and the millions of stars soon had my whole being at peace. No longer did I have the feeling of being cut off. I now had the profound sensation of being somewhere special. This pleasure was complemented by gazing at the myriad stars, and locating the constellations that still remained in my memory from my sea-going days. Orion in particular brought back fond memories, as I sat in the cockpit locating each star that made up the outline of the mighty hunter and his dog Sirius. I must admit to a smile of pleasure at the many memories that came to mind.

In mythology Orion pursued the Pleiades and for his trouble was eventually slain by Artemis, and was then placed in the sky as a constellation. Not such a bad ending I suppose; at least he is so obvious that he cannot be ignored. Turning to look astern I located the Plough bright and clearly pointing to the North Star, the only fixed star in the heavens. This star over the centuries had been a sure beacon to navigators in the northern hemisphere in providing a means of determining their latitude.

The day had progressed favourably. Sufficient distance had been gained off-shore to be clear of any coastwise shipping, should there be any. There was no sign of steaming lights to landward, or anywhere else for that matter. As the evening was nearing an end, the sea air gave the sleepy suggestion that it was time for me to lie down and get some rest.

While preparing for this voyage there was one important adjustment made to the radar. To do this a technician fitted an alarm to the radar that would sound when a target came within the pre-set guard range. This worked marvellously when along side in the marina but, when switched on out on the briny the alarm sounded loud enough to wake the dead, and continuously with no target in sight. So this was item two to malfunction. For the rest of this voyage I would be hoping that this alarm system fitted on other vessels would be working to give warning of my presence. To rely on a sailboat's navigation lights to be seen from a large vessel was tempting fate. Although very bright, they were low to the water and tended to be difficult to see, especially with a boat rising and falling in a sea, and even assuming that the large vessels in question would be keeping a good lookout for small craft.

It was considered impractical to undress and climb into the forward bunk due to the struggle that would ensue should I have to get out in a hurry. The layout of the berth was designed to take the full width of this section of the boat, and as one would lie feet forward, to throw off the bedding and swing one's legs round to clamber out and get dressed takes time, and at my stage of stiffening advanced years, it was considered prudent not to take advantage of this comfort but to lay out the cockpit cushions on the main cabin deck and fully booted and spurred, so to speak, take my rest thus.

One more thing I did before lying down for the night was a trip to the bathroom. There had been considerable movement with the boat generated by the waves during the day. Most of the time with an easy pitching and rolling, and the infrequent jerk when the boat hit a wave at an awkward angle, this is known in the trade as hitting a milestone. Sod's Law and true to form this is what happened when I entered the bathroom and was thrown off balance, falling heavily against the door. The door was of louvered construction secured against the weather by a wind hook at the bottom section. With a great weight coming into contact with an immovable object with some force, the obvious happened: the door broke. Several slats came out of their sockets and rattled onto the deck but apart from that the door remained intact and usable. As I was the only one on board and had no need for the privacy of a closed door the situation was left as it was. I made a mental note to make repairs when circumstance became more favourable.

Returning to my place of rest I set my mental clock to wake up at frequent intervals during the night and soon fell into the arms of Morpheus.

Setting the mental clock, as it turned out, was quite uncalled for because the position I was lying in on the hard cushion, combined with my body weight caused the elastic in my underpants to dig into my upper leg causing enough discomfort to bring me awake. The only way to solve this problem, as I was wearing the survival suit, was to turn over when one side became a bother and ease the soreness, turning over again when the lower side became a bother, and so on through the night. In between the turning over, I got up to check that all was clear and free from danger. Not a bad alarm system, come to think of it.

*

When daylight started to lighten the horizon my new day commenced. First, I took a look around the watery wilderness for any sign of shipping. Satisfied that there was no danger, the kettle was put on and tea made. Two cups of tea then breakfast. This sequence of events became the norm for starting the days during the rest of the trip. And a more perfect way to start a day I cannot imagine. The reader must forgive me for the frequent reference to this morning ritual but it was a very important part of the trip and of my mental wellbeing.

After checking my position by satellite I realised that with the weather being favourable it was unnecessary to continue on a course south of west to cross the 100 fathom line. A change of course would make it more convenient to cross the line further south and thus save some distance. An alteration of course to due south was thus made, and so brought me on a track parallel with the Washington coast and, a healthy distance off shore.

A high pressure system, called the North Pacific High, covers a vast area of the north Pacific with the winds flowing out in a clockwise motion from around the centre. There are several permanent high pressure systems situated over the oceans of the world, which provide well known tracks for sailing vessels. So it was then that steady progress could be made on the eastern side of this high with winds from a constant direction, giving the most favourable point of sail. Now I could relax and enjoy the solitude, feeling the caressing wind and the movement of the boat, both adding to the pleasure of just being here.

The accident with the bathroom door weighed heavily on my mind this morning. It wouldn't take too much to totally destroy it, should the same thing happen again. As mentioned I didn't require privacy, but when transiting the Panama Canal the extra people on board would. I was expecting to make the transit on arrival so there would be no time to make repairs should the door be totally demolished. Ah, yes! If only our expectations came to fruition. Wouldn't it be a wonderful world?

The best solution I could come up for the time being was to use the bathroom as little as possible, and as there is no time like the present, I moved to the stern lockers and kneeling there with one hand for myself and one for the job, took a pee over the stern.

Soon it was time for elevenses, then soon after a sandwich and a cup of tea. After lunch a much welcome snooze, for half an hour, to replenish the batteries that had been run down with constantly getting up and checking for shipping during the night. Pottering about until dinner at six I created a daily routine that became pleasurably time consuming and comfortable.

The loss of freezer capacity was a nuisance but had to be accepted and the choice of another pork item was considered to be safe. It was thawed out and floppy but didn't smell. Each time that I approached the choice of meat I became a little more despondent at the sight of all this waste of produce. Before much longer I would have to bite the bullet and dump all of this lovely grub. There was no point in taking chances and becoming ill.

The peas had thawed also, but were still firm enough for a meal. With carrots and potatoes a meal fit for a king was prepared. With a glass of red wine to wash it down what more could one ask for in the art of culinary delights? At least there wasn't any chance of the wine being in short supply soon. All of the wine was home brew, sixty litres in plastic waiter bags. Bottles were considered to be too fragile to carry on a boat. In the sea going environment with a boat bouncing about in the waves carrying bottled wine was asking for trouble, not to mention all the space that they would take up.

While I ate the evening meal, the wind increased to 25 knots, causing the boat to heel more than desired. Rather than scrabble about in the dark taking in a reef in the mainsail the boom was let out to spill some wind. A fisherman's reef as it is called. The boat behaved most favourably under these conditions. Spray was starting to come on board with the increase of wind, the tops of the seas being whipped away to splatter the full length of the boat. The SatNav put our position on the same latitude as the mouth of the Columbia River. So it was satisfying to know that good progress was being made under these conditions and the spray became just something to put up with, a minor irritation when out on deck.

While sitting in the cabin waiting for a suitable time to lie down for sleep I was awakened from my reverie by the sound of water, not a pouring sound but rather water falling. Curious, I got up to investigate, only to find that water was coming into the galley by way of the cabin heater chimney. Odd, I thought, the chimney cowl has a canvas cover to stop this sort of thing. Going out into cockpit and looking forward made it obvious what the problem was: both the canvas and the cowl had disappeared.

This problem had to be addressed now; it was not an option to have water coming into the boat via a chimney or anywhere else. Giving a mental expletive I went below, donned the safety harness, and got the necessary tools and a small piece of plywood suitably coated with sealant. Making ones way forward on a bouncy boat requires two hands and great care. However, by first shoving the drill, and plywood piece ahead of me along the cabin top, and waiting for lulls in the spray and the heavier movements of the boat,

I arrived at the scene of action. The task didn't take long, for I needed only to drill and screw down the plywood piece. I was soon back down below, wondering what would be the next problem to arise.

I wasn't kept waiting too long to find out. At half past three in the morning I sensed something was amiss, and by glancing at the compass readout above the chart table it was obvious there was a problem. The boat was seriously off course. I could only wonder why this would happen as the Hydrovane steering had been most reliable. The only reason that came to mind, and this was conjecture only, was if the wind had increased it would cause an increase of pressure on the opposite bow, causing the boat to come round to the wind and set another course. Whatever the reason the boat was heading towards Hawaii, and no matter how much I'd enjoyed Hawaii when visiting there, it was not my intention or wish to visit this trip.

It was quite possible that being awake at such an early hour had made me a little dopey and in attempting to get the boat back on course I kept getting the steering set-up wrong. And off we would head towards Hawaii again. For a while I left the steering to the autopilot while I thought the Hydrovane set-up procedure through. It wasn't difficult really to come to a conclusion. I'd been failing to apply counter rudder on the main steering. I guess it was too early in the day for conscious thought. However, it seemed that my theory of wind pressure on the bow could be right. It was quite cool out in the wind and it was a relief to go below again to lie down and maybe doze until the next call out.

Daylight came, and the sun rose on a bright clear day. The usual routine of tea and breakfast, then potty time, all passed by and I could relax. After such a hectic night I felt the need to have an after breakfast snooze. Just half an hour's repose worked wonders. So in the light of this experience a regimen of relaxing whenever the occasion allowed came into being. It also became a matter of conjecture as to whether I spent more time horizontal or vertical in the pursuit of this theory.

The noon position gave the distance over the previous twenty-four hours of 110 miles. An achievement not to be sneezed at: in fact quite a good run when one considers a daily estimate of 100 miles as a yardstick. Even the dolphins had trouble keeping up.

This daily progress wasn't achieved again for the rest of the week; the wind became erratic in intensity, although fortunately the direction remained favourable. On only one day was the 100 mile criteria reached. The least distance covered in one twenty-four hour period was just 48 miles. No matter. Progress was being made and I wasn't in a round the world race. Saturday noon put the position 160 miles due west of Crescent City, Oregon.

Saturday evening I sent a progress report by e-mail with the Satellite phone link to the pre-arranged contacts. They then would forward the message to all interested parties. This may seem a convoluted way of letting people know what I was up to, but it was decided during the planning stage that with the cost of satellite communication, and my indecisiveness with modern technology, it would be better to let just two people handle the distribution.

During the following week the weather became much warmer and I could finally get out of my Andy Pandy survival suit. The freedom of movement and the joy of feeling the sun and breeze unrestricted by this heavy article of clothing was a pleasure indeed. Lying down on the cushions with a lack of restraint by bulky apparel also allowed me an adjustment of my underpants elastic. A positive plus and much appreciated. All was not well with this sleeping arrangement because when I needed to get up to check on the current situation, I found that it was difficult with my stiff old bones to stand upright easily. I achieved it only with much grunting, oohing and aahing! Obviously some other arrangement had to be considered, a place of repose somewhere that called for putting my legs down to stand, rather than having to roll over onto my knees before attempting to come upright. The forward bunk was out of the question for reason previously mentioned. The after berth was being used for storage, so that wasn't an option. This left the settee. I viewed this possibility with some dismay. It was curved, only the width of a chair seat, and wrapped around a table. The design called for this table to be lowered to make up another bed, should that be called for. This then could resolve the present problem, only to create more problems. Not only did I take my meals at this table, it was also used for writing up the journal and many other uses. However, I seemed to be faced with Hobson's choice. At least this option of kipping on the settee should be given a trial run.

The next morning I was asking myself why I didn't sleep on the settee from day one. It was a most restful spot. The only problem that arose was when needing to change sides. The settee was too narrow for me to roll over, so it was a case of getting up and changing end for end. The plus side of this action was that I could check on the situation outside while on my feet.

The days progressed pleasantly; the weather was fair with the sea slight. Once a routine had been established the days just flew by. Boredom, as one might think, would be a problem under these circumstances, but boredom never happened. I must qualify that statement, however. Boredom did crop up now and again but this had nothing to do with the circumstances of being alone on a boat in the middle of the ocean. Rather, strangely to say, from doing the crosswords. These had been given to me by a very good friend with the admonishment to do them if I became bored. As it turned out the crosswords created a reverse reaction. The first crosswords were reasonably easy, although the lay-out of the blocks were not in the accepted format of being equal on each side, and top and bottom of the square. But, no matter, these puzzles would exercise the brain. Or so I thought. After completing the first one and moving on to a second and third I realised that some of the clues were being repeated, and so it became a test of memory. This was true with each puzzle right through the book. It must be said though that I now know that a dace is a fresh water fish. An interesting development evolved over the ensuing weeks because of having a go at these crosswords. Whenever I felt a need to be bored, irritated, cross or whatever, I would pick up the crossword book and start a puzzle. I could then become frustrated and toss the stupid thing to one side with a curse. This seemed to work wonders with my perverse psyche.

Before I knew it, it was Saturday again and time to make a report, but when it was entered into the lap-top and ready to be transmitted by satellite it would not go. Several attempts proved to be futile. The only recourse now was to phone the help line, and, after half an hour of being walked through a re-installation of the program the message finally went, leaving me wondering what else would happen to make my days fruitfully frustrating.

Sunday was, strange though it may seem, considered to be my day off. Unless called away to make refreshments or meals, checking on the probability of shipping, etc, I kept the phone handy. This had a two fold purpose: the ring tone was very low, not helped by my standard of hearing: and, this was the day set aside for friends to call should they so wish. The day then was taken up with reading, of which there was a varied selection, or listening to CDs, of which again there was a varied selection, or just sitting and thinking. Or just sitting. Surprisingly the day didn't drag and boredom never happened. Contentment must have had a hand in this I suspect. The problem with sending the report bothered me though, and I spent some time thinking on the subject.

As I must admit when it comes to technologies I am a dummy, and not a little suspicious of what goes on in the little box of tricks called a computer. So it was about this time I got to wondering if my last report had got through as there had been no confirmation of this, and I must admit with the way this trip was panning out with all the hiccups a touch of paranoia could be creeping in. There was only one way to find out and that was to phone base. Well! What do you know? The satellite phone didn't work.

What to do now? Obviously, if I couldn't have communication with the base then they would not know if I was still above the waves.

The position of the boat at noon was south of the latitude of San Diego and a hundred miles from the coast of Mexico. Should I go back to San Diego to have the phone fixed? To carry on to Panama was out of the question. The distance was too great to be without communication and keep the folks back home in the dark worrying about my safety. After pondering the situation and with much perusing of the chart, I decided that my one remaining option was to make for Cabo San Lucas at the tip of Baja California, an estimated five days away, still a cause for concern for those who would be waiting for the weekly news, but the best option.

It was during this period that a bit of luck came my way. A vessel steaming south was overtaking at a distance of five miles on my starboard side, and after several attempts answered my call on the VHF radio. The officer of the watch called the captain who graciously agreed to pass a message via e-mail to base. This kindness certainly took a load off my mind.

Had I known the true outcome at the time I wouldn't have been so complacent. As it turned out the message was not received and the non-recipient hadn't been unduly concerned about my lack of contact anyway. I was not a little miffed after all the worry about lack of contact. I could not accept that the message would not have been sent. More likely the recipient didn't recognise the sender's address and didn't open it. Doesn't it make you want to curse the spam and virus merchants for all the trouble they cause?

But that was in the future.

Having made this change of plan and accepted that a diversion from the original was now the order of the day, I settled down to the prospect of a few days' break in the Cabo. I had spent a vacation there a few years previously and apart from being pestered by the Timeshare people, quite enjoyed the place. At least I knew where to go and how to approach the harbour. The next few days passed in a relaxed and trouble free manner. The weather remained clement, the seas slight and the sails full. If I had been of a poetic nature no doubt I could have waxed eloquent on the joys of cruising in relaxing surroundings. 'Just give me a tall ship, and a star to steer her by,' that sort of thing. Although being of a practical turn of mind

I could hardly have set out on this venture with such limited equipment.

In due course I sighted the coast in the region of Cabo San Lucas just after daybreak and set a course to close the land. During the night a tear had appeared in the leach of the genoa. Probably it had got caught on the spreader, but as it was only a small tear, it didn't concern me all that much. With the repair kit on board it would be attended to while alongside. However, the wind was starting to blow quite strongly and as the land was getting close I took the sails down and started the engine. This was most timely as the wind increased alarmingly and by mid morning was up to forty knots from the north. The wind direction running as it was along the coast started to bring up a rough sea with quite a swell running, throwing spray across the deck as each wave slammed against the side. These conditions had me manning the steering, because with the rolling and pitching I did not consider it prudent to engage the autopilot. With the push of a wave against the bow threatening to throw the boat off course I had to anticipate and put the helm over to meet the pressure. The wheel was constantly in use as the boat bucked and gyrated to the action of the sea.

In this situation one could use the flyer's maxim transferred to a nautical environment: flying by the seat of ones pants. Wonderful as an autopilot is it cannot anticipate a wave action, and to have the boat broach to a wave would be most undesirable.

Within the hour the land provided a lee and it was then easy motoring along the easterly trend of the coast, around that magnificent rock that has a hole in it, Los Arcos (the arch) and then on a reverse course to the harbour of Cabo San Lucas and the fuel dock and marina. I was twenty-five days out from Pender Island.

CHAPTER THREE

CABO SAN LUCAS

The Spanish Conquistador Hernan Cortez, in 1535, was the first European to come to this part of the world after subduing the Aztecs to seek a fortune in gold and silver that was supposed to abound here. He was disappointed in this assumption, but left his name to the sea on the east side of the peninsula of Lower California a sea that stretches all the way back to where the Colorado River exits to the sea, a distance of 700 miles. Lying as it does at the southern most point of the Baja, Cabo San Lucas remained very much a backwater until after the Second World War, when American celebrities from the movie industry discovered that they could access this part of the world by plane or with their long distance pleasure boats and take advantage of the abundance of marine life which provided a sport fisherman's paradise. From then on, and after the road was built, there was no looking back. As a tourist attraction the Cabo just took off, and is now a vacation spot for those who seek the sun and the beautiful beaches, and the world class sports fishing.

None of these pleasures were for me though; mine was just a stay of convenience, an interruption of the original plan of proceeding directly to Panama. As it turned out this break in the original arrangement proved to be pleasantly relaxing. The climate at this time of the year was dry and warm. The tourist season was coming to an end so there would be a marked downturn of people bent on enjoying themselves. This of course was no concern to me as I was here for more mundane matters. Namely, to contact the Satellite phone people and seek direction as to where to send the offending object, refuel, fix the tear in the genoa, and boost the charge on the batteries. I also wanted a meal that comprised meat that didn't come out of a tin. The original fresh meat had long gone to the fish that is if it was still fresh enough for them. It certainly wasn't for me. There had been another little mishap during the previous few days that also needed attention: the plug for charging the phone and the electric shaver had gone into destruct mode and was completely useless. So that would have to be replaced. A car cigar lighter is such a useful item but, so delicate that the moist atmosphere takes its toll on the connections and soon corrodes them. The way things had been going this diversion to Cabo San Lucas was a blessing in disguise.

The approach to the fuel dock couldn't have been simpler as it was directly inside the entrance and at the end of the marina floats. Willing hands soon had the boat tied up and refuelled. I took the short walk along the floats to the office for the assignment of a berth, payment for the moorage, and there I was, all secure and ready to do the necessary paperwork for the inward clearance. First, though, I considered a call to the satellite phone people, but was stymied from the word go. In the Marina Office I had noticed a telephone in the lobby, and it was with this that I proceeded to make the call, only to find out that one needed a call card, that irritating invention that seems to have frustration attached to it. In the same building as the Marina Office was a store that catered in a small way to the boating trade and luckily they also sold phone cards. The call I had to make was long distance, and an 800 number. The call went through alright but before you could say Jack Robinson the call was cut off through lack of funds on the card. Obviously, the 800 number didn't mean anything. The store owner proved to quite helpful, and also spoke excellent English. He sold me another card. This, although a little more time was used before I was cut off again, still didn't get me to the person that could deal with the information required. The store owner, whom I shall call Alex, as that was his name, came to the rescue once again and suggested I ask the Marina manager if I could use his phone. After all, it was a collect call. For some reason that I didn't quite grasp this alternative was not forthcoming. Something to do with telephone system being an internal set-up and would not accept long distance calls. At this point it became more important to have the inward clearance into Mexico and, I took the Marina manager's direction to the Port Captain's office, which he pointed out, was just over there, a five minute walk. When over there, there was no indication of the place I wanted. Not being shy about asking directions even in a foreign country, I approached the guard at the gate of the Naval Base, and in my best Spanish, asked, "Que es el Porto Capitan's offico?" At this question surprising though it may seem he looked blank. Maybe it was my Yorkshire accent? While I was figuring out how to rephrase the question, another armed guard sauntered over who, when I repeated my question, also looked blank. He must however, have caught the key words and things brightened up.

"Ah! Capitan del Porto?" he asked, looking pleased with himself.

"Si." Now we were getting somewhere, I thought.

Up went his arm and pointed in the direction of the town. This didn't gel with what I had been told at the marina and arguing wasn't a consideration. So I took myself off in the direction indicated, none too happy at the way things seemed to be developing.

It was a hot afternoon and walking was becoming uncomfortably warm, with my skin taking on a definite glow. To return to the boat would not solve anything. Soon I came to what proved to be a small market selling tourist merchandise, the sort of thing that holiday makers buy as a memento, put in a cupboard on arriving home and promptly forgot. Big wide Mexican sombreros magnificently studded, and curly brimmed, that sort of thing. Wearing such apparel in northern countries would bring unwelcome attention and would definitely be out of place. There were a few men hanging about who looked like locals, and it was to them I directed my next question.

"Do you speak English?" I asked, not wanting to confuse these good people with my Spanish.

"Yas, I spic a leetle," a tall man answered.

"I'm looking for the Port Captains Office," I said, much relieved at finally getting somewhere.

"Come," he said, "I take you," and he walked away towards a car. Just like that, no preliminaries.

Slightly surprised at the way things were developing I hesitated, but only for a second. This was a chance not to be passed up. Quickly catching up with him and on the passenger side of the car, I noticed there was no handle on the door; it was to be opened from the inside. With a feeling of slight dismay at this introduction and the general decrepit state of the vehicle I climbed in, wondering if I was taking the right course of action.

Churlish I may have been to harbour these thought at the outset because it wasn't long before I was becoming very impressed with this Good Samaritan. It was quite a distance to the Port Captain's building, and the thought of walking there and not knowing the way gave rise to daunting thoughts. During the journey he asked me not to tell anyone that he was taking me, because if the taxi drivers found out he would be in big trouble. After all this kindness, how could I?

Not only had he driven me to my destination but insisted on coming in as an interpreter. This was most fortuitous as the clerk didn't speak English and it transpired that we would first have to go to immigration, and then return with the necessary papers before he could give me clearance. So off we went on, to me, another mystery tour. The process of legally entering Mexico was far from completed because waiting in line while bureaucracy took its interminable time, I was presented with a form and told to go across the road to the Bank and pay up, then come back to complete the paperwork. So off we went, at least down to the street where my companion suggested that he must go about his business. Not in a million years could I fault his decision; he had been very attentive to my problems which had taken so much of his time and, I would be able to handle the rest of the procedure alone. To show how much I appreciated his help I suggested that he be given something for his trouble.

"No, no, nada, nothing," he protested,

And so started an argument that I later realised was the polite way of settling a debt.

"Come now," I said, "you have taken so much trouble on my behalf, you deserve something." And I took out my wallet.

"OK, a couple of dollars."

"A couple? How much? You tell me."

At this he held up his hands and shrugged. "It's up to you."

I was becoming a little exasperated at this game and said, "I have no idea what the right amount would be." Then, "Ten dollars? Would that be OK?"

Another shrug and a hand gesture of acceptance, "Sure."

And so with a hand shake we parted company. I was most grateful for his help but, wondered if ten dollars had been enough. No doubt he would have been too polite to question this amount. It was pointless pondering the subject so I took myself off to the Bank.

It seemed as though everyone and his uncle and aunt were lining up waiting for service and as it was well into the afternoon, I was becoming anxious whether this business of clearing inwards, and negotiating the outward clearance, would be completed this day. As it turned out it wasn't to be. After the immigration side of this procedure was satisfactorily completed and the necessary papers presented to take to the Port Captain, this wasn't the end of it. Next in this chain of bureaucracy it was required of me to go to yet another department before the clearance could be given. This as it turned out was close by the marina and the office I should have gone to in the first place. Well we live and learn, don't we? It was hot and I was weary so I engaged a taxi. As it turned out, although the office was open, the man in charge had gone home and I was requested to return in the morning. I said to myself, enough for this day, dismissed the taxi and returned to the boat. By the time I would have returned to the Port Captain's office they would most likely have been closed anyway.

While on the boat I noticed an almost continuous procession of buses passing around the Marina office. They would travel along the road from town, disappear behind the marina building then re-appear from the other side and return towards the town, stopping only long enough to pick up passengers should there be any. What made me curious was that there were so many buses, nothing like a regular schedule, when a person would wait for ages then two buses would turn up. Here it was more like a regular procession, approaching from town, circling the building and speeding away again. To satisfy my curiosity, and after the solitude of the boat and my own company I was now getting to like people, so I wandered up to Alex's shop and made enquiries. True to form Alex was most helpful and explained that these buses were independently owned and operated, and apparently anyone could go and buy an old bus and run a service in and out of town. The beauty of this arrangement was there was no long wait and the fare was only six pesos. Deciding to try out this mode of transport I went back to the boat and took a shower, got dressed up, and presented myself at the bus stop. A vehicle of uncertain pedigree, painted yellow with the words, 'School Bus' showing through an attempt at being camouflaged soon pulled to a stop. The word, old, in old bus was an understatement. Ancient would be nearer the mark. But, for six pesos who was complaining? A bone shaking ride on a seat of torn vinyl with a coil spring threatening to pierce ones bum was the consequence. But then, the alternative of a taxi for ten dollars wasn't even to be considered.

During my quest around the town for inward clearance I had seen an Internet café and it was to this that I made my way. Not only was there internet, there was, joy upon joy, a telephone, a telephone that worked by dialling without the insertion of a card. Just make the call and pay at the desk, at least a nominal fee for the collect call as the café owner had to make a living. Matters seemed to be taking a turn for the better now. Within no time at all the satellite phone people had been contacted, the problem discussed, and I was given an address where to send the offending article to be forwarded to my e-mail. The next call confirmed that no message had been received from the vessel contacted during the previous week. At this I was a little bit miffed, after all, brotherhood of the sea and all that jazz. But as previously mentioned this attempt at contact could have been considered spam. Ah well, as I hadn't been missed, the business had become matterless anyway.

Much enlightened by getting matters moving, and fortified with a happy heart I sought out a suitable restaurant. There are many eating places to choose from in downtown Cabo so I chose the first one I came to and I was soon tucking into a delightful meal of baked red snapper on a bed of rice, with just a suggestion of assorted vegetables. The fish was served whole, complete with the staring eyes, or I should say, eye, as the fish was lying on its side. As I was famished the stare was completely ignored and the flesh soon scraped down to the bones. After three weeks at sea to tuck into a meal that was protein rich and hadn't been prised from a can was a delight indeed. All washed down with two bottles of Tecata beer. Lovely.

It had been a long hot and tiring day so taking a short walk in the direction of home base to settle the meal, I then caught the first available independently operated bus. Much to my relief this bus, albeit hurtling along the road at an alarming rate, was much less of a bone shaker. Even the seat was in one piece.

And so it was that I retired for an early night and in the comfort of the forward berth. Much pleased with the latter events of the day, and thoughts on tomorrow, I fell into a sound sleep.

*

Without the necessity of having to frequently awaken during the night to check on shipping, weather, and make sure the boat was travelling in the direction it was supposed to, I enjoyed a sound, full night's sleep awakening only when it started to get light. After a normal start to the day with tea, breakfast, and the usual routine I was out on deck appreciating the prospect of yet another warm sunny day, and washing the torn sail with fresh water prior to the repair.

While waiting for the sun to dry the genoa I filled the time by packing up the satellite phone ready for posting. Nothing would be open at this time of day, neither the post office, nor, any Government offices which still had to be dealt with, so matters took on a leisurely pace. Apart from repairing the sail once it was dry, there were the water tanks to fill and the batteries to charge from shore power.

With modern materials a preliminary sail repair is quite an easy task. There is still the repair that can only be tackled with a palm and needle but, in the case of a small tear more often than not this can be dealt with by what is known as sail-maker's Duct Tape. This is a fabric that comes in varying widths with a peel off covering that reveals an adhesive backing. All that is required is to cut to length, round off the corners to prevent the tape lifting, remove the peel off backing and stick the tape over the tear, and Bob's your uncle, repair completed. This is a stopgap method, and only recommended as a repair until the services of a sail maker can be engaged. In the present circumstance with such a minor tear this patch would have to suffice as my time here in the Cabo was limited and any delay was for the purpose of getting the phone away for repair. So it was then, with the minor chores out of the way, and the morning progressing, I took myself off to the first place of call to pay another fee, collect the piece of paper for the Port Captain's office and catch the bus into town. Now that I knew the correct procedure and destinations the frustrations of yesterday were not repeated. Matters took on a flow of their own, and when I walked into the office the clerk noticed me and left the person that he had been attending to and came over and took the offered paper. The office was quite crowded and would otherwise, had I not received immediate attention, have promised a long delay. This attention, much to the looks of annoyance from the other people waiting for attention pleased me no end. My irritations had been suffered on the previous day so there was little sympathy for their discomfort. In a matter of a few minutes, not counting yesterday, my Inward and Outward Clearances had been attended to and I was free to leave Mexico for Panama. But first the phone to get off, buy a cigar lighter to replace the duff one, and dowel and glue to fix the broken bathroom door. When these chores had been satisfactorily completed it was back to the boat and away. Or at least that was the intention.

However, fate was taking a hand again.

After posting off the phone and returning to the boat with a happy heart in preparation for departure I noticed, while checking the engine oil, that there was a considerable flow of water alongside the engine bed coming from the back of the boat. There had been a slight ingress of water prior to this but nothing the bilge pump couldn't handle. This leak had emanated from the seal where the rudder post came through the hull. This was a weak area of the steering system as the tiller bearing was only about nine inches above the bottom seal. Above that there was two feet of rudder post. This arrangement had been fine in relatively still waters but out in the ocean with the rolling of the boat the spade rudder had worked like a loose tooth on the seal causing it to leak. What to do? The boat ideally should be hauled and the leak fixed from underneath. As an alternative if Alex had a quick drying adhesive in his shop that might solve the problem.

After much discussion on the subject and dismissing the products offered as being unusable, Alec had a bright idea. He phoned his friend the boatyard owner and had a word with him to see if he could fit me in for a haul out. What transpired during the conversation and what arrangements had been made, I couldn't say, as I don't speak Spanish. When Alex got off the phone he looked thoughtful, then, as though a brilliant idea had formulated, advised that I go and talk to his friend the boatyard man. What else could I do but concede to this suggestion? He had gone to this trouble on my behalf and the problem had me worried. So it was then that I returned to town to have a word and see if it would be convenient for the boat to be taken out of the water.

This turned out to be a wasted effort as the yard man was quite emphatic about not putting me ahead of his other customers. This left me wondering why Alex had sent me on this wild goose chase. It would appear, and I came across this helpfulness time and again in the Latin American world, that in their eagerness to be helpful they would suggest anything to try and solve a problem. As they say, you live and learn. And these situations are not to be taken with offence. Just make one's own decisions on any given suggestion. Or better still don't even ask in the first place.

When I returned to the boat the afternoon had progressed to the point were it would be pointless leaving until an attempt had at least been made to stop the leak. So it was then that an arrangement was made to stay yet another night.

A liberal application of fibreglass cloth and thick epoxy putty with enough hardener to set it off rapidly was then applied around the area of the leak, after drying this appeared to do the trick. This then had to suffice. So, with an incongruous thought that water is best kept outside of a boat I left for another meal in town. The good thing about all this, and I do try to look on the bright side, is that I could look forward to missing yet another home cooked meal, which was a blessing.

CHAPTER FOUR

CABO SAN LUCAS to PANAMA

..........to suffer.
The slings and arrows of outrageous fortune.

Hamlet Act 111

Another good night's sleep put me in the mood to get my act together and get on my way, but first another trip into town to purchase a few extra provisions and a final check for any messages that had come in, and one or two to send off. Friends had expressed the wish to transit the Panama Canal with the boat and act as line handlers. This arrangement would be most welcome and to see friends again would break up an otherwise long spell away. Also the line handling would cut the cost of the transit a little. As there was to be no communication from the boat between the Cabo and Panama, all I could do was send an estimated time of arrival (ETA) from here.

Before noon goodbyes had been said, not to Alex though as he wasn't around. His wife did wish me a safe journey and hoped that I would return, which was nice to hear. I hadn't thought much on that subject but, meeting such friendly people maybe in the years to come could be a possibility? So it was that, before noon the lines were cast off, I motored out of the harbour and cleared Los Arcos headland. In no time at all the sails were up, the engine switched off and I headed in a south-easterly course towards the bulge of Mexico in the vicinity of Manzanillo, with the intention of keeping well off the coast and coastwise shipping. With the peace and the quiet of moving through the water at a brisk pace a feeling of freedom from civilisation took over again. There is a great deal of truth in the saying that one can only find peace away from the land, and I could almost feel the blanket of tranquillity closing over me. With the warm wind on my skin and the slapping of the waves against the hull to thrill the senses, life was good. Heeling slightly on a port tack with the wind on the beam I gave over the steering to the Hydrovane.

A fair wind and a trouble free passage would bring me to Panama in a matter of three weeks. How optimistic can one be? But then the future can only be experienced, not foreseen. With these pleasant thoughts I prepared and consumed lunch, then took a refreshing snooze. Having a lie down in the afternoon for ten, maybe fifteen minutes, surprising though such a short siesta may seem certainly worked wonders, a pleasure to be indulged in at every opportunity.

The land by the Cabo was soon becoming a blurred mass and by late afternoon as I sat in the cockpit looking back there was no distinguishable shape at all. Once again there was only the boat, the sea and me.

Over the next ten days sailing parallel to, but out of sight of the coast of Mexico, life was sublime. A fair wind on the port beam gave a perfect point of sail; progress was being made at a reasonable average of just less than one hundred miles a day. The weather was warm enough me to take a shower out in the cockpit. The Solar Shower had been filled with fresh water previously and left out in the sun all day on the coach top to warm. They are a great invention these showers; a plastic bag with a shut off valve at the end of a spout, then hung off the end of the boom gives a most adequate means for a body wash, and most importantly with a slow delivery from the spout, is a water saver. In this situation though there was one point that needed attention. With the boat rolling easily in the swell the bag would swing about in a most erratic and alarming manner, requiring one's attention to avoid being slapped by the bag while soaping down, particularly so when ones face is covered in soap with the eyes closed. With a little practice this oscillating action can be anticipated and with a deft movement one can duck.

My birthday rolled around on this stretch of the voyage, and as one does on these occasions there is a need to do something special, or if not special, then different to the everyday run-of-the-mill routines. Glumly I perused the provision cupboard, and there wasn't much that could be done for a change in the food line. The excitement of corned beef, or spam for that matter, had long been exhausted. Pondering this problem for some time I decided that maybe a serving of fried rice with a fried egg on top, if nothing to write home about, was at least different. So this sumptuous repast was put into being. This I took with a glass of red wine to wash it down. It made for a feast that could not to be scoffed at. The thoughts, as they do on festive occasions, go back to other times when I celebrated with people around, and today on my seventy-first was no different. Last year was a milestone of sorts when friends helped in the celebrations. But, today? Undaunted and there being no-one else, I gave a hearty rendition of, 'Happy Birthday to Me', and felt greatly elated at the experience.

Evening was coming on and the light fading, so taking a cup of coffee out to the cockpit I sat and reminisced while keeping a sharp lookout for any traffic that might be in the area until darkness blanketed this part of the Pacific. No shipping had been sighted, not this evening nor any previous evening since leaving the Cabo so, after only a little thought on the subject I opened Peter Binner's bon voyage gift of the bottle of Glen Morangie. Strict instructions had been issued about when this should be opened, and not until Panama. Also this act was contravening my own rule of partaking only in a glass of wine with the evening meal, no beer, no hard liquor. Well it was my birthday so why not, and rules were made to be broken, so it was a case of, 'Cheers, Ron,' a lift of the glass and a sip of the single malt with a hearty happy birthday. Needless to say this forbidden fruit was a nectar indeed and most enjoyable, more so because of it being forbidden.

To paraphrase Newton's Second law of Motion, for every action there is an equal and opposite reaction. The following morning the residual euphoria from the previous evening was replaced by glumness on the sight of the genoa. During the night and unnoticed in the dark during the checks, a tear had appeared along the leach seam. This was only a few inches in length and apparently not getting any worse. The old adage, 'a stitch in time saves nine,' came to mind but this was the middle of the ocean with a brisk breeze blowing. The tear was close to the leach seam which presented difficulty in sewing. Should the tear become worse then it would only go as far as the next cross seam, so I decided to leave the problem until there was a lull in the wind. As progress was being made out of the Pacific High, I made a reasonable assumption that there would be the anticipated lull before picking up the trade winds off the lower part of Mexico.

As I progressed to the south the coast tended towards the southeast, then easterly. In the next two days the wind changed to the trades which required a change of course to follow the trend of the coast. This put the wind forward of the port beam and the mainsail adjusted accordingly; the boom was hauled amidships to flatten the mainsail and the genoa trimmed to sail as close to the wind as reasonable, with the wind at sixty degrees on the port bow. There had not been the anticipated lull in the wind to allow the repair, and as the tear on the genoa leach had remained static I was pleased to let the matter rest.

The noon position having been taken and plotted, I anticipated a good day's run and went below for lunch and the afternoon snooze. The rest of the day and through the night was a relaxing time, just a steady progress towards my destination. The usual chores had been carried out, which involved reading the latest book while seated in the cockpit: 'The Conquest of Mexico,' was rather appropriate I thought as we were still paralleling the coast of this country. After preparing and eating dinner I had a relaxing interlude in the dark listening to a music disc. There was quite a selection of CDs on board with a wide variety of music ranging from classical to jazz. Shirley Bassey was there, too, and Kiri te Kanawa at the other end of the singing scale. It became a much anticipated relaxation, these music evenings, and something of which I never tired. That is how the evening progressed until the time came to check if any dangers threatened on the broad ocean.

On the warm balmy evenings when the stars came out I would stand on the top step of the companionway and lean with my arms on the hatch opening just gazing into the night with my thoughts dwelling on the good things, and good people that have been part of my life, the gentle warm wind almost a sensual caress on my exposed skin, directing my thoughts to matters not to be mentioned. Life could never hold such contentment as those moments. All too soon it would be time to go to bed or, should I say, time to go to settee to rest.

*

During the night the frequent checks produced no worries and even the steering behaved. However, something strange was going on that was difficult to pin down. While taking my rest between visits to the great outdoors, with my head on the pillow, I was hearing voices. These were in the form of a conversation between a man and a woman the actual words undistinguishable but the inflection unmistakable. When I lifted my head they stopped and started again when my head was set to the pillow. Not given to fantasy I didn't put this down to visitations from outer space or other such imaginings. Having said that, these thoughts must have come to mind I suppose. Rather I surmised that it had to do with the movement of the boat, and the bilge water swilling from side to side, or at least that is what I told myself, and I would fall asleep trying to interpret what was being said, nosey that I am eavesdropping on other people's conversations. Be that as it may there were far more important matters to consider than the possibility of supernatural beings.

To conserve the batteries it had been my habit to limit the use of electric power by switching off any unnecessary circuits, particularly during the night.

So it was then that when checking the position the following noon I found that the boat was in almost the same position as the previous noon. This was a most odd turn of events which caused me great deal of consternation. The wind had eased to around ten knots since the last fix but we were still moving. Rechecking the GPS didn't give any indication of errors from that department which was also checked against the hand held GPS. Puzzlement indeed and what to do? At least the problem wasn't electrical. The boat was not going the way that it should, in fact, not making any progress towards the appointed destination at all. The reason for this anomaly was only revealed much later in the voyage. At this time, however I could not come up with an answer except to carry on for another day and see if the situation improved.

The following noon indicated a little progress in the right direction but still very unsatisfactory. Obviously this point of sail was not suitable for getting us to Panama, or anywhere else for that matter, as the trend of the coast would increasingly bear towards the east and bring the wind ahead even more.

It didn't take me long to come to an alternative decision. In fact, under the circumstances the only way to go was to put the wind on the beam again and the best point of sail, head south until I met the Southeast trades from the southern hemisphere which, when they cross the equator, blow from a southwest direction. This would entail a much greater distance to travel because with the coast tending away to the southeast and the boat travelling towards the south, the distance between us and Panama was getting wider. The way I saw it there was no alternative, unless I was prepared to doodle about here hopelessly trying to close the coast. The other positive thought was that I could cross the Inter Tropical Converge Zone sooner and faster. The ITCZ is the area between the two trade winds and much influenced by squalls and heavy rainfall. So I then set the course to the south and with my spirits lifted the boat heeled on a port tack picking up speed.

Not all was a bed of roses though. A problem had developed with the cigar lighter purchased in the Cabo; this it turned out was defunct. This was an important piece of equipment as it was this that the inverter plugged into to charge the lap-top. As the laptop was redundant due to the satellite phone being ashore it was no problem in this respect. However, the electric shaver also plugged in to this receptacle to be charged, and with this being redundant my beard would inevitably develop. Facial hair is not considered desirable in my case and I was not keen on developing a full set of hair on my face, not for vanity, but rather for the feel of it. When looking in the mirror I would have the uncanny feeling of looking at another being staring through a hedge, not a desirable state of affairs but, alas, one to be borne under the circumstances.

The next day the wind died sufficiently for me to get the genoa down to make repairs to the tears that had appeared over the last few days. The sailors duct tape that had been applied in the Cabo had not held so the morning was spent stitching a patch over this particular area, and folding and stitching a patch over the leach. It was quite a nice interlude sitting out in the sunshine doing the needlework and taking on a tan. As it turned out this interlude didn't last, as the wind started to pick up before the jobs were completed, and so the sail went up again with the resolve on my part to return to playing the seamstress during the next lull. I was thankful that during the period between the first tear and when it had been possible to make a repair there had not been anything alarming like a violent ripping of the sail, just tears that caused some concern but which held.

The gloriously sunny weather lasted for some days more, a time of relaxation which I enjoyed principally because it was not necessary to wear much in the way of clothing. Even the wind was warm, so I wore just a pair of underpants, and why even this limited clothing one might ask? After all there was no-one to be bothered by my nakedness should I be so. But one should preserve some sort of decorum I suppose. This state of affairs sure saved on the laundry.

All good things must come to an end though, and before many days had passed the sky clouded over and darkened ominously. Rain appeared towards the eastern horizon and the wind rose to twenty-five knots. This was a sure indication that ITCZ was nigh. As evening was coming on and in anticipation of squalls arriving during the night and, being reluctant to fight with the sails in the dark, I doubled reefed the mainsail and reduced the genoa to a third of its area.

In the planning stage for this voyage, amongst the many preparations that I made for this, that, and the other, a plastic sheet with a spout stuck in the middle had been fabricated. This rig was to be arranged to collect rain water and direct it via the spout into the water tanks. In preparation for catching the approaching rain this plastic sheet I secured in position with the spout inserted into the filler pipe to the water tanks. The filler cap was on the side deck between the rails and the cabin top. Alas, this proved to be impracticable as the wind got under the plastic sheet, ejecting the spout from the filler pipe. So to Plan B: the sheet was moved into the cockpit, spread out with fastenings secured to the rails on either side of the boat. The spout was now in a bucket. This too wasn't entirely satisfactory as the spout wouldn't stay in the bucket with the wind flapping the sheet about. As a variation on Plan B, I filled a plastic bottle with water and placed it in the sheet to hold it in place. This proved admirable for the purpose. The spout stayed in the bucket.

And so the rains came with the squalls, intermittently as squalls do, and flashes of lightning were followed by the crash of thunder. This heavenly display made for a diversion of sorts: with each flash I counted the seconds before the thunder gave the distance from the lightning. The closest lightning flash was twenty miles away which perversely gave me a feeling of disappointment as a flash of lightning immediately followed by a deafening crash of thunder usually gives me a mental jump and an adrenalin surge. My, but what one will do for kicks?

The bucket that collected the rain water which when sufficiently full was transferred to the water tanks gave me alternative entertainment during an otherwise, apart from the heavenly displays, quiet evening. Unfortunately there was an uncalled for side effect to this manna from heaven. The working of the boat in the waves had opened cracks between dissimilar materials, i.e. the wooden window frame and the fibreglass coaming, thus causing leaks. With the wind driving the rain through what must have been just small apertures, this ingress of water ran down behind the settee back to accumulate on the seat, soaking the cushions. As the leaks were small they took quite some time to create puddles. I placed the cushions on their edge, and mopped the puddles, and waited for the rain to cease, which it did, as is the case with squally weather. Then it blew again bringing more rain, with the gust at times reaching forty knots. How pleased I was with having the foresight to reef down the sails before these gusts made life difficult. What with the window leaks and my tramping water in from outside after checking for shipping and such during the lulls, the cabin became quite damp. Apart from these nuisances the boat was making good progress, and I comforted myself with the thought that it wouldn't last forever. As the days passed though, the noise of the wind and the lashing of the rain on the windows, and the leaks, and the mopping up, became quite tiresome. Ennui crept in too, and under such depressing circumstance this wasn't unusual. One evening after the meal I was sitting listening to the Mozart's 21st Piano concerto, the 'Elvira Madigan,' the rain had eased off a little, and it occurred to me to get up and check around for any shipping. I debated whether to go out on deck or not; if anything was there I probably wouldn't see in the rain anyway. I decided stay where I was. Why go and get wet when it was much better to stay inside where it was damp. From this another train of thought developed: was it possible for a human to be affected by rising damp? Couldn't say that I'd heard of such a case. When I was an apprentice on cargo ships in the tropics it was not unknown to get athletes foot from sweating, but then that is a far cry from rising damp. I had to give an inward smile though at the thought of maybe getting athlete's foot of the butt. Such thoughts I considered to be the result of apathy and a tired mind and I wondering how much longer it would be before getting back into finer weather.

A few days later there was an occurrence that shook out any feelings of ennui and had me in a state of energetic alacrity. It happened during the afternoon: the rain had eased with only the odd shower during the morning and early afternoon, and the sun was shining spasmodically through the clouds, promising a passing of the squalls. I was relaxing in the cabin reading about Cortez doing his Conquistador thing in Mexico when my senses were directed to an increase of wind. The wind had been reasonably steady at twenty-five knots but with a glance at the wind indicator I saw the needle was showing gusting to thirty-five. At this wind speed the tops of the waves were being blown into a spray and the boat speed had increased also. The waves were about twelve feet which was no cause for alarm as they were running faster than the boat, which is how it should be. The problem that could develop, however, would be if the boat started to run faster than the waves. In such a situation when the boat went into the trough it could broach to and be swamped. This would be a most unpleasant situation to be in. The main sail was double reefed and the genoa reduced, but obviously this wasn't enough to slow the boat. The option that faced me was to impede progress sufficiently to keep the waves passing under the hull and moving faster. The recommended practice was to trail a drogue behind, thus arresting the forward motion. This I didn't have. Similarly, trailing a heavy line, the sea anchor rode would do but that would have to be manhandled back on board when more clement weather returned. The next option was to heave-to, an option under the present circumstances regarded to be the most favourable and the quickest. Another glance at the wind indicator showed the wind had increased to forty-five knots. In these situations as speed is of the essence but not so speedy as to take an unnecessary risk. Taking the time to don the safety harness I was soon on the coach top dropping the main sail and lightly lashing it to the boom. Back in the cockpit the wheel was put hard over to bring the boat's head into the wind. Nothing happened with this manoeuvre, the boat just kept on going ahead. In the matter of only a few minutes I was in the cabin firing the engine, then back to the cockpit to engage the gears to bring the boat around. Well, imagine my surprise. The boat had turned itself around during my absence and was riding the waves with the sea on the port bow where it should be. After all the frantic energy expended, not to mention the adrenaline surge, I was gobsmacked that the boat had first refused my efforts, then gone and done what was required. Does this boat have a will all of its own? Considering the other occasions when it had tried to make for Hawaii, I couldn't help but consider that possibility. Having said all that I must admit to a profound exhilaration while on the coach top securing the main sail. The boat had skidded and sheared in the following seas, the full force of the spray whipped off the wave tops to sting my skin, the scudding clouds and the warm sunshine all contributed to my elation.

After this expenditure of energy and mental gymnastics the wind dropped back to twenty-five knots. A state of affairs I was not about to act on immediately, first a cup of tea and waited to see which way the cat would jump. After half an hour the wind had settled and I resumed progress towards the south.

During the unpleasant interlude of the ITCZ yet another event happened to mar the pleasures of boating. As is my wont the engine was run for an hour every third day to top up the batteries; the solar panel didn't seem to have any effect in this line of work. On the last attempt to fire the engine nothing happened except for a grating noise. At this I deduced that the cranking battery was flat. On checking this battery and the four house batteries with the hydrometer all showed a full charge, and yet the electric panel volt meter indicated less than nine volts. This was indeed a puzzle compounded by the fact that when it comes to understanding the mysteries of electricity my knowledge is basic indeed. This was of great concern; apart from not being able to charge the batteries there was the problem of not motoring into the anchorage at Panama. But that was sometime in the future and now I had to try and find a possible fault between the batteries and the panel. If this could be solved then maybe the engine would fire. But, niggling at the back of my mind was that the fault might lie in the batteries being duff. After doing all that my limited experience would allow I had to admit that from now on until expert help was available it would be a case of conserving what electrical energy remained.

And so the days passed. In time the ITCZ was crossed and the squalls and gusting winds and the rain were behind. The cushions from the settee were dragged out into the sunshine to dry, and the forward hatch opened up to allow a flow of air to pass through the cabin, hopefully to dry it out. The wind had eased considerably and the reefs were taken out of the sails. The genoa had suffered a little more and the mainsail had also torn. The ties on the reef points had ripped down the sail only to be stopped by the battens. The three tears were only six inches in length so nothing serious there and they couldn't go any further. On the luff of the mainsail are slides that fit into a track on the mast to keep the sail tight against the mast. Several of these slides had broken and it was with not a little dismay that the luff now had bellied out in places, allowing the wind to pass with a resultant loss of efficiency. The redeeming feature of this problem, if one could call it that, was that the broken slides could be replaced by redistributing the good ones to more strategic positions. To do this the sail only had to be lowered without taking it right off the mast to do the change over, as is the case with the foresail when making repairs.

The return of the sunshine and fair winds compensated immensely for the previous unpleasant weather conditions and, with a lifting of the spirit I anticipated reaching the south-west trade winds. All thoughts of the past boisterous weather were gone. It was at this time that I was joined by several boobies, the feathered kind. For the most part they settled down in a raft to ride the waves when night came on, but some squabbled and fought each other for a perch on the forward rails of the pulpit. One particularly cheeky character found a perch on the aft rails and stayed there for days keeping in tune with the rolling of the boat. How this was possible eluded me for the rail was smooth and the bird had webbed feet, but he did, and made this balancing act look easy. These birds are about eighteen inches in length with brown feathers. The area around the eyes is purple, and the eyes stare unafraid. The beak gives the impression of the nose on Pinocchio after telling a few lies. A most interesting bird which never moved from its position on the rail even when I passed close enough to poke him. Not that I did for he was far too cute to frighten off, and company of a sort, the first thing to look for when I came on deck.

In the fullness of time I reached the trade winds and put the boat on a course for Panama. I had previously directed the course to the south so the distance to Panama had been greatly increased.

Good sailing weather was anticipated but, with a distance of sixteen hundred miles to go would take some time, adding considerably to the length of the voyage. And what of the friends who would be expecting my arrival on the announced twenty-one days? There was no way to contact them to abandon the idea of joining the boat for the transit, which became one more worry. And I hated to think what they would be thinking: stuck in Panama on an enforced holiday not knowing what had happened, whether I was dead or alive. All I could hope for was that, having no contact, they would not even start out.

There was one bonus to put on the list and that was we were now south of ten degrees north latitude which meant there would be no tropical storms to worry about. These monsters, thankfully, do not operate in the band of ten north and ten south latitudes.

The trade winds, for the most part, remained constant with the occasion lulls that allowed the foresail to be taken down and repairs attempted. The genoa had suffered during the squally weather and was now in a most parlous state with the leach torn away from the rest of the sail. The sail had also torn part of the way along the bottom edge of two of the seams. Despite this, the sail still held together and was pulling the boat along efficiently, considering the injuries it had suffered. The sail-makers duct tape had long since come away and disappeared, suggesting the stuff had no meaningful repair qualities. Household duct tape had been tried on the last attempt at repair and that too had come away and was flapping around in the wind like a demented crow. The patch that had been sewn on was holding out magnificently but the sail was showing signs of coming apart around it. In the time allowed between the winds picking up again I attempted to repair the seams which were coming apart. And, also, to stop any further progression of the tears I stitched across the seam. This particular lull lasted about two hours before the winds picked up again. Well satisfied with the effort and keeping a watchful eye on the sails behaviour I progressed eastwards, with the boat rolling easily in the swell.

Just after dark I sighted the bright lights of a fishing boat on the starboard quarter. At this time the wind had eased again and my boat was not making much forward motion above keeping steerage way. I deduced from his speed and direction that he was laying the long nets that have been the subject of so much controversy during the past few years. These nets are made with indestructible monofilament which catches anything and everything. The fishermen claim that they are fishing for squid only but, can they claim this to be true. Any other species of marine life is also in danger of getting caught up in these nets and unable to free themselves, die. There have been reports of nets, which are miles in length, breaking free and becoming so loaded with dead marine life that they sink, and when the catch has rotted away they rise to the surface again to carry on trapping. And so the process is repeated, and as the monofilament is indestructible it can go on ad infinitum, a truly terrible example of man's greed and indifference to the creatures of the ocean.

While I pondered these problems the fish boat gradually reduced the distance between us and was getting quite close. Something happened to my thought processes at this juncture, which I'm hard pressed to explain for I went below to put on a pair of shorts. No doubt I thought that if he was to bump into my boat I'd better be presentable. A crazy idea, even in the subconscious, but I had been on my own for some time so it should be allowed that a lapse in sanity could happen under these circumstances. However, he moved off across my stern and stopped some distance away, while my leisurely pace to the east increased the distance between us and I could take off my shorts again.

During the course of the following week all power from the batteries died. This was a nuisance for quite a few reasons. There was no readout from the instruments; no GPS, wind speed, and no gyro compass. Without power the bilge pump wouldn't work and to empty the bilges which were making quite a lot of water at this time I had to resort to the hand pump. No problems there, at least for the next few days until that also quit operating. On investigating and taking out the suction hose I discovered a hole allowing air to be sucked in with the result that the bilge water was not being lifted. The application of that most wonderful duct tape soon had the fault repaired and the bilges kept low, at least for a few more days when the pump acted up again with no evidence of a hose leak. It was then a matter of baling the bilge with a saucepan, transferring the water into a bucket, and then emptying this into the kitchen sink. Wherever the leak came from it got progressively worse as we headed to our distant destination, and before long the bilge was being baled three times a day. The water didn't at any time come over the floor boards but it was close. The leak from the rudder seal had been inspected closely since leaving the Cabo but there wasn't enough leakage to justify the amount of water entering the boat. So it where did it come from? There was nothing to do but keep baling until I arrived in Panama and the services of a haul out would hopefully reveal all.

It so happened that in planning this trip I'd had the foresight to buy a hand held GPS. If this had not been so I wouldn't have known where I was on this planet. Just head east by magnetic compass until land was sighted, I suppose. Ah! The joys of boating are not experienced by many. One must admire the early explorers who just wandered about the oceans looking for new discoveries not knowing what they would find. Not to mention the shipboard diseases. At least I wouldn't get scurvy.

There wasn't much that went wrong after this. But then there wasn't much else that could. Just the solar shower disappearing one night. This had been sitting on the coach top between the hatch coaming and the grab rail. Quite difficult one would imagine for a bag of water to escape from these restraints. But it did. No doubt a free surface effect had been set up inside the bag with the boat rolling in the swell and working itself over the grab rail and, plop, over the side it went. At least that is what I surmised. A loss but not critical, as there was always a bucket to get an overall body wash from. To be quite honest I should have anticipated this happening because on a previous occasion I placed a four litre bag of wine on the kitchen counter only to have it plunge to the deck and burst open when the boat rolled. A different situation and conditions, maybe, but one should learn I suppose.

The loss that was felt more critically though was the flashlights. These had been bought as a set of four. Bright yellow they were and of varying sizes, from big chunky to pencil size. One by one they gave up the ghost, for what reason I never did fathom. Occasionally, by giving them a good shaking, a glimmer would appear then give up again. The batteries were up to snuff so that wasn't the problem which was just as well. During the pre-voyage shopping spare batteries I had purchased in quantity. Alas, these had suffered from the all pervading damp and became quite useless. This loss of flashlights was particularly annoying as this was the only means there was of checking the compass course on a dark night. All these little anomalies paled into significance though when the self lighting picot for the stove failed, no doubt due to the dampness. That in itself was not critical as there was always the BBQ lighter, at least until that fell apart. Even then, as I had by now developed resilience to all these petty happenings, all was not lost. Ha! Ha! I said to myself there is one more means of lighting the stove. And, I must say here that this wasn't going to beat me, no way was I going to do without a cup of tea. There was an alternative should the stove be out of action as there was an electric kettle and the generator. But more of that later. Having planned well ahead for lighting the stove,

a box of matches had been put on board in a watertight plastic
container. Carefully opening the box and taking out a match and
placing the box on the counter, as lighting the stove is a two handed
affair, one hand to press and hold in the knob for a few seconds the
other to light the gas, I successfully lit the match. Just as the flame
was approaching the gas, the boat took a violent roll, putting me off
balance and causing me to drop the match, and would you believe
because of this wave action the box of matches was thrown into the
sink. At this I must admit to a small gesture of despair by throwing
my hands up and crying out, 'Why me Lord?'

There was no answer from above. But, I had a few
derogatory thoughts on the subject. Why ask anyway? The Lord
moves in mysterious ways, and in my case, with violent movement
of the waves.

However, all was still not lost. Maybe the propane stove
was out of commission until something brilliant came to mind about
the problem of lighting the gas. In the meantime there was still the
portable generator and not only an electric kettle but, and this is
were forethought brought its rewards, an electric frying pan,
purchased at the great expense of two dollars at the local thrift store.
These then were put to use to prepare that nights dinner. The clouds
of black, smelly smoke that emitted from the fry pan thermostat were
a little alarming, probably the damp again, and although the
thermostat didn't work, I cooked a reasonable dinner of stew.

These items were put to good use for the next couple of
days, the frying pan to cook dinner, fried rice with peas and carrots
being the meal of choice for this were the most suitable for this type
of cooking utensil. And, although the thermostat did not work it had
stopped smoking. The kettle boiled the water for the ubiquitous tea,
a beverage that one cannot live without. Using the generator for
these tasks was all very well in an emergency such as this but, the
propane stove should be handling the cooking and, should the fuel
supply for the generator run out I would be in a right pickle. Apart
from any other consideration the stove provided more scope with
four burners and a capacious oven. After mulling over the problem
for a day or two the bright idea then struck me about how to light
the propane. Why didn't I think of that before? Dragging out one of
the batteries from below and baring the ends of two lengths of
electrical wire, I attached one length to the positive side of the
battery and the other length of wire to the negative side. Striking one
wire against the other produced a spark of sufficient intensity to
light the gas. Eureka! The manoeuvre though called for a little
contortion as two hands were needed to strike a spark and a knee to

hold in the stove knob. With a little practice balancing on one leg against the roll I found this manoeuvre to be eminently successful. We were back in the cooking business. A mental pat on the back for this act of inventiveness was duly applied.

The sin of pride it seems carries a penalty, for having proudly cooked and eaten the first meal on the regenerated stove I went out on deck for a bucket of sea water for washing the dirty pots, when the boat took a heavy roll. The mainsail boom swung over causing the sheets to catch me unawares. Off balance I was thrown violently against the coaming. Obviously the wind was not strong enough to create sufficient pressure on the sail to resist the force of that particular wave. The pain this caused in my lower back was such that I didn't dare move. I just sat still wondering if anything was broken or any organs damaged. Well, I couldn't stay in this position forever, so easing off the coaming and gritting my teeth against the pain I managed to get below onto a more comfortable seat. Although it hurt like the blazes I came to the conclusion that nothing was broken. Why not was a puzzle, from the force with which my back met the coaming would suggest that something would have to give, but thankfully that this wasn't the case. The result of all the milk I drank as a child building strong bones! Unless of course as they say that Yorkshire men are, 'strong in the back, and thick in the head.' Whatever, this incident had me taking pain killers, something that I had almost never done. Funny though, how a situation like this can bring to mind an amusing anecdote. On this occasion it was when I was at the chemists having a prescription filled for pain killers, foresight again. There was a bit of banter going on between the chemist and me, with me claiming not to take pills but rather put up with pain because of a high pain threshold. There is no bragging element to this statement; it is just that taking pills of any sort goes against my principle of not wanting to become reliant on them. This conversation was being avidly followed by the girl assistant and the Chemist became impatient with my attitude and told me with some asperity that the pills would be needed if I got toothache.

"I don't get toothache," I stated.

"Everybody gets toothache," said the chemist with a hint of exasperation.

As she had her back to me, and the conversation was threatening to get out of hand, I just clacked my dentures at the assistant. We both had great difficulty keeping straight faces at this.

Sometimes the devil gets into me.

Now these painkillers came in handy and I silently conceded the argument to the chemist.

Over the next few days the weather remained constant and the boat required only a little sail handling. When this chore did have to be dealt with, it required gritted teeth and very careful movements. Time heals all things, as they say, and in due course apart from the occasional muscle pull which brought on an involuntary, 'Aaagh', life progressed. After a few days I gave up the painkillers as it occurred to me that when I took them the pain would become subdued, then when the affect of the pills wore off the pain seemed to be worse. There was nothing for it but to take careful movements and grin and bear the discomfort.

When the land came into view towards evening some days later, my pleasure can well be appreciated. It had been a very long time since I had sighted land. The boobies though had departed; I had become used to having them around as they had been company of sorts. A cheery, 'Good Morning,' when I came to the cockpit at daylight to the bird on the cockpit rail never met with any response, only a blank stare from the beady eyes. Well, they had gone now and I silently wished them well. Possibly they would meet up with another boat and provide company there.

The speed of the boat being as it was we soon came abeam of Punta Mariato, the headland at the southwest corner of the Peninsula de Aguero, and only one hundred and fifty miles from our destination. The end of the journey would soon be in my grasp.

Oh, dear! Will I never learn not to look forward in naïve anticipation?

*

Several ships were sighted closer to the shore, more than likely having transited the Canal and heading out into the Pacific. These observations prompted my decision to continue my present course and keep the distance off the coast and the shipping until abeam of Cabo Mala on the southeast corner of the Peninsula de Aguero, when a course change to the north into the Gulf of Panama could be safely carried out and be clear of the traffic from the Canal.

Through the morning and into the afternoon I made progress at a reasonable speed eating up the miles to Cabo Mala, then to make sure that the big boys wouldn't get in the way, directed the course a little to west of north. This alteration would also bring the coast in a better position for viewing. After all the time spent on the trip down from the Cabo San Lucas just having the ocean to look at, a change of scenery was most certainly the order of the day. Not only was there the dense jungle to admire, there was the added bonus of examining all the rubbish floating by. The amount of flotsam drifting in the Gulf of Panama was something to behold. Had there been a fast flowing river in the vicinity that brought down trees and other rubbish from the interior, then this would have been understood. But, this rubbish was man-made, mainly: plastic bottles, plastic bags, plastic milk containers and cartons of varying sizes, and much to my amusement, a condom heading west. At least that was the way it was pointing. It would seem that not everyone in this Catholic country followed the dictates of the Pope regarding birth control. He obviously doesn't advocate recycling either.

By mid afternoon the wind died to nothing, not a breath. It was as though the boat was sitting in a sheet of glass. Well, with no engine there was nothing else to do but wait it out until a breeze picked up again. The vagaries of the wind in the Gulf of Panama are well documented so I was prepared for a wait, or not, and trusted to whatever. If lucky the wind would pick up again with an evening sea breeze.

That evening, just after sunset, there was a slight breeze, and we were moving, at not more than a drift, but at least there was movement and in the right direction. This gave the boat steerage so it was possible to direct the boat, which was a blessing indeed as it took a direction between a headland and a small islet, then passed close to an outcrop of rocks, which now had a low swell breaking over them. As the sea was generally calm I took this wave action to be a result of ships' wakes. Needless to say, with our movement no more than a drift I watched these rocks with no little apprehension until we had safely drifted by. Even though it was very dark by this time there was enough light from the shore buildings to make out the white of the breaking surf.

At this time of day it appeared that the locals chose to do their fishing, not commercial, but rather a couple of guys in a small boat with bright lanterns, no doubt to attract the fish. What surprised me while sitting on the aft lockers with my feet on the wheel steering the boat was that there was no recognition of my being there even though at times they came close enough to be almost touching. I'm sure if I had said, 'Boo', they would have jumped, so engrossed they were in their activities. Although I had no power for navigation lights, it was a bright tropical night, the clouds having gone to allow the stars to come out, and therefore I was not exactly invisible. It was getting on for midnight before I reached open water and all the other boats had left. Even the little breeze had died away and we were stopped again, so I felt secure enough to lie down and get some rest. Through the remainder of the night it was a case of coming awake at more frequent intervals than out in the ocean, for after all there was no possibility of sound sleep under these conditions.

Daylight comes fast and early in these latitudes so I was soon able to assess the situation. Although there was no breeze to speak of there was a slight movement of the boat parallel to the shore over which I had no control. At this point the drift was close to another group of rocks below a lighthouse. This had me making plans about what to do if the boat struck. There would be no force to drive the boat onto the rocks, there being neither wind nor swell. So I hoped the boat might just bump and be pushed off again with the boathook. There was nothing to do but sit and wait for events to develop. If this situation called for abandonment it wasn't more than a short clamber up to the lighthouse, and maybe get help from there. My mind also mulled over what could be rescued under these circumstances, and I wondered what the reaction would be from the lighthouse keeper when a soaking wet sailor appeared at his door toting his goods and chattels. As it turned out none of this planning needed to be put into effect as the drift took the boat clear, very close but clear nonetheless, causing a relaxation of tension and my sigh of relief. This part of the voyage was fast becoming an experience garnished with much anxiety. Having cleared this particular potential hazard I continued to drift in the direction along the coast which presented a view of yet more outcrops. Another nasty situation seemed to be developing. Within the half hour though, a movement of air sufficient to lift the sails out of their torpor came off the land. Casting away all thoughts of keeping out of any potential ship running me down, I directed the boat away from the shore, thinking that at least ships can manoeuvre, rocks can't. The gods must have been looking out for me, for when I was at a safe distance off the shore the wind, or should I say air movement, died away again. And there the boat lay, drifting towards the ocean again. The next twenty-four hours set my progress back some ten miles. Then progress towards Panama for a while, then drifting back, then progress one way then the other across the Gulf. This went on for ten days just being at the mercy of nature, but thankfully I was in no danger from either rocks or ships. On the eleventh day that lovely southwest trade wind picked up again, blowing right into the Gulf. And off we went again as fast as the tatty sails would take us towards Panama. That evening put my position twelve miles from and in sight of the signal station on Flamenco Island at the entrance to the Canal. Then the wind died again leaving us drifting. Daylight comes quickly in these latitudes and so does darkness. And so it seemed did the local fish boats. These, and there were many of them apparently trolling, progressed up and down in procession on each side of me throughout the night. Working on the principle that they could see me on their radars, and were slow moving, should they bump me, it would bring me awake. I lay down to doze a little after midnight.

Well before sunrise the fish boats had departed, gone to wherever fish boats go after a night out. Now it was time to head towards the anchorage below the signal station. Having given some thought about how to make contact with the port to announce my arrival, I had brought the anchor battery from its place forward and connected it to the house circuits. This gave power to use the VHF radio, and thus contact with shore. Much to my pleasure this worked admirably and contact was made, loud and clear. Odd though, as on being directed to the anchorage, I was instructed to then go ashore and phone.

"Who should I phone?" said I. A reasonable question I thought.

"You will find out when you get ashore," came the answer.

This puzzled me, but then, when in Panama do as the Panamanians do. No doubt all will be revealed in the fullness of time. And true to form there was plenty of time.

There was only a light breeze, but the boat was moving in the right direction towards the anchorage below the signal station and to the east of the Canal approach channel. There were a great number of ships at anchor, but no ship movements that could be observed, so the slow speed of the boat would not be an impediment to them. With chronic lack of progress over the last days I couldn't help but think that my beard was growing faster than the progress of this odyssey.

The wind, breeze, air movement, whatever, died again and so drifting once again became the norm. Then a little puff, just to tease, then calm again. But, wonder of wonders progress, slow though it was gave a closing towards the destination.

After starting out at four this morning from the night's position until I came into the anchorage took twelve hours, a distance of three miles. But then the fates hadn't finished with me just yet. At the very moment that I was ready to go forward to drop the anchor a reasonably strong breeze sprung up, pushing the bow onto a heading away from the direction required to make the anchorage. From previous experience the bow would not come across the wind to take another course, and to put the wind on the opposite bow required a jibe manoeuvre, or in other words bring the wind across the stern. By the time this had been completed the boat had been blown out of the anchorage and into the approach channel to the Canal. The wind dropped and there I was were sitting becalmed waiting for another breeze. Feeling a little pissed off by how events had carried me out of the anchorage just when success was in my grasp, my attention was attracted by the sound of a ship's whistle giving five short rapid blasts indicating that danger loomed and I should vacate my position to somewhere safe. This ship had the right of way of course; after all it was the Panama Canal and he wanted to get to the locks. But then what could I do? Well I suppose I did what anyone else would do under the circumstances. I spread my arms aloft, hands outstretched in a gesture of helplessness. At this, much to my anxiety the ship increased speed and headed in my direction. Crikey! After all this time during the past weeks keeping clear of all shipping I was now to be run down only a matter of minutes from my goal. Life at this moment seemed to be vindictive. All that I could do was watch the relentless approach of this monster and gulp to keep my heart from choking my now dried out mouth.

The distance between us was closing rapidly, the ship bearing down in what I considered a most dangerous manner. Then a slight alteration of course took him to the other side of the channel and across my bow. As this wall of steel passed close enough to spit on I could see the rails were lined with crew expressing complete indifference to my predicament. The strangest thought came to me at this. A line from Albert and the Lion came to mind when I looked into the eyes of these people as if reading their thoughts: 'There weren't no shipwreck nor drownings, in fact nothing to laugh at all.' A strange thought but maybe I had been too long at this game? What really miffed me was that no one came from the bridge to see if they had missed or not. As I lay rocking in the wake of this ship I thought how callous of them. At least if someone had come out to check I would have waved in acknowledgement of his courtesy.

The vagaries of the wind being as they were in the Gulf of Panama they came up again and from the right direction to blow the boat slowly back into the anchorage and out of the way of any ship that might be using the channel. It was with a slump of the shoulders in a gesture of profound relaxation and relief that I had finally arrived and the anchor was down in a safe berth, albeit with tatty sails, mainsail tied to the mast with rope replacing the non-existent slides, no engine, batteries flat and this, that, and the other out of commission. The initial estimate of twenty-one days had stretched to

fifty-one which must be a record of sorts. The last one hundred and fifty miles took an incredible ten days
                    But, I was 'appy. I'd arrived.

CHAPTER FIVE

PANAMA

.......if you can wait and not be tired by waiting.

Kipling.'If'

So this was where Balboa waded into the sea and proclaimed the whole South Sea for Ferdinand, King of Spain. Vasco Nunez de Balboa (1475 to 1519), a Spanish colonist, conquistador and explorer, was the first European to see the eastern shore of the Pacific Ocean. It is also claimed to have been he who named this vast ocean, Pacifico, due to the calmness of the waters, although some say it was the Portuguese explorer Magellan who gave this name. My money would be on Balboa based on the assumption that the Gulf of Panama, which he was looking at, would be much more 'pacifico' than the waters off the Strait of Magellan, i.e. the Southern Ocean. Nevertheless, this proclamation opened up the whole western coast of South America to exploration and the conquest of Peru which provided vast wealth in gold and silver to the Spanish Treasury.

Although born into an impoverished noble Spanish family with little or no influence Balboa managed to aspire to Governor of Panama under an elderly nobleman, Pedro Arias de Avila. Avila was an extremely jealous man who resented the growing popularity and influence of Balboa with the Indians and local Spanish population. In 1518 Governor de Avila falsely accused Balboa of treason, speedily had him tried and sentenced him to death. On 21st January 1519, with four friends, Balboa was beheaded. Unlike de Avila, who has passed into obscurity, Balboa has been remembered. The Panamanian currency, shows his portrait although nowadays only in the small coins, the American dollar being the currency of choice, and the city at the southern end of the Canal, bears his name.

*

It was pleasant lying at anchor observing the activity on shore. The anchorage was just off the causeway that stretched from Balboa to Flamenco Island; although this was no longer an island as it was joined by the causeway to the mainland. During the building of the Panama Canal this island was a popular excursion and picnicking spot for the wives and families of the American engineers and executives working on the construction of the Canal. John Stevens, an American railroad engineer in charge of the construction, used the spoil from the diggings to create this causeway. Over the years various shops, restaurants, nightclubs and marinas have cropped up at various points along the roadway. This was a Saturday evening and it was interesting to see a procession of vehicles coming along the road, reaching the end, turning and heading back towards town. This I surmised must be an outing of sorts where the local populace drove out in the cool of the evening to take the sea air. It would seem that the tradition of going out to Flamenco Island was still alive but these days by road rather than by boat. One mode of transport that was plying the causeway was a vehicle that at first sighting gave me the impression of an awning with several people under it moving with no apparent means of propulsion. It became a lot clearer once I trained the binoculars in that direction. It reminded me of a horse drawn carriage from movies of the Old West: Paint Your Wagon comes to mind where one of these carriages was bringing in the ladies of pleasure to No Name City. The carriage in question was similar to these I observed this evening but lacking horse propulsion. The canopy was, open on all sides, and people were seated with their knees pumping. This phenomenon I observed more closely the following week while I was on the causeway and the knee pumping of four adults became clear. This was the means of propulsion: four bicycle pedal arrangements geared and linked to the back axle. The contraptions were a rental item to give pleasure to whoever wished to put in the effort to ride the causeway and view the surrounding waterside scenery, a neat idea, but hot work in this climate.

There were not many boats in the anchorage; one sailboat close by appeared to be the size of a rich man's play thing. I was later to learn that it was a hundred and ten feet in length and quite an impressive boat it was too. Judging by the activity on board it carried a crew; at least these people were observed to be active and not sitting around having sundowners or whatever it is rich folks do while on their gin palaces.

The evening was still, with not a breath of wind, but what's new, and it was most pleasant standing on the top step of the companionway leaning on the coaming just watching the activities of the people around and about. Restful one might say listening to the muted sounds of the traffic on the road and the bursts of laughter from the people. Not having seen people for so long it was a kind of companionship, but with the added pleasure of not having to make contact. A long time spent in one's own company makes one a bit of a recluse I guess.

It had been a long day and the anxieties, excitements and now the relaxation had made me weary and ready to turn in, happy in the knowledge that I could sleep the night through without the need to regularly check on any imminent dangers. Tomorrow would be soon enough to go ashore and make the phone call. At about this time loud music started up in the near distance which seemed to come from a group of buildings at the turn around below Flamenco Signal Station. So be it. There was no way this was going to interfere with my rest. With the hatch closed and the doors pulled to, the music faded to an undulating murmur, and in my weariness it was no bother at all.

*

True to expectations I had fallen asleep in record time on the settee, a habit I guess. The forward berth was available and ready for use with no need to get out in a hurry, but then old habits die hard. Had I taken the berth then there wouldn't have been the shock that met me on waking. It was still dark when I awoke but with bright lights shining through the windows. This gave me an initial fright as mentally I was still out on the ocean and these lights struck my mind as an approaching fish boat. Not for long though as I soon realised the lights were from floodlights on the shore. The adrenaline rush though had me rattled for a moment or two. The few hours of continuous sleep had been most refreshing and although it was too early to be active the remainder of the night was spent musing over cups of tea about what actions should be adopted to clear inwards. The first of these chores, after checking in over the telephone, would be to get a new battery to fire the engine, as I was still convinced that insufficient oomph! from the batteries was the cause of the problem.

It wasn't long before daylight came and the daily routine started. After breakfast I hauled out the dinghy and inflated it in preparation for going ashore. It was while I was doing this that a man in a kayak passed by. Without a break in his paddling he gave a cheery, "Good morning," and the advice to move to a safer anchorage away from the rocks. Should the wind get up from the north I was in a dangerous place. From my past experience with the wind, or lack of same, this advice seemed to be a bit over the top. However, I conceded to his better knowledge of the area and resolved if a wind came up I would so move. I told him this and the reasons why. With a wave he paddled on his merry way disappearing around the adjacent headland, leaving me to finish inflating the dinghy and put it over the side, ready to take me to the first dry land my feet had been on for some weeks.

Where to go to telephone my arrival was still a mystery. When I contacted the signal station again this didn't resolve anything and I was told that I would find out once on shore. Indifferent to say the least, I deduced the attitude to be, but, nothing ventured, nothing gained as they say. And so I row ashore to a landing on a shallow stone strewn beach and, with much difficulty, having to nurse my still painful back dragged the dinghy up the beach out of the reach of the rising tide. Well aware of my luck of the recent weeks, I took the extra precaution of tying the painter to a convenient bush. Belt and braces one might say. It would be most frustrating to return to see the only means of getting back to the boat disappearing over the horizon. Satisfied that all would be well I clambered up the low bank slipping and sliding on the loose surface to gain the top with the assistance of clumps of grass and undergrowth, then walked towards where habitation might be found.

On reflection, the row ashore and the effort of dragging the dinghy up the beach, having prompted this it seemed that my back pain had lasted more than was welcome. Surely in the time that had passed since the accident there should have been an improvement? The thought was dismissed just as quickly as it came; there wasn't any evidence of a broken rib or damage to the internal organs that I knew of. Therefore it must be bruising which, I hoped, would go away in time. The nuisance value was that I was unable to perform a task without a sudden relieving movement, and a, 'Bloody hell', to bring the task to an abrupt stop. This was particularly so when I hauled on a rope or worked a winch, which was a principal activity on a boat. I couldn't let these inconveniences be any deterrent to continuing the voyage though, so just grin and bear it was the order of the day.

There were buildings close by the landing, cleanly attractive in their newness, a short distance and across the road from where the traffic had been observed on the previous evening, These low two story buildings were spread out over a wide expanse separated by open gardens and parking spaces, empty of vehicles at this early hour, all looking as though recently built and pleasingly attractive to an eye used to staring at an empty ocean. The restaurants and shops housed in these buildings gave the impression that this was a resort of sorts. There were a few people about, service staff no doubt, cleaning up after the previous nights reveries, and it was to these that I made my way. After accosting a person or two who seemed that they might help I finally found someone who spoke English, and he very kindly walked with me across a parking lot to a building and pointing through the glass fronted entrance gave directions up a flight of stairs to the Port Captain's office situated on the first floor. At this level a balcony formed three sides of the building above the entrance hall. Looking across to the far side and behind a glass fronted office I noticed two men in conversation. One was seated behind a desk, the other in a chair at one end. It was to this place that I made my way, hoping to gain some information about becoming a legal visitor.

Luck was on my side; the notice on the door stated that this was the office of the Port Captain, and even though it was Sunday the Port Captain was in residence. However, over the period that I was to stay in Panama I came to realise that the gentleman that occupied this office was not actually the Port Captain. Such a luminary was to be found in the main offices in Balboa. But of course I was not to know this at the time. Justino, as I came to know him, was more of an assistant who attended to the business of clearing vessels inwards that visited the Flamenco Marina and Resort. This place, situated at the end of the causeway was where five weeks would be taken out of my voyage, not that I realised this at the time. I was still planning on just hauling the boat getting the sails repaired, having the batteries checked or replaced as necessary, and transiting to the Atlantic side.

In time as my acquaintance with Justino developed I came to realise what a nice helpful man he was. He showed a mixture of shyness and kindness, deferential almost, which from my past experience with officialdom was an odd combination. These qualities were evident because the help he gave was far beyond the parameters one would expect of his job description.

As I entered his office and approached his desk he stood up and smiling, held out his hand. The handshake was firm and friendly which was comforting as all too often, when a handshake is soft and limp this is sure sign that the giver is indifferent to the receiver, and so speaks volumes regarding his approachability. The second man who had been seated at the end of the desk stood to be introduced as the Port Health Inspector, and speaking in Spanish to Justino, nodded and smiled to me. He then took his leave, slinging the strap of a canvas satchel over his shoulder.

Taking the proffered chair. I said, "My boat is anchored," indicating with a wave of a hand in the general direction of where it was. "I arrived yesterday evening from Cabo San Lucas." Then I placed the clearance from the Cabo on his desk.

"Si!" he acknowledged and nodded.

"I wish to clear Inwards," I said, a little nonplussed at what seemed to be his indifference. But then, as I was to learn, in Panama one takes a languid approach to life's tasks. He only appeared to be indifferent. It was an adopted macho attitude which one often meets in dealing with the male population of Panama.

"Also," I said, leaning forward in the hope that this move would demonstrate my seriousness, "I need to haul the boat. You know, take it out of the water."

"Si!" He nodded again.

I waited.

"Come," he said. "We go your boat, then immigration." After gathering the papers he handed them back to me.

Ah! A sign of progress, I thought, but I was curious about the procedure. Nothing ventured? When in Panama do as the Panamanians do.

So it was then that we left the building and headed across the parking lot. Not to his car or in the direction of the boat, as one would think, but after skirting another building the marina boatyard was before us. It was a most impressive sight which filled me with pleasure for the boat could be hauled out here and I would not have to go to the trouble of trying to sail along the shipping channel to Balboa. As we approached the marina office building a gentleman driving a golf cart came up and stopped, got out, then moved to go into the office. Justino hailed this gentleman in Spanish, and he came over.

"Buenos dios."

"Buenos dios," said Justino, and then spoke again at length as though explaining something important. In my ignorance of Spanish I could only speculate what it was about.

The new arrival, a man of medium height with thinning light brown hair and moustache, turned and addressed me in perfect English, accented with an American inflection.

"You want to haul your boat?"

"Why, yes, if that is possible," I said politely and greatly pleased at such a prompt response to my problems and with no struggling to make someone understand. Then noticing the name tag inscription, 'John Cole, Director,' I deduced he actually was an American.

"It won't be until tomorrow. I don't have a crew today with it being Sunday."

"That's fine," I said. "But I don't have any power, the engine quit on me."

"No problem, I'll send a tow." After a short pause, he announced, "It will be a dollar fifty a foot, a day. Ten dollars for water and electricity."

I nodded acceptance. 'Forty feet means, sixty dollars a day, plus ten.' I'm no slouch when it comes to sums. Especially when I have to pay.

"Do you have a sail maker in the yard?" I asked, as he was climbing back into the golf cart.

"No, but I can call one in if you want."

"Sure, thank you."

Then as an afterthought, he added, "We're quite a new facility and don't have our own trades here. In time maybe, but not at the moment." Then reflecting as though he had forgotten what he had come for he got out of the golf cart and walked to the office.

"The tow will be for you at eight tomorrow," he called over his shoulder.

"Lovely. I'll be ready." I was much relieved at the way the boat's problems were being addressed with such ease.

He walked away with what appeared to be a sense of urgency towards the office. During my time here Mr. Cole was the only person I met who showed any sense of urgency, but then he wasn't Panamanian.

Justino and I then proceeded to the beach.

Launching the dinghy again became a painful exercise. Justino in his willingness to help would enthusiastically pull on one side, while I was holding on to the other trying to favour my back and having acute pain with each movement. Eventually, after many instructions to him to take it easy and not pull against me, we managed to get the dinghy into the water and rowed out to the boat.

"Coffee?" I asked when he was seated, waving the kettle to emphasise the question.

"Si."

I wondered if our conversation would progress beyond this one word. Up to now communication had been conducted by gestures and English from me and not much more than the one word, "Si" from him. Not to worry though, we were making progress with the clearing inwards.

While waiting for the kettle to boil, Justino busied himself with the paperwork. Then curious, sipping the coffee, I wondered why he was so quiet and spare with his words. After all he was reading the forms that were written in English without too much trouble.

"You said we would go to the Immigration," I stated.

"Si."

"Would it be possible for me to send an e-mail? You know, internet."

"Si."

Flush with success at this communication lark I added, "I also require a battery," I might as well make the most of his largesse.

"Si, no problem," he answered, smiling.

Well, he may not speak English, but he certainly understands the language, I thought with relief. Therefore it wasn't going to be too difficult to get my requests across the language barrier.

Inward clearance now issued, coffee drunk and passport tucked safely into a shirt pocket, we made our way back to shore, dragging the dinghy back over the stones of the beach to a secure mooring once again to the shrub, but it was not without much gritting of teeth, and admonishments against Justino's painful enthusiasm. The word sorry or its Spanish equivalent doesn't seem to be used much. Justino just gave a surprised look and an acknowledgement of, "Ah! Si." Until the next time.

The journey to Balboa in Justino's tired old car was a revelation. The way it would cough and splutter had me wondering whether we would make it to immigration but it did. The route took the full length of the causeway, some two miles, before we came into the city of Balboa, a community built by the American engineers to house their Canal workers. Fine, clean houses they were too with large overhanging roofs to shed the tropical downpours. There is little American presence now that the Panamanians are taking over responsibility for the Canal and these residences looked unused, I found this a little odd as the buildings and grounds seemed well maintained and I wondered why they weren't occupied.

The visit to Immigration didn't take long. A stamp in my Passport and we were on our way. By this time I had given all direction over to Justino. I just contented myself to being driven around Balboa and out to a place called Albrook which proved to be a new and vast complex of railway station, bus terminal, food stores, shopping mall and joy upon joy, an internet location. Bless you, Justino, you are a kind man. Under the circumstances I didn't think it to fair to keep my Guardian Angel hanging about so it was sufficient for me to just send a quick message to let the folks back home know that I had arrived and was safe. A more detailed announcement could be sent when more private time was available. The shortness of this visit at least prompted a response from Justino that proved that he could speak English.

"You were only two minutes," he announced, surprised.

A little taken aback, but pleased that communication was possible between us I contented myself with just explaining that the recipients would know that I was safe.

Outside the noise of the traffic was deafening. The road through the complex between the terminal and the buildings on the other side was roofed over causing the traffic roar to be amplified. Background noise from the roaring busses added to this maelstrom of noise. Everywhere there were people, crowds moving every which way. With the volume of traffic and the crowds of people all wanting the right of way it was easy to understand why the police controlled the pedestrian crossing. There was no doubt without some control mayhem would have ensued. I've never seen such a surging mass of humanity, or so it seemed after my recent solo existence.

I had explained to Justino that a battery was required so that the engine could be fired. So it was into the superstore that we directed ourselves. This place was a veritable Aladdin's cave. There seemed to be everything that one would wish for contained under one roof. But, it was lunch time and I was hungry. So minding the adage not to go shopping when hungry we repaired to the Deli before embarking on a shopping spree.

"What would you like, Justino?" I asked viewing the menu board.

This question only seemed to cause embarrassment as Justino just waved his hands around in refusal. "Ah! No, no," he said.

"But you must eat something," I said, surprised at his response.

"OK! Maybe the fruit salad," he answered, rather reluctantly I thought, and I hoped this wasn't going to be a contest between us on the subject of food.

It didn't seem much to me but, if that is what he wanted then so be it. I let him order for both of us. After all he had the language. What I had asked for turned out to be a sandwich far larger than I'd anticipated, so half was offered to Justino. At first he refused, but after my insistence that it was more than I could manage, he accepted. Was I being introduced to Latin American politeness? Justino had no qualms about sharing this feast once the courtesies had been observed while I, reflecting on his meagre fruit salad, felt better for the sharing.

Apart from purchasing a battery the advantage of being in such a store, prompted me to stock up on grocery items. One purchase that filled me with joy was my favourite scotch, Famous Grouse. Not only did they stock such a treasure, a free scotch glass was part of the promotion. No doubt I was going to have a good selection of scotch glasses by the time I left Panama.

Returning to the marina Justino insisted on helping get the groceries on board which I found to be a very kind gesture and felt for all the trouble he had gone to on my behalf he should have some remuneration.

But first there was the battery to connect up and the engine to run. If this could be accomplished then there would be no need for a tow to the boatyard. Much to my chagrin nothing happened. Nada, (Spanish creeping in now; must be the climate). Dead as a dodo. Now what? Checking the battery connections didn't change the situation. Obviously, something beyond my limited knowledge of things mechanical was the problem. As there was Justino to ferry ashore I might just as well seek out John Cole and order a mechanic. If I wished to transit the Canal in the near future then expediting the repairs was of the essence.

This was explained to Justino.

"Si!" nodding his head in agreement. "Bueno."

"Can I give you something for your trouble, Justino?" as I took out my wallet mindful of his assistance in matters grocery.

"No, no, no problemo," he said, waving his hands again in refusal.

It seemed to me that this performance had a familiar ring to it. Although it has to be admitted that Justino was a different kettle of fish to the gentleman in the Cabo, this initial refusal to accept remuneration for being helpful can only be construed as Latin good manners.

"Come now, I must give you something for all that you have done," I said as I opened my wallet.

After a moments hesitation, with again the hand gesture, and obvious embarrassment he suggested, "Ten dollars, okay?"

That was a small sum to pay for his attention to my welfare bearing in mind had he not taken me to the Immigration and shopping I would have been at a loss what to do or where to go, but, if that is what he wanted who am I to complain?

"Please, don't tell the taxi drivers," he asked with concern.

His request was understandable when one comes to think about it.

"Si," I said with a grin. Cheeky, I suppose, but the urge to reply in his language was irresistible.

*

John Cole I tracked down in the eatery cum bar on the corner across from his office eating a pizza. As the weather had turned hot and humid and the Bar was air-conditioned it made sense to sit with him for a while and have a beer. The beer was very cold but also very thin without much strength to it, a disappointment after being so long without. A buzz to satisfy the senses would have been welcome. John promised to arrange for a mechanic for the next day and as he was ready to go home we parted and went our separate ways.

This busy day was not over yet though for when I left the Bar the Port Health Inspector was waiting and wanted to go on board the boat for an inspection. So once again into the breech, so to speak. This dinghy launching and rowing people out to the boat was proving to be something of a behaviour pattern, and let's not forget the back pains from the effort.

Senor Health Inspector was a different personality from Justino. Where Justino was deferential in his dealings, Senor Health was only interested in completing the formalities with no distraction, not even a cup of coffee. The paperwork was completed in no time at all, and then came the questions and instruction.

"Have you any animals on board?" he asked in English.

"Only myself," I answered smiling, introducing a moment of levity, and unable to resist a tease at his seriousness.

He only looked blank at this facetious comment. Couldn't blame him for that.

"No," I said.

"There is only you on board?"

"Si." Seemed as though the Spanish was getting to me. "Yes,"

"There have been cases of dengue fever in Panama."

This statement took me a little aback as I was under the impression that when the Canal was being built all these fevers had been eradicated by the spraying and draining of the mosquito's breeding areas. Still, I suppose there was nothing to stop them returning. While pondering this, with half an ear I was listening to

Senor Health extol the virtues of frequent spraying of the cabin, and to inform him should I see any mosquitoes.

Gathering up his papers he pushed them into his canvas satchel and stood ready to leave, waiting for me to play the part of the ferry man.

Finally, after taking him ashore, I could relax a little or so I thought. As I was sitting on the settee with a cup of tea contemplating the events of the day and thinking of the morrow and what that would bring, a breeze came up strong enough to dispel a little the afternoon heat. What better time than this to move to another anchorage as advised by the kayaker.

Oh, dear! No sooner had the anchor been brought on board and the foresail unfurled than the breeze died away. So what's new? While contemplating whether to drop the anchor again or wait for another puff, the decision was taken out of my hands. From the aforementioned gin palace an inflatable dinghy had put out and headed my way.

"Need a tow?" the occupant asked.

"Would I? That would be kind of you," I replied with relief.

A tow line was quickly rigged and the dinghy started to take up the slack. Unknown to me, as my concentration was on the dinghy, the bight in the towline had hooked onto the anchor locker gooseneck vent. The dinghy took off, the towline slack came up with a rush, and the gooseneck vent parted company with its fixture, up and over the side, tracing a graceful parabolic arc up into the evening air to go plop, never to be seen again. There was only time for me to shake my head in exasperation at this latest calamity and say to myself, "Not again," before having to pay attention to the rapid progress to the new anchorage. Boy! Could that dinghy pull?

Well, this day came to end as most days do; anchored in a safer position, albeit at a greater distance from the landing place should I wish to row ashore again, I enjoyed a pleasant relaxing dinner complete with wine, music from the CDs. After the evening had taken on its dark shroud, I had a nightcap of The Famous Grouse, much appreciated after the enforced abstinence of the previous weeks. This was the life.

*

The tow arrived shortly after eight the following morning as promised. As I was an early riser I had finished the morning routine, and had checked the bilge which had not risen appreciably, which I put down to the fact that the boat was not moving, and therefore no water had been forced into the boat from the rudder seal. My, how one can be deluded by false assumptions, which would be all too evident at a later date.

The boat that was to do the towing came alongside and the crew soon had a line on board. There was little I could do except stand around as everything that could be done was done by the boarding gang. They handled the job admirably with little or no verbal instruction among them. Much to my relief they even pulled up the anchor; with the state of my back this action pleased me no end. The boat that was doing the tow was a powerful launch, as long as my boat and rather big for the job at hand I thought. As I came to know the yard and its operations better I learned that this launch was intended for nobler tasks than towing disabled yachts. Its size, power and range enabled it to deliver supplies to vessels off-shore.

Before the hour was up the boat had been towed around Flamenco Island, between the breakwaters enclosing the marina proper, and positioned under the hoist. The positioning of the lifting straps was an interesting exercise. On previous haul-outs in Canada the owner of the boat instructs the people responsible for hauling the boat where to position the straps to avoid fouling underwater obstructions, such as propeller shafts and transducers. In this yard a diver went under the hull to position the straps. One other interesting feature that I noticed while the boat was being transported from the lifting dock to the hard stand was a large sign fixed on the side of the Travelift announcing that no personnel were to be on board vessels being moved. Bit late for that I thought as no one had instructed me on that fact, and with the boat centred over the dock one would need wings or considerably more agility than I possessed to get off. Well, if the yard ignored this rule why should I care?

It became even more evident that the Flamenco Resort and Marina was still in the development stage at least the repair yard part of it. Refinements come last I would suspect as once in position on the hard and the Travelift departed, there was no ladder to get off the boat. Fortunately, there were still yard personnel hanging around who at my request dragged a painter's tubular scaffolding over and positioned it at the stern. A ladder would have been nice but, beggars can't be choosers. The scaffolding was awkward to negotiate with only a single plank on the top section and diagonal tubing for a foot hold on the way down.

On inspection the underside of the boat was a revelation, which left little doubt as to why progress through the water had been so slow. Just below the waterline for full area of the hull was entirely covered with gooseneck barnacles, heaving and writhing in protest at being removed from their environment. So much for anti-fouling paint that had been applied only six months previously.

Among the people hanging about admiring this maritime phenomenon were two young lads who, their spokesman said, would remove the barnacles for fifty dollars. Of course one should always negotiate even if already decided on an offer.

"Fifty dollars?" I asked, not keeping the disbelief from my voice.

He wasn't to be deterred though, "Si. Him," pointing at his buddy, "And me, twenty-five dollars each. We clean everything."

It was at this point that I realised what had been niggling at the back of my mind since being lifted out of the water. There was no power washing facilities which is normal in any yard that takes boats out of the water. There being no better way to clean off barnacles, seaweed and the like this deficiency was viewed with dismay. However, on reflection it did give employment to the local casual labour force to perform this task by hand.

I looked at this writhing mass and the work that would be required to remove this growth; also the awkward positions that would be needed to be perform this task decided the matter. My back gave a little twinge in confirmation.

"Alright, fifty dollars."

"Another fifty dollars and we paint for you. He very good painter," he said, indicating his mate, whom I gathered was the silent partner.

"First clean, then we will see. Okay?"

I saw the lads started on the removal of the barnacles when John Cole turned up with the mechanics and the sail maker. There might be a paucity of facilities, but there was no faulting John's organisation in this yard. As neither of these gentlemen could speak English, John very kindly did the translations about what was required. They then came onboard and were shown to their respective areas of expertise.

I struck a deal with the sail maker on the price to first repair the genoa for which he wrote out a rough contract with the request for six hundred dollars up front, for materials I was given to understand. When the genoa was finished we would negotiate for the mainsail repair. This system of cash hand-outs either before or after a job of work was completed became all to clear during my stay here. It was the favoured mode of payment if any work was to be carried out. No cheques, no credit cards, only cash, and then no bill higher than a twenty due to fear of counterfeiting. This, over time, became an imposition and inconvenience, but something one had to go along with.

I didn't have that sort of money on the boat and told him so. This didn't faze him as he had a taxi waiting and we could go to the Bank. Unknown to me at this stage was the fact that my PIN number on the Credit card had crashed. So after numerous futile attempts at the ATM I finally managed to get the daily limit of five hundred dollars. With this he had to be satisfied until I could get the balance on return of the repaired sail, when he would be paid. With this mutual agreement he was dropped off at his place of business and I returned to the yard to be presented with the bill for the taxi which included the sail maker's original journey out to the yard.

"Cheeky bugger," I thought.

John had seen my arrival and came over to tell me the worst.

"The mechanic says that the engine is seized."

"What," I said in disbelief, "how can that be? It has always been most reliable." It occurred to me that I was in denial; the engine had to be operational. This belief in a such a piece of machinery was ridiculous I know but, these past few weeks since it had failed to fire I had believed, in my ignorance, the problem was with the batteries.

"Well they have tried to turn it over and it won't move. They are waiting to show you."

"Bloody hell!" I thought with a twinge of gloom. "What next?" Then just as quickly so as not to tempt fate, "Don't ask," was the mental response.

Back on board a demonstration of the problem was enacted for my benefit. A long handled box spanner had been fitted to the fore part of the engine and an attempt to turn the shaft proved that it was indeed immovable

"Can't they fit a pipe over that to get better leverage," I asked hopefully.

This request was passed on by John and the reply returned. "They say that no matter the engine is seized," he said.

"So what do they suggest," I asked, feeling the gloom deepening.

After discussion in Spanish I was advised that the engine would have to come out and taken to their Workshop.

Well, what could I do but agree. They were the experts and accredited by the yard management, so they wouldn't be conning me I thought with unreasonable suspicion. At least there was some satisfaction in that revelation. This day was not going too well so far.

As these gloomy thoughts were going through my head I realised that John was speaking to me.

"They will bring a truck tomorrow. I'll arrange for the crane."

One of the mechanics was speaking again. Chubby and indolent was he, and subsequently I came to understand that he was the one with the experience who never laid his hand on any tool except to pass it to the younger guy who did all the work.

"When they get it to their workshop and open it up you will be required to go and inspect it," John translated.

"Why on earth should they want me to do that? Just fix the thing," I said feeling things were getting to be a little too much.

"You'll find that no-one will do anything without authorisation. They need to cover themselves," he said.

Digesting this information didn't take long as I was becoming well aware of the need to go with the flow.

"Alright. Let's get the ball rolling," I agreed.

*

"Will you be transiting the Canal?" a voice behind me asked. I had been watching the lads scraping the barnacles and listening politely to the chatter of the one who had proposed the job. It seemed to me that he chatted up the punters while the quiet one did the work. Still if that was their arrangement who was I to interfere. I was having enough put on my plate now to bother with other people's work ethic.

"Sorry," I said, turning to a slightly built man of middle age and noting his grey hair and beard.

"Will you be transiting the Canal?" He asked again.

"That is my intention."

"Could you use a couple of line handlers? My wife and I are making our way to Cartegena."

I was a little off balance at this time with not knowing when the engine might be ready, and as yet I hadn't registered with the Canal authority to do the transit. I had far too much on my mind to make yet another decision, especially catering to some strangers needs.

After explaining to him that I had no idea when I would be ready to go but, if and when I was ready and they were still interested then we could get together and talk some more. After all, one normally has to pay for line handlers, and as four are required to perform this task in the locks, it would make sense to make use of two free ones.

"How can I contact you?"

At this he took out a pen and wrote his name and the hotel he was staying at in a small notebook, tore out the page, and handed it to me.

"Okay, Gerry," I said after glancing at the paper. "My name's Ron."

"I gathered that from the name of your boat," he replied knowingly, grinning his pleasure at being so observant.

I smiled in agreement. "Dead giveaway isn't it?"

He then fell into telling a rather interesting story. His wife and he had travelled from New York by car and decided to see the world while they were still capable. The car would be sold and they were waiting in Panama for the next part of their adventure, if possible a passage to Cartegena. During the course of my travels I was to meet with quite a few people who had cast caution to the winds and got out of the rat race to go where life took them. Well, there was no way I could fault that, only applaud. After all wasn't I in the same business.

Before long he went to meet his wife, whom he said was around somewhere, no doubt meaning the general vicinity of the Flamenco Resort and Marina.

I wasn't left alone for long for yet another person approached and introduced himself as Luis, a taxi driver who was frequently in the yard and should I require a taxi to go into Balboa or Panama to let him know. Being the new boy on the block and not knowing the routine vis-à-vis transport this solved a problem for me as I needed to get to an Internet facility that evening and contact the folks at home to inform them of the situation here. An arrangement was made and he would pick me up at 6 o'clock outside the office.

The barnacle scrapers had finished their job to satisfaction, cleaned up the debris, and were paid. After many assurances that should I require the boat painted they were first class painters and would do a first class job, they took their leave. At last the source of water ingress could be examined and a plan of action determined. The bottom rudder post seal had, with the working of the rudder, broken off parts of the epoxy securing the seal to the hull, which in my estimation when repaired would only be a stop gap solution. What was needed to resolve the problem of the rudder post working on the seal was a bracket arrangement at the top of the post to resist the rudder movement. It now became a case of which project had priority: the engine, sails, or possibly new batteries. New sails should also be factored into this wish list, somewhere down the road. These items were at the top of the list. In my limited financial state careful consideration to this was the order of the day. A wind generator was also a must if the batteries were to be kept fully charged without recourse to the engine, but not this week. The "must have" seemed to be growing. With efficient batteries the bilges could be kept low as the bilge pump would be operative. This fact carried the day. A repair to the hull in way of the seal would have to suffice. I had so many worries it is not surprising that I thought that the reason why so much water could have entered the boat might be something other than the rudder seal. The outside of the boat had been inspected with no evidence of ingress apart from the rudder seal, so I had convinced myself that this was the source of the problem.

*

The workers finished at four thirty leaving the yard deserted but for the security guard and the occasional boat owners still working on their boats. Just to my right there was a seventy foot yacht undergoing painting below the waterline. During the day three young men of a northern origin who, due to their Caucasian features I guessed must be crew, periodically climbed on and off the boat going about their business. Although I was taking an interest in what went on in the yard I was loath to approach people, content to just keep a watch on what went on. Must be from spending so much time on my own. The boat was called Dynasty, which, if one used a certain inflection on the last syllable could sound ominous.

Ahead of Dynasty was a large cabin cruiser with the crew still working, removing the anti-fouling paint with a noisy power tool, sounding something like a power planer but not as big. Judging from the way it was being held upside down under the hull I couldn't help but feel for the operator. His arms must have become numb from holding the machine for so long in such a position. Curiosity as to just what was going on had me thinking I should go and investigate sometime. At the moment though I had enough on my plate to worry about what other people were up to. Once matters settled down and I could see which way the cat was going to jump would be soon enough to be nosey.

To my left was another cruiser of Panamanian registry. The interesting thing about this boat was the people engaged for maintenance. Only once during my stay in the yard did I see them activated into any sign of labour, and that was when a well dressed gentleman, presumably the owner appeared to inspect progress. For the rest of the time they just lounged about under the boat. They must have been planning on a long stay judging by the arm chairs which were positioned under the boat in the shade for their comfort. Nice work if you can get it.

All this surrounding activity I viewed with a beer to relax with. Now it was time for me to make a move. First take a shower and get cleaned up before venturing into town. The facilities for taking a shower in the yard were conspicuous by their absence. Toilets? Yes. They were something to be thankful for, and a relief, if one would accept the pun. I did not have to manage on the boat. But no showers; these would be built in due course I was informed. This I had a hard time understanding. Surely when the toilets were built it would not have been too much of a problem to include shower facilities. While they were at it they could have also included laundry facilities which were promised for sometime down the road. It would seem my wish list had extended to the Flamenco Resort and Marina facilities.

This is how matters stood at the end of the first day high and dry in Panama. It had been a hot day and to get cleaned up was a priority. Obviously, to be successful in this enterprise caused a direction away from the norm. There was plenty of water in the tanks, but the freshwater pump had decided to go into destruct mode, probably in sympathy with all the other mini disasters of the past few weeks. Under these circumstances the need to get a shower became an obsession. Away from people, out on the ocean alone the lack of hygiene is of little importance but now, faced with mixing with other humans, there was no chance that I was about to be smelly. There was no alternative but to take a bucket bath. The easiest way to get water now was not from the tanks but to go ashore to the standpipe and carry a bucket of water back to the boat, stand in the shower stall and perform the ablutions that way. Having enough water so as not to run out while still soapy took some planning, and to climb out of the boat and trot across the yard covered in soap suds was not something I would relish, not to mention scaring any of the locals that might be about. It is amazing really what planning can go into a simple task like getting clean. A new fresh water pump was a definite must, one which I made a mental note to attend to on the morrow. There was a Marine store in the general area of the Yard so we would see what was offered there.

Otherwise all went according to plan with the bathing and I was shortly ready at the appointed place awaiting the taxi driver, Luis. This was to be my first lesson in Panamanian reliability. Whatever arrangements are made for whatever time, don't believe it.

Either add an hour onto the time or ignore the arrangement entirely seems to be the norm. In this particular instance after waiting for half an hour it was fortunate that Gerry, the erstwhile transit line handler, came by with his wife and car, in this otherwise deserted place.

"Want a ride, Ron?" he called out the window.

"Thanks, but I've arranged for a taxi."

Gerry gave an ever widening grin at this remark. "Been waiting long?"

"Half an hour or so," I replied.

"You will be better off coming with us; otherwise you will be here all night."

Somewhat puzzled, but not wanting to pass up the chance of a ride, I walked over to the car and got in.

"Hello," I said to the lady in the passenger seat.

Gerry made the introductions.

"I don't like the idea of leaving," I stated, expressing my concern at abandoning the arrangement with the taxi driver.

Gerry and his wife both gave a short laugh.

"When you have been here a while you will realise that arrangements mean nothing," said Gerry. "He is probably doing his thing, don't worry about it. Where do you want to go?"

"Well mainly an Internet location, then get a meal." I ran my fingers through my hair. "And a haircut if possible. I'll soon be tripping over this lot," I said.

"No problem, all three are right by our hotel."

On this assurance we fell silent and took an interest in the passing scene. Coming off the causeway Gerry directed the car towards Balboa with the explanation that at this time of day the traffic was much lighter than the direct route into Panama. He took us through the streets of the old American canal family residences, which was impressive in the orderly cleanliness, and the quiet peaceful atmosphere.

Gerry's attention must have been distracted by the scenery for he hit a speed bump without slowing. Sitting in the back seat the force of this contact with the immovable object caused me to rise up slightly; the pain this caused to my injured back brought forth a loud and involuntary cry of anguish, startling all of us. Between gritted teeth, in an attempt to ease the discomfort, I explained the problem. To his credit, Gerry slowed at each new sleeping policeman and eased over with exaggerated care.

Soon after leaving Balboa we passed through the older part of Panama with its rundown buildings, intense traffic and streets crowded with locals going about their business, such a seedy change from the Balboa sector, Gerry pulled up outside a barber shop advertising two dollar haircuts.

Gerry was pointing across the road giving instructions. "There's our hotel. The Hotel Lisboa."

"Mmhuh!" I answered, still favouring my back and not wanting to risk speech.

"Round the corner there are a few places to eat. Quite reasonably priced too. And right here is the barbershop."

"That's very good of you," I said showing my appreciation for not of having to seek out these places for myself. "Your help is much appreciated."

Even though I had the door open ready to make my exit, I was considering the flooded gutter and the best way to keep my feet dry. Gerry hadn't finished talking about them being line handlers. His wife's comment that we were three feet from the curb and the gutter was flooded brought him back to the real world.

"Sorry," he said. "Just a minute. I'll pull up."

This solved the problem of keeping my feet dry allowing me to exit the car and assure them that when the time for transit came I'd be in touch. And so we made our farewells.

Shortly after I was sitting having my ears lowered, always a relaxing time listening to the clip of the scissors and watching the hair roll down the sheet to fall onto the floor. The hairdresser was a young lad, early twenties I would think, and keen, as though he had been allowed to perform on his first customer. Who knows? Maybe I was. For when the hair had been cut he insisted on having a go at my beard, much against my protestations. It was my intention to shave it off at the first opportunity, besides it was time to eat, and with my blood sugar problems, a task that should be attended to without delay. But, he was already getting on with the job. I couldn't fault the guy's enthusiasm and to resist at this stage was to leave with a partly trimmed beard, which would have been ridiculous. I had to admit that he made a good job of it, taking the hair from the cheeks but leaving it full along the ridge of the jaw.

From here a routine developed that would be followed whenever I came to town to eat and deal with e-mailing. Across the road outside the Hotel Lisboa I would alight from the taxi, walk around the corner to eat dinner, and then go back to the Internet next door to the Hotel. These duties having been attended to, I just stood at the curb and hailed a taxi to go out to Albrook and the Super 99 supermarket to buy the groceries for the next leg of the voyage. Altogether, this system was convenient to the extreme as it saved organising a suitable vehicle to transport the amount of food required in one go. Also, I could eat the evening meal cooked by someone infinitely more capable than I, and check any messages in the inbox. On this occasion I made contact with the satellite phone people to arrange for the phone to be returned. However, they assured me that they could find nothing wrong and that the unit was in good order. This made me feel rather sceptical as it didn't perform prior to Cabo San Lucas.

I now learned that none of my friends had attempted to turn up in Panama. I was disappointed that they would not be coming, but relieved that they had the sense not to venture out when there had been no contact from me for so long.

*

The following morning dawned bright and clear, promising another warm day. I took my usual morning tea into the cockpit to sit and watch the yard come alive. The workers wandered in with no sense of urgency, just drifting towards the place of the day's employment. It was with some amusement that I watched the guys that were presumably to work on the boat to my left gather to lounge around in the shade under the boat, and remain in a state of repose until, to the best of my knowledge as, the end of the day. In counterpoint to these layabouts the work on the large power boat over on my starboard bow had resumed as soon as the personnel and equipment had been assembled. It was a strange feeling to sit observing other people's activities and not be observed myself, at least no one deigned to look my way or acknowledge my presence.

Sitting in the cockpit sipping tea I realised that my back wasn't hurting anymore. Strange, I thought, as I eased my back to find out if this was true. Much to my delight it was. Could it be that Gerry's speed bump therapy had done this? Regardless, it certainly was a pleasure to be able to walk, and to work without the need to favour this part of the anatomy. Thank you, Gerry.

Although I had work on the boat to do I was loath to start. Today the engine was to be taken out and I didn't wish to be part way through a job and have to attend to the requirements of the mechanics or for that matter, be absent buying a freshwater pump. Apart from the obvious repair to the rudder seal which required mixing epoxy and applying fibreglass to the injured area, there were also areas of the top side paintwork to attend to where the original paint had come off in sheets, exposing the filler coat, and giving the topsides paintwork a look of being inflicted with the mange. The hull below the waterline needed a coat of antifouling paint, but this required an investment that would have to be deferred until my finances were known and could be allocated in order of priority. At this time the cost of repairs to the engine was as yet unknown. No doubt all would be revealed by day's end.

Still there was no way I could sit around all day so armed with a scraper I started the task of removing what loose paint remained on the topside, ready for a patch painting. There didn't seem to be much point in giving an overall coat of paint when the original would likely shed away again with wave action. Although the paint I had used was a well-known brand, of an internationally approved quality, or so they claimed, and the same manufacturer as the anti-fouling. I resolved to not to be taken in by their claims again.

After lunch John Cole came over.

"See you've had your beard trimmed. It suits you," he offered, looking critically at the barber's handiwork.

That being a matter of opinion to which I didn't subscribe I made no comment.

"No sign of the truck for the engine?" I asked. The concerned tone of my voice must have sounded more like a statement. The mobile crane had arrived sometime previously and was parked close by and I hoped I wasn't going to be charged waiting time.

"I'll find out what's happening," he said. He pulled out his cell phone to make the call in rapid and unintelligible language. The call ended, he closed the phone and with an air of someone who is familiar with the train of events imparted the information.

"The truck was taken out on another job this morning, and hasn't returned."

John cocked his head to one side in an attitude of one anticipating a response of an unexpected nature. He must have noticed my lips tighten in exasperation.

"So we wait all day and they can't let us know what the situation is," I said, not trying to hide the annoyance in my voice. "So what now?"

John shrugged not so much as an apology, but rather to express that this is Panama. This is the way it is.

"They will come tomorrow, ten o'clock."

'Yeah! Right.' I thought.

The uncertainty of the way events seem to be happening didn't exactly fill me with happiness. Visions of being a captive in Panama's apparent hairy fairy life style were looming large. My impatience at wanting to get through the Canal and across the

Caribbean before the Hurricane season got underway was heavy on my mind and needed to be addressed.

In the meantime other people had wandered over requiring John's attention and leaving me with my thoughts, half listening to the chatter. The conversation ended and without another word to me John got into his golf buggy and drove off. This I realised was a factor of life in John's day. If ever a man had nervous energy it was him. This seemed so opposite to the people who worked for him. A good man, and one whose good will and energy I came to rely on in the coming weeks.

Not wanting to hang about I left to see what was on offer with fresh water pumps.

*

They didn't come for the engine the next day either, making some other excuse, so it was another inactive day. Not entirely wasted though as an interesting conversation came up with the owner of the large power boat. Having wandered over to see what kind of tool was being used on the antifouling area it transpired that it was similar to a power planer, which accounted for the high pitched whine. This tool shaved off a predetermined thickness of paint, cleaning to the aluminium plating only. What I found to be particularly interesting was the person operating this tool. He was of Central American origin but put to shame the lack of enthusiasm regarding work in the local populace; in the two days that I had been there he had worked continuously with only the occasional break for refreshment.

When I remarked on this fact to the owner, an American, he expressed disgust for the local work force, using for an example the guys lying about under the other boat. He had brought his man down with him from Costa Rica, where he lived, as crew and general dogsbody and praised him for the effort he was putting in to maintain the boat.

During our conversation I remarked on the unusual keel the boat had; this was boxed shaped, maybe eighteen inches in height and the same in width, running the full length of the boat, some thirty feet. When I was told that it was full of mercury that really threw me. It must have cost a fortune to fill that cavity. The owner explained that the boat had been built for the Coastguard as a rescue vessel and, as it was built with taxpayer's money, expense was no object. A little cynical even if true. The weight that the mercury provided was to create a self righting effect should the boat turn over in a heavy sea. The boat had been bought by its present owner at Government auction. Should he ever decide to scrap this vessel his outlay most certainly would be more than returned by the contents of the keel. I have no idea of the price of mercury but it is widely known to be very expensive.

So the day passed with little activity on my part. The projects on the hull were considered, only to be shelved until I could get a good run at them without being interrupted, the engine guys being uppermost in my thinking. These people were not the only ones I was waiting for. The electrician was conspicuous by his absence which I had occasion to remind John. It was a matter of urgency to have the electrical system checked. The trip down from the Cabo had created many doubts, not to mention frustration brought on by my ignorance of things electrical, as to why power was not available. A continuity check on all the circuits was high on the list, something that required equipment that I didn't possess. For my part I hadn't been exactly remiss in this enterprise, and the yard electrician had run a power line to the boat which made it possible to put the batteries on charge. After twenty-four hours there had been no appreciable result. When the refrigerator was switched on the volt meter needle fluctuated most alarmingly indicating that it was grabbing at low and insufficient voltage. To my limited knowledge this suggested that there was something definitely wrong. Either the batteries were duff or there was a circuit grounding, draining the batteries.

Well the day hadn't been totally wasted as I bought and installed a very efficient fresh water pump that was unlike the original in construction. Whereas the original relied on an accumulator tank to supply air pressure, the new one operated when a tap was opened and marvels of marvels had no part of its construction that would rust or rot out, being all neoprene.

By four thirty when the yard activity started to peter out, all hope of a truck coming to take the engine was abandoned. John Cole very kindly offered to go by the mechanic's place of work to check on what the hold up might be. And for this I had to be satisfied. So left to my own devices again I got myself cleaned up and went into Panama for a meal, to check for any messages at the internet café, then to Albrook to grocery shop. On returning to the boatyard I decided to have a beer at the corner watering hole. Stopping for a beer before returning to the boat to sleep developed into a nightly routine and I became well known to the staff to the point of being addressed as Mister Ron. "Ah! Good evening, Mister Ron," became the cry. "You want pasteurised beer?" This greeting was a result of

me passing a beer before my eyes on an earlier visit and stating that
it was, "Past your eyes." It was a pleasure to see the delight this
simple little jest gave these young people.

*

During late morning the following day, much to my delight,
the truck arrived for the engine. The vehicle that did the transporting
gave me doubts as to what sort of engineering outfit I had got tied
into. The size of this vehicle would have been more suited to
transporting cattle. The logo on the door didn't suggest anything to
do with engineering trades either. But, who was I to comment on
this? My little engine would be quite happy for the ride, and I
certainly was not going to complain. At last things were starting to
happen.

The mechanics of removing the engine and, indeed
everything that was do with bringing this injured machine back to
good health started an all too familiar process. Of the two bodies that
came to attend the operation, one was the chubby fellow previously
mentioned who sat around giving orders, and the young lad who
provided the sweat and the labour. No doubt this was the accepted
system. Probably Chubby was the qualified mechanic and the lad his
apprentice. More respect for Chubby would have been generated on
my part had he become more involved than occasionally passing a
spanner.

Some days the climate in Panama can be exceedingly hot
depending on whether there is cloud cover or clear skies, a breeze or
still air, or a combination of these factors. Today, fortunately for the
lad, it was cool, for working in such a tight space as the engine
compartment disconnecting the engine can be quite a trial. All went
well though and the mobile crane was soon lifting the engine out of
the boat into the cattle truck. By noon I was left engineless, to ponder
my next move. First lunch then tackle the rudder seal.

With the engine ashore with its problems being dealt with I
felt a certain calm in my daily routine. All the other problems would
be taken care of when the occasion arose. It had been established
during the last contact with home base just how much my wealth
amounted to. Nothing to go daft about in this revelation but at least
it gave a certain solvency to my life and I could deal with bringing
the boat back up to operational perfection. Or close to it. This fact
was a comfort as I could now keep a close watch on spending. There
was one irritation in the scheme of things: my debit card seemed to
have thrown wobblers by refusing to produce cash from ATMs. This

was a nuisance but not critical as I could get cash back from the supermarket when paying for groceries, enough for pocket money to pay for small purchases in day to day living.

My mind at ease, the days passed pleasantly and took on a certain leisurely pace. The sail maker returned with the foresail suitably repaired, although the material he had used didn't look much like sail cloth. To my fertile mind this material conjured up visions of old army blankets. Beggars can't be choosers though and I had been made aware of the scarcity of people in the trade of sail repairing. Since the departure of the American Canal workers sailboats were to all intents and purposes non-existent. The sail maker was a big man in both build and voice, forceful in speech and demanding in tone. This didn't faze me though as he didn't speak English, only loud rapid Spanish which, I couldn't understand, so I just closed my ears. This bombast and other similar attitudes met with on other occasions, mainly with taxi drivers, I took to be the local interpretation of manliness. The way certain taxi drivers would lean out of the windows to gesture and verbally accost the local females, who I might add, took not the slightest interest, was embarrassing. If this behaviour was a sign of manliness I wondered what they would be like when they grew up.

Later on towards the end of the week I was summoned to view the engine which had been opened up for my inspection. What that would achieve was lost on me; the cylinders were full of water which had caused the engine to malfunction, but looking at this didn't help solve the problem. Just an explanation would have sufficed if that was the only reason for bringing me all the way out to their yard. They had sent a taxi to bring me to see the offending object. A driver who spoke English whose help in negotiating a price to fix the engine was most welcome. All spares were to be extra, which I thought to be fair, and I gave my consent to proceed. Had I known then what was to transpire an alternative arrangement would have been made. But then hind-sight is ever infallible.

During this sojourn at Flamenco Resort and Marina I had made the acquaintance of an American marine engineer whose services I would have much preferred. His name was Joe Brassiere, or at least that is how his last name sounded and judging by the ribald comments from others of his acquaintance this could well have been. Joe was highly respected for his professionalism and work ethic, all much desired, but in my ignorance of yard practices not to be for my benefit. The mechanics allotted to my problem were on contract to the Marina and therefore John Cole was honour bound to recommend their services. Because Joe operated independently, his services could be engaged by arrangement with the management on request from the customer only. None of this was known to me at the time which was a great pity for at the very least a communication would have been established, and without the run-around I would receive from the people appointed to my project.

In the fullness of time the 'electrician' presented himself. Ah now things are beginning to happen,' I thought. Alas, the language problem cropped up again. Not for want of fluency though; this gentleman was quite voluble in his needs which he wrote down for me to take to the Marina store to purchase for him. My explanation of the problem and what was expected was another kettle of fish with which I was soon to be acquainted.

Needless to say he hadn't budged by the time I had returned, but give him his due he was soon on the job. A nagging doubt as to his qualification to fix the electrical problem soon had me regretting employing the guy.

The house batteries were located under the settee and required a bit of manoeuvring to get at, although for one person to work there was quite acceptable. Two bodies getting in each other's way was not desirable. So I stayed in the cabin and waited. Before too much time had elapsed he emerged pleased with himself and sweating profusely, which was not surprising as it could get quite warm in such an airless location. Through his voluble Spanish I was given to understand that the work had been completed. I was sceptical that he had not done any more than clean the battery leads. This point was not raised at this moment because of something else that had taken my interest so I just let him rabbit on sweating profusely, while I watched a bead of perspiration hanging off the end of his nose like a dewdrop ready to fall off a leaf, willing it to drop. In due course nature had its way and the dewdrop dropped to be replaced by yet another gathering in readiness to follow its predecessor, and strangely with no effort from its owner to do any sweat mopping. Fascinating though this show was it was not getting on with the job. Besides, I'd not understood a word he had said.

"Battery. OK?" I asked, interrupting. Knowing full well that it wasn't

"Si. Batterier Bueno." This was accompanied by more voluble Spanish. By this time I got the impression he was trying to convince himself.

Time to interrupt him again.

"No, Bueno," I said, switching the volt meter to show the needle bouncing up and down the scale like a thing demented.

"Ahh!" he said, knowingly, "No Bueno,"

"Bloody right mate. No Bueno," By this time I was becoming annoyed with this person. Obviously he hadn't a clue about electrics, boat electrics anyway. All I wanted now was to get rid of him.

"How much do I owe you?" I asked, pulling out my wallet. I felt that he wasn't worth anything but was not prepared to create a scene.

The twenty dollars he asked for was small payment to get rid of him.

After he had left I pondered the situation for a while then came to the conclusion that new batteries might solve the problem, but I was very reluctant to do this not knowing if the existing batteries were salvageable.

As luck would have it, John Cole was about to come on board to check on the progress. My irritation with the departing, 'electrician' was still needling me coupled with my frustration at being no further on with the electrical problems. In no uncertain terms I told John what I thought of the guy and that I would go and buy another battery.

"Don't do that just yet, let's find out if these batteries are dead," he remarked wisely.

That threw me for a moment, "How can we do that?"

"I'll phone the House of Batteries and tell them to come down. They have the equipment for testing batteries."

John was on the phone for a few moments only when he turned to me and asked, "What sort of batteries do you have?"

When I told him he explained that they would bring batteries in case the original ones were finished. I was relieved at the possibility of my troubles in this regard being solved, and John received my profuse thanks.

Before the afternoon was over the old batteries had been declared defunct and new batteries installed. The added bonus to this wonderful experience was that the fridge would operate and the beer could be cooled. I was now a much happier camper. As an added assurance the charger was connected to make sure the batteries remained topped up to the maximum charge. A loss of power when the means to avoid this were readily available would be stupid at least, not to say criminal. The more I thought about batteries the more I desired a wind generator. Had I not listened to false witness before embarking on this adventure more than likely the problems resulting from lack of electricity might never have arisen? But that was hindsight again. Sadly, this item would have to wait for sometime and place in the future, the ever spectre of low funds was rearing its ugly head. The next most pressing item on the agenda now that the power was restored was to connect the water pump and to purchase and install a cigar lighter. The one to provide the means to shower, and the other to charge the shaver to get rid of the hair on my face, the inverter for the lap-top and the Satellite phone when this was returned. Life was taking on a much rosier outlook; finally a fully operational boat was in the offing.

*

The following day the repair to the rudder seal was made and suitably boosted in a belt and braces mode; covering the whole seal and backing onto the hull with fibreglass cloth and epoxy putty. Satisfaction guaranteed, at least until a brace for the rudder post could be fabricated. Comfortable with the results, I approached John about returning the boat to the water. It seemed to me that waiting on the hard at seventy dollars a day was somewhat ridiculous, when I could anchor off to wait for the engine. A much better solution was proposed that would facilitate getting on shore with less effort than having to row the dinghy from outside the breakwater; tie up to a mooring buoy inside. There would be a charge, however. But what is new? And ten dollars a day seemed reasonable compared to the seventy on the hard.

Nothing happens immediately in Panama, so it was another three days before the tide was right. By this I mean that the high tide had to coincide with the working day, time and tide waiting for these men presumably.

These waiting days were not wasted however; during this period I took the opportunity to register for transit something which I still planned to do. No sooner had this been done than information filtered down that the Canal was closed to small craft due to one chamber at Miraflores being closed for maintenance. This put a completely different outlook on my plans. The hurricane season wasn't going to wait for me to get clear so it would be the height of folly to try and dodge these terrible winds. Also there were other considerations to patch into this equation. Should I make a timely transit and an Atlantic crossing then that would put me into the English ports getting on towards late in the year, thus creating a knock on effect. By that time I would have done the rounds of friends and family, winter would be on the threshold, making a passage south undesirable. Besides, the engine hadn't been returned and who knows when that would be, and having covered the cost, would there be enough funds to pay for a transit? Change of plan: I would sail west and make the circumnavigation the other way via the Marquesas, and Tahiti.

The information of the closure was confirmed by John. We were discussing the delays of the return of the engine and what information John had received on this subject when we were approached by a couple who had come into the yard seeking passage as line handlers to the Atlantic side of the Canal. John informed them of the closure and left to phone about the engine. It was then that I mentioned there was more scope for getting a berth at the Balboa Yacht Club as this was where the boats congregated awaiting transit, should the Canal be opened again at a time suitable to them, that is.

"Will you be going through?" the woman asked.

"No, I'll be going the other way, Marquesas, then on to Australia."

"Ooh! I have a son in Brisbane. Could I come with you?" asked the woman eagerly.

"Sorry, I travel alone," I said without a second's hesitation, ignoring her enthusiasm but not without a twinge of regret at the crushed look she gave me.

"Pity," she said, walking away.

My reaction had been spontaneous. Instinctive I suppose, because after all I didn't know her. For all I knew she could have been a psychopath or something. Had to admit she was a comely looking woman. Besides if the man she was with was included in the request the boat would have been too crowded for comfort.

On John's return he had good news. He had spoken to the girl in the mechanics office who had told him they had gone to customs to clear the spare parts.

This information was indeed good news; as the engine would soon be returned and the saga could be resumed. Right?

Later that evening while sitting having a 'pasteurised' beer I noticed two of the crew from the Dynasty sitting outside. During the time in the Yard the only conversation that had passed between us was the time of day; or good morning. Rather limited but one has to respect others privacy. On this occasion they were not working. What better time to make their acquaintance? Once the formalities were over a friendly rapport was established. Of the two, Geoff soon went his way leaving me with Damien and, later by Damien's girlfriend. It developed into a most pleasant evening. Damien had a wealth of experience for one his age, which I put at mid to late twenties. Footloose and fancy free was Damien, seeing the world by crewing on other people's boats. He had taught English for a year at a school in Korea, lack of qualifications didn't seem to be an important factor for either party. The world is certainly a young person's oyster. Because of this chance encounter, there were many enjoyable evenings I spent in the company of Damien and his girl friend, Vivien. Vivien Lee would you believe? Her mother was Panamanian, her father Chinese.

There was another fortuitous happening that came out of this decision to make the acquaintance of the Dynasty crew. The following day, Geoff, with the skipper, came on board my boat for a look around. Stan, the skipper, stared at the cabin deck with what I took to be a look of dismay, and well he might. The cabin deck had suffered grievously from the marine environment. I will admit here that the material I used, house wood flooring, was not the best choice but at the time it seemed acceptable. However, the top veneer had peeled away due to the damp and was looking quite tatty and forlorn.

"Would you like some teak decking?" asked Stan. "Our decks have been replaced and there is some planking left over. You can have it if you like."

"What would you want for it?" I asked.

"No! You can have it. It's extra to what we needed. The fibreglasser wanted it but sod him, I'm not doing him any favours." His voice carried the tone of one that was displeased with the person in question. "A bottle of scotch, if you like" he added.

Needless to say, the teak decking was on board my boat quicker than a rat up a drain, long before Stan had a change of mind. Beautiful wood it was too, not a knot or shakes in the lot, and more than enough to completely replace the whole of the interior decking. Today was indeed my lucky day. As it so happened there was a bottle of Famous Grouse on board which changed hands before the transfer of decking was completed, an added incentive to deter any change of mind on the part of this benefactor.

As I was still waiting to have the boat in the water, what better time than this to make a start? The project would have to be done in sections to facilitate walking about while the glue dried, so I tackled the main cabin deck first, ripping out the old planking with gusto.

Stan's good will had not yet expired. While engaged in this project he and Geoff came by and asked, as they were going into Panama would I like to go along and get some supplies, caulking, that sort of thing? This day it seemed as though I was really on a roll.

As it turned out there was no caulking left as Stan had cleared them out for his project but for just one tube. No matter, I purchased a back saw and Set Square, thinking the caulking could wait for a later date.

Elated at being able to replace the old decking I soon had a completed section of deck to admire, and what a pleasure it was too, regardless of the lack of caulking. Progression to an efficient and fully appointed boat was being realised.

While working on this arrangement the sail maker returned with the mainsail, full of himself and bragging by gestures and voluble Spanish on what a good job he had made of it, until I pointed out that he had sewn across one of the batten pockets and therefore the batten could not be returned to its rightful place. Also, he had repaired the tears in the way of the reef points but made no provision for passing a line through the sail for reefing. The bragging ended but not the voluble Spanish which he directed to his young assistant. Grievously hurt I would have guessed, at this lack of professionalism, his assistant looked long suffering, no doubt having gone through similar situations before. So it was back to the sail loft to make adjustments. When he did return there was still the problem of mast slides; these apparently were unobtainable in Panama. The sail maker had made an effort to redress this problem and had tracked down a few slides that were too large. These required reducing to fit the mast slide, which was easily done by sandpapering the nylon edges. With this method a sort of Heath Robinson arrangement was cobbled together. That solved the problem of some of the slides but there was still the connection of the slide to the sail. This was resolved temporarily by using small shackles. After settling the bill with the sail maker I ordered suitable slides from the United States.

That evening Damien and I took the short walk along the causeway to a restaurant to meet Vivien for a meal. The restaurant being close to the waters edge was open to the cooling sea breeze which made for a most enjoyable evening. Vivien being fluent in both English and Spanish took a lot of effort out of ordering. In fact being the owner of her own business she was quite happy making decisions which Damien and I were quite content to go along with as it left us to have our banter. At the close of this most delightful evening with these two young people, the first social evening spent in company since leaving British Columbia, it was suggested that a friend of Vivien's should be roped in for a nightclubbing foursome to which I begged off, excusing myself on the grounds that tomorrow early the boat was going back into the water. Damien and Vivien liked to party into the small hours night clubbing, which to me in my advanced years was very low on the agenda of things to do, in fact not a consideration at all. A pleasant constitutional stroll back to the Marina set me up nicely for a nightcap of 'past your eyes beer' at the local watering hole.

*

There was some delay in the launching for when the Travelift was positioned over the ramp the heavens opened up with a tropical downpour scattering the attendant crew to seek shelter. This deluge lasted for some twenty minutes until the operation was resumed with the crew chattering excitingly over the experience. As a result of the rain the air was much cooler and cleaner, a pleasant change from the previously muggy weather.

To my horror and distress when the boat was returned to the water and safely tied to the buoy the bilges were fast taking water. The leak from the rudder seals was obviously not the only means of ingress. To cap this frustration the bilge pump wouldn't work either. Well as they say in the boating world, 'if it isn't one thing it's five others.' This state of affairs could not be tolerated and the source of the leak would have to be investigated. I soon realised that the best way to detect a leak was to use a reverse process, i.e. take the boat out of the water again with the water still in the bilges and observe where the water came out.

As mentioned earlier, nothing happens in Panama just when you want it to, so it was a few more days before a second haul-out would be carried out. As luck would have it I came across Joe in the yard during this waiting for the second haul out, and I related the problem with the electrics, and the bilge pump in particular. Although mechanical problems were his forte, he was pleased to have a look and see what was what. Now that is what I call a professional. The result of this investigation revealed that the float switch was kaput, and the three way control switch iffy. So, a new float switch was purchased and fitted, the switch cleaned up, the wiring checked out. All this effort by Joe on my behalf left me very pleased with the way progress was made in the matter of electrics. It also restored my faith in human nature, re Panama. There was one other matter that had to be resolved which would have to wait until suitable equipment was available. Were the batteries discharging to ground?

Shortly after rowing Joe ashore I was informed that there was a parcel for me in the office. You can imagine my delight that the Satellite phone was now returned and communication with the outside world was again possible. Back on board and the phone connected to the aerial I made a call to base back in British Columbia which went through, loud and clear without a hitch. My star of confidence was rising. The indicator on the phone showed a low battery reading, which was no problem, just plug it into the socket and all would be well. Except that the phone wouldn't take a charge. Several attempts with the different charging leads gave no satisfaction and it was with the star of confidence fast sinking towards the horizon of gloom that I realised that there was still a fault with the system. With dejection and frustration fighting each other for dominance I realised that the offending article would have to go back again. Time was now pressing as I fully expected to get away from here within a few days. So the phone was boxed up, Luis' taxi engaged and out I went to the Fed-Ex office. The phone people were contacted that same evening to be told in no uncertain terms that their product was non-functioning, and would they please do something about fixing it.

*

It was during this waiting period on the buoy that I was called to the office to be confronted by a tall sophisticated looking gentleman whom it turned out was the accountant for the engine people. A dour gentleman he was too, emanating disapproval. At what, one could only guess. He didn't, or more likely wouldn't, speak English. I say this because it has been my experience that the better class of educated people in the Latin American countries do speak English, and very well too. So it was left to John to do the translating. It transpired that before any spare parts would be ordered I would have to sign a letter of approval, which the Senor presented, silent and aloof in a most imperious manner. No excuse was offered as to why we had been told, many days previously, that they had been to the Customs to pick up these very same parts. Not to mention that I had already given verbal approval. Apparently, no-one is trusted to pay up even after giving their word, which I found irritating, not to mention this latest delay while the spares were ordered and waiting for them to come from England. As I was totally in the hands of these aggravating and suspicious people there was no alternative but to grin and bear the situation. Needless to say, I was not in any way endeared to them for their cavalier attitude. I signed his form, and he departed glum as ever. In fact I decided that he should be dubbed Senor Glum for future reference.

So the days passed lying on the buoy, with me pottering about and working on the cabin deck until they came to haul me out again.

When this happened I made sure I was in such a position on shore to observe where the leak came from. There was no doubt about where, as the water just streamed out from the fore part of the keel where it joined the hull. It would appear that sometime during the passage down from Canada the keel had worked in the seaway, loosening the connecting bolt allowing ingress of water through the bolt hole and into the hull. To tighten these bolts at this time was impossible; the construction of the boat precluded this. The only alterative would be to seal the leak from the outside. No doubt the leak could start again sometime in the future, but until a return home and a comprehensive haul-out this method would have to do.

I shuddered at the thought what such a haul out would entail as this would mean cutting out bulkheads and decking, in fact ripping out most of the interior to get at the six by nine inch white oak keel bearers. These then would need to be cut to free up the bolts; all eleven of them. Drop the keel, then reseal to the hull. A daunting thought to say the least.

As the source of this leak had been missed on the first haul-out I could only surmise that when the weight of the boat had rested on the keel the gap, as small as it must be, had closed up.

The provisional repair to this leak didn't take long and while the boat was out of the water a fresh coat of anti-fouling was applied. The finances were healthy enough to put this project into fulfilment. The original coating was serviceable but with the amount of fouling it had attracted, I didn't trust it to the expected six week passage to the Marquesas

The time required to make this repair and apply the antifouling to a satisfactory conclusion didn't take more than a day which in this, the original manana country, didn't mean diddly squat. Regardless of frequent requests to be put back in the water I was still there a week later. This, however, turned to be an advantage as the engine came back towards the end of this period all nicely painted. With the boat out of the water putting the engine back was much more convenient for the use of the crane. The delay in putting the boat back in the water, and then the engine turning up when it did had me deeply suspicious that matters were being controlled behind the scenes. My needs seemed secondary to the controllers' desires. Ah! Well, go with the flow, as they say, life is much less frustrating that way. Besides, I was becoming as laid back as the locals by this time.

One would think that with the engine back in the boat, it would just be a matter of connecting up all the parts, put the boat back in the water, test the engine and away we go. No way, not here in Panama anyway. The mechanics, Chubby and his lad, were quite content to connect the engine onto the bed and connect the propeller shaft before taking off again.

Just so the reader has no doubts about the actual situation, the lad did the hands-on part of the operation with a little help from me in guiding the engine through the hatch into position on the holding down bolts, Chubby being content to give voluble verbal directions accompanied by much waving of hands towards the crane operator. This approach to work ethics would seem to be the norm here but, Chubby made no effort to help the lad and I developed a low regard for him.

The haul out had happened on a Friday, with a promise of being returned to the buoy on the coming Monday. It was on the following Friday before being it was water borne again. With the extra cost of sitting on the hard on my mind I took up the matter with John with no satisfaction. What had been going on behind the scenes over the delay I was not privy to, and was given no satisfaction. John, kindly waived the cost of the tow over to the buoy, a small gesture to compensate for the wait on the hard for which I had to be thankful.

Lying on the buoy proved to be a relaxing time, each morning I would take my tea out the cockpit to enjoy the early morning. Without fail, Derek would pass by at speed in his dinghy on his way to work in the boatyard. Derek, an American, had arrived in Panama from Hawaii fifteen years previously and never left. His boat, a catamaran had been converted into permanent living quarters and was moored close to the shore on the far side of the marina. He had married a Panamanian girl and was thus allowed to work in the country. They had a child together who, at the time I were there, was about six years of age. Imagine my surprise, when one afternoon relaxing in the cockpit, this child of such a young age came hurtling past in the dinghy in full and sole control. She obviously knew what she was doing as she very professionally put the dinghy alongside, embarked her father and came hurtling back to return to their boat. The do say that women mature quickly in the tropics.

There was a job that I had been putting off for some time. Emptying the holding tank so the macerator pump could be inspected, Joe had assured me that there was power there, which suggested something mechanical was the cause. Derek had told me there would be no problem with dumping the contents of the holding tank over the side as no-body cared anyway. So, putting aside my reluctance I began siphoning the contents into a bucket then throwing the slop over the side. I soon lost count of how many buckets there were, maybe twelve at a guess, before finally emptying the tank. Not a pleasant task, what with the smell. The siphon hose had a bulb to draw the delivery, so I considered myself lucky I didn't have to suck. The cause of the problem was that the cutter, which broke up the solids, had jammed with hair, which when one considers this, is not a very clever feature of this type of pump. However, the pump was working again.

During the following week the engine was connected and a speed trial into the Bay carried out to my satisfaction, with one complaint: the engine alarm wouldn't shut off. Being Panama this problem would have to wait for another day before being attended to. At least matters were progressing towards a departure date which, with all things being equal, couldn't be far off. Alas, this was not as close as one would have hoped; another delay of a different stripe was in the offing.

On checking the e-mail that evening I was informed that the satellite phone people had found the fault and had returned it to the manufacturer under warranty, and it would be returned within ten days. This was good news of a sort, but no cause for jumping with joy and therefore I adopted a wait and see attitude and hoped that the phone really would work when returned.

Senor Glum appeared again on the next day with Chubby and his lad. With John interpreting I was given to understand that a trip to the Bank was the order of the day for funds to settle the bill. Cash only, no Credit Cards. To this request I objected as there was still the matter of the engine alarm. To my delight it was agreed that this would be seen to the very same day, so while the lad worked on the engine with Chubby supervising, and me in attendance, Senor Glum was left to cool his heels on shore. It was mid afternoon, and hot, before the job was completed, which didn't improve his outlook on life judging by his look of disapproval:

Off we went to the bank or should I say banks as the one in Balboa which I usually dealt with was closed, necessitating a tour of Panama to find another branch. If this traipsing around hadn't been so tiresome sitting in the same vehicle as these people, it could have been entertaining. The bank would only allow a withdrawal of five hundred dollars in one day to which Senor Glum, if this was possible, became even more annoyed, but which delighted me. Through all this seeking of funds I was kept out of the conversation, due to my lack of Spanish. I gathered though that my travelling companions, by the tone of their conversation, were not at all delighted. Finally we ended up at the mechanic's place of work to report to the owner. These people had given me the run-around during the past few weeks so the shoe was now on the other foot. It gave me a great deal of pleasure to inform them that as I could only draw a daily amount of five hundred dollars they would have to wait until there were enough funds accumulated to settle the bill, and would they kindly return me to the Marina. No sooner had I left the office than I was asked for my Credit Card. 'Ah! I thought, they do take plastic.' Not so, they only wanted to check my credit. The cheek of it? Now if they had the facility to check a person's credit they obviously could take credit cards. So, what were they up to? Tax dodges maybe? The half hour ride back to the Marina with Senor Glum was carried out in total silence, in an atmosphere that was fraught with resentment. Cutting the air with a knife came to mind. What could be the guy's problem? He wouldn't even respond to my thank you when I got out of the car.

The accumulation of funds was performed on a daily basis as there was a maximum amount that I could draw at any one time. The bank opened at eight o'clock, which was an ideal time for me as I could be there before they became busy. The procedure was to present my credit card and passport to the girl at the front desk, who would check my credit rating and then give me a slip with the amount to present to the cashier. Who would then count out the required dollars.

On the second day the girl asked me if I was married. A strange question I thought, and wondered what that had to do with drawing cash. It did occur to me later that the question was a form of invitation. If the answer was no, then one is free to ask the person for a date. Being a little slow on the uptake I didn't follow through with this. She was a very attractive woman, in her early thirties, I would guess, but my recent past precluded any interest in taking up another relationship. On the following days the subject was not raised again. Just a good morning greeting of friendly recognition.

During the time it took to accumulate the amount to settle the bill, strangely enough, Chubby and his lad attended to the engine. Just what they were doing was beyond me as the engine had been run to satisfaction. The alarm wasn't silenced satisfactorily but they didn't appear to be tending to that, rather the lad was disconnecting parts of the engine and re-assembling. It crossed my mind that they were probably making sure I didn't take off without paying. This presumed suspicion of their motives towards me seemed to have become mutual.

In the fullness of time the funds to settle the bill was accumulated, but another problem arose. Having spoken to Justino at the Marina requesting outward clearance I was informed that this would take place in Balboa and we set out in Justino's car to the office that we attended on arrival, calling at the Bank on the way for the last of the engine fee. For whatever reason the Immigration Officer was quite angry when he inspected my passport, and kept saying, "Diablo, Diablo." This I understood was Spanish for devil. He didn't seem to be using the word as an expletive but rather, with throw away gestures of the right hand, was trying to tell me something. For whatever reason Justino had made himself scarce and was unavailable to explain what this irate gentleman was on about. Could it be he was telling me to go to, the devil? Surely not, for this was official business. The official appeared to realise that we were getting nowhere and the problem was solved by taking me outside to speak to a taxi driver that happened to be there. The driver, having listened to the immigration chappie, turned to me and speaking very good English advised that he would take me to Diablo, which housed another section of the Immigration Offices. There I must pay a fee and come back here to complete the formalities. So that is what all the Diablo business was about. Diablo was another area of Balboa.

This taxi driver obviously wasn't going to miss out on making a little money out of this trip which took a mere five minutes there and five back, with a wait long enough to part with a considerable amount of the day's banking. Having been long enough in Panama to know taxi prices what this guy charged was double the going rate. Obviously I protested, but his mate adopted an intimidating manner suggesting that the request was reasonable. For my part I didn't fancy being duffed up for a mere five dollars so with as much grace as possible under the circumstances, coughed up.

Then once again I presented myself to Immigration Part One, had my passport stamped and was directed across the yard to another building housing the Port Authority. The desire to gain officialdom's largesse to be allowed to leave Panama required a lengthy form filling session. The door to this office had been left open which allowed me to see Justino in the hallway sidling out through another door. Although he didn't acknowledge me his look was apologetic, enough for me to keep silent, feeling that a word from me would not be welcome.

The form filling itself was not a lengthy affair, if the typist had attended to the matter without interruption it would have been over within just a matter of probably ten minutes. But this was

Panama where social graces and good manners are paramount. Amongst a certain level of society that is, and if the occasion suits. The preliminaries to the form filling were conducted by me putting down under the secretary's guidance details of the boat. And I should say at this point she didn't speak any English either, no more than the Immigration chap. So the directions for information were conducted by understanding boat measurements and details in word sounds and descriptive gestures. This information was then taken to the typewriter to be made into an official format. Another person then entered the office and sat down, starting what was to be a long conversation with the typist who, one presumed, had the aforementioned social graces. One must be polite and pay attention to the speaker. The form filling stopped with only an occasional peck at the keys when the conversation had a lull. I deduced from the papers he was holding and his air of familiarity with the office that he was an agent for some other boat, and well known to the typist. By the intense tone of the conversation I deduced that the subject was one of some importance, as either one or the other of the participants would strengthen their verbal delivery, not in the sense that there was a conflict of opinion but rather an important point on which they both agreed. Nothing they said had any interest to me as I hadn't a clue what they were discussing. All my emotions were directed at getting my form completed and leaving. Certainly I could have been rude and reminded the form filler that I was still there and would she kindly complete my bloody form. But, that didn't seem to be the best approach and I decided to wait it out. When the discourse finally ended and the form completed, to my surprise and chagrin, it wasn't a clearance that had been filled out but an invoice regarding the dues connected with my nearly five weeks stay in Panama. Now if that wasn't adding insult to injury I don't know what would be, particularly as the bill came to a tidy sum, just about cleaning me out of the daily bank allowance. With yet another visit to the bank looming on the morrow I paid the bill with the compensating thought that the girl in the bank was quite pretty and friendly. My, but what the mind conjures up when faced with a financial injury.

The next move in this saga of attempting to leave Panama was to be directed to the next office to present the proof of payment and receive the permission to leave. At least I could be thankful it wasn't the Cabo and have to tramp all over town to complete these formalities.

*

Thankfully, Senor Glum was not awaiting my return holding out his sweaty palm for his due. At this, perversely, I entertained a twinge of regret. It would have given me some satisfaction to send him on his way to return the next day. After all, having put up with the run-around from his company for the five weeks and being held against my will, being petty would have been some compensation.

Justino showed up though, regretful at abandoning my cause. It transpired that his boss had sent him to an arriving ship to transact its clearance inwards. He did, however, offer to take me shopping for groceries prior to my imminent departure, for which I was grateful. To have a helping hand and ready transport was preferable to struggling on my own and engaging taxis.

All was not peace in the old homestead though, for later that day when a relaxing beer would have been welcome the kitchen tap riser split, spewing water at great pressure across the galley. It seemed that the new water pump was not lacking in efficiency. So a trip to the hardware store for a new riser took precedence over a relaxing beer.

By the time the new riser was fitted it was evening and time to meet with Damien for a beer, and an amusing banter session. Good company was Damien and a welcome relaxing change from the day's trials. Vivien, Damien's girl friend, joined us later when, I'm sad to say we, were both a little affected by the intake of beer. For my part I had trouble getting into the car, which was commented on by the office girls the next morning that ignored my protestations that it was due to stiffness brought on by old age. The effects of the beer can't have been too bad though because after Vivian dropped me off in town I managed to down a meal and return to the boat without incident. Rather I would suggest that my mood was due to elation at the coming departure: besides, I have difficulty getting into cars anyway even when I'm not influenced by outside forces.

*

Nothing is ever perfect in this life, and I make this comment thinking of what happened the following morning after being to the bank for the balance of funds I was enjoying a cup of coffee in the cockpit watching the day develop, when I was abruptly brought out of my reverie by the sound of water under pressure. With the previous day's occurrence still fresh in mind I dashed below to find that the tap riser under the bathroom sink had split, no doubt in sympathy with the galley sink. It was off to the hardware store again for parts and spent an unpleasant interlude crammed into the sink unit doing contortions again.

No sooner had this problem been solved than Chubby and his sidekick turned up to tinker with the engine. The boat was on a mooring and it was up to me to ferry these characters from the dock, and believe me it was quite a pull. Chubby being on the heavy side can only be described as unwelcome ballast. For the next two hours it was my dubious pleasure to hang around watching the poor lad, with sweat pouring from him, doing whatever with the engine, which to my mind was in good shape anyway. Chubby spent the whole session just sitting watching, offering the odd comment. And, the cheek of it asking me for a beer; needless to say this request was sharply refused. It truly was a very hot afternoon and I could have downed a beer myself, and my sympathies were with the lad who looked as though he could use a beer if only to replace the lost fluids. I would have willing shared a beer with him, but he couldn't be given one without the other, and there was no way the idle Chubby would be offered. This refusal of refreshment served a purpose though, as they shortly reassembled what they had been pottering with and requested a ferrying to the dock.

Senor Glum had been sighted earlier in the day hovering around the office area and as I was anxious to depart this place I gathered up the wherewithal to settle his bill and ferried his off-spring ashore. True to form Chubby had left his gate pass on the boat, again, so it was up to me to row back and get it. Truly I would be glad to see the back of this person.

The transaction was carried out under the amused, interested eye of Christina, one of the office girls who were on duty that day. Not that her interest was of an official nature rather that she happened to be attracted by the amount of money that was changing hands. The banks were not issuing notes of a higher denomination than twenties due to a counterfeiting scare so the pile was quite impressive. The amusement came when having handed over this considerable number of dollars I asked Senor Glum for change of fifty cents for the remaining forty-three cents. One would think that for a mere seven cents it was not worth the bother, but then after all the delays sanctioned by this engineering firm an urge to be devilish possessed me. Imagine my glee when he didn't have the change but had to ask Christina. I'm quite sure that if Christina and I had exchanged glances mirth would have taken over. As it were only we two that saw the humour in the situation.

John Cole had come into the outer office at this moment and must have wondered what was going on. With a stack of bills on the counter to have three people sorting out a few cents must have looked odd to say the least.

"John;" I said, "Would you tell him that although the engine is satisfactory, the alarm sounds continuously."

After an exchange in Spanish, John said that they would come back tomorrow to fix it.

By this time I'd had all I cared to take of their hedging and interminable delays and there was no way that I was going for that one. The alarm wasn't that much of a bother and I only mentioned this to let Senor Glum know that their attention to detail was nothing to be proud of.

"No way," said I. "I'm leaving first thing tomorrow."

Ignoring the Senor who was busy stuffing the settlement into his pockets I directed my next statement to John.

"I'll go over to the fuel dock now, John, then come and settle up with you. I'd like an early start in the morning."

"OK. Your bill will be ready."

However, even yet matters were not going to run smoothly. Returning to the office to settle the marina dues I found that my credit card would not be accepted. It appeared that I was temporarily broke, at least for this particular bill, until my pension was paid into my account in three days. A further hold-up of three days in Panama was not the option that I was prepared to choose. The other alternative was to pay with my back-up credit card, one that was kept in reserve, which when funds were removed could not be replaced without considerable problems. In this situation there was nothing for it but to bite the bullet and dip into this reserve.

"What time will you be leaving, Ron?" asked John.

"As soon after first light as possible. Well, after my morning ritual anyway, can't set out without the morning tea."

John nodded, accepting the importance of this statement. "I'll be in the yard at seven, make sure you come and say goodbye before you leave."

I must admit to being touched by this, but then, our relationship during my stay had been one of goodwill, and to leave without saying goodbye would have been churlish to say the least. It had been my intention to say cheerio this evening, but then at the outset of a six week trip what does a couple of hours difference make?

*

At the promise of finally getting away from Panama I felt elation, but also a twinge of regret. Having been there for five weeks the place and people must have got to me. Their laid back attitude to life I found to be opposite to my get a move on approach. But then, by the time I came to leave their relaxed way of life seemed to be the way to go. Too late to change though; as one gets older one tends to get a fixed attitude and set in one's ways, and in the morning all this would be in the past. So move on and be happy.

The last evening was spent pleasurably in the company of Damien and Vivien over dinner at the restaurant down the causeway, and then much against my wishes I conceded to their pressure to visit a nightclub. The reason for giving in to this alien pursuit was due to the fact that the nightclub in question was within the Flamenco Resort and only a few minutes from the boat. Needless to say the racket was deafening, drowning out all possibility of conversation. It wasn't long before I slipped away for a farewell 'Pasteurised' beer at the regular watering hole, then went back to the boat for a good night's sleep.

CHAPTER SIX

PANAMA to MARQUESAS

*'......a procurer of contentedness; and that it begat habits of
peace and patience in those that professed and practiced it.'*

Izaak Walton. 1593-1683

Having made the goodbyes to John and his staff, rowed
back to the boat, deflated and stowed the dinghy, I got away from
the mooring at 0730 motoring out of the marina and around
Flamenco Island into the Gulf of Panama to find a breeze. This was
not long in coming as by eight o'clock it was soon blowing briskly at
fifteen knots out of the south-west. A sure sign that the trade winds
were here to greet me, the sails were soon hoisted with the boat then
making an exhilarating progress. That feeling of peace and
contentment gradually took hold of me again as we headed out from
the constraints of shore-side living with its crowds and noise. I was
beginning to believe that I didn't care much for people, nice and
pleasant that they can be, or for that matter their environment. The
further away from Panama I went the greater the feeling of
happiness became. The solitude of sailing truly was the life to have.

True to form though, as this was the Gulf of Panama, the
wind died away around noon. From the past experience the vagaries
of the wind in this part of the world could not be relied on for
making any appreciable progress, but this did not worry me unduly
as I now had an operative engine. Normally, when the wind fails one
just sits and waits for it to come up again. After all to use fuel
unnecessarily is folly. Of course there is always an exception to any
rule, and in this particular case it was a wise move to fire up the
engine and get clear of the busy shipping lanes and out into the
Pacific proper.

The gremlins hadn't given up just yet though. The engine
fired and was put into gear. As there was no wind the Hydrovane
steering was inoperative which didn't present a problem as there
was the Autopilot. The idea was to engage this method of steering
while I made lunch. So far, so good, at least until it came to setting a

course by the gyro compass, when something about the compass struck me as odd. The compass indicated the direction we were travelling to the north which was a hundred and eighty degrees out of whack. Something amiss here, but what? Well may I ask? And that is all I could do as I don't know anything about electronics either. All was not lost though as the autopilot was keeping the course it was set for, probably as fooled as I was by the compass. There was no way I would go back to Panama to try and find someone who could fix it; from now on the courses would be set by magnetic compass.

An anecdote came to mind at this time, one that Joe had told about a boat owner engaging a local to fix a problem with his electronics. He ended up with his in destruct mode, requiring a new unit shipped down from the United States. Not for me, thank you; the magnetic compass would be fine until such time that a representative of this particular system could be engaged.

Lunch passed pleasantly while I was in the cockpit with the boat chugging along famously. This venue for lunch was so I could keep a watchful eye on the gyro compass to see if maybe it would sort itself out, but alas no satisfactory results in that direction.

The wind came up again within the hour, so it was off with the engine and back to sailing. This lasted until the following noon when we were comfortably in the steady south west trade winds. In twenty-four hours the boat covered the same distance as it did in ten days when I was trying to get to Panama. There is certainly something to be said for having a clean bottom and an operating engine. Truly life had taken a turn for the better. All that was needed now was to get across the equator into the south-east trades, of which this wind we were experiencing now was a part, and then it would be just a case of boogying along to Heva-Oa in the Marquesas with the wind on the port quarter, a most admirable point of sail.

*

For the next few days with the wind constant on the starboard beam I made a course towards the bulge of Ecuador. This was not the original intention but for some inexplicable reason this boat would not travel in the direction asked of it when the wind was forward of the beam by more than two points. This situation had also evolved when I was trying to make a better course coming down from Cabo San Lucas. Obviously the sailing qualities of this design left something to be desired. Enough said of this phenomenon, remarkable though it may seem, but one must work with what one has. Once again distance would be added to the overall trip, something to write about I suppose, if nothing else.

Some sixty miles short of the equator and too close to Ecuador for my liking I brought the boat around on the other tack with the hope of passing south of the Galapagos Islands. This tack was held for the next few days when I realised that, due to the crab like qualities inherent in my boat, we would pass to the north of this archipelago. Hawaii was in that direction but as mentioned before, much as I like Hawaii this trip was to be elsewhere. So it was a case of turning back the way I had come and try to make more distance to the south before changing tack.

During this interlude of backing and filling I sighted a ship heading on a reciprocal course. As it came closer it altered course slightly to pass nearer, no doubt to get a better look at this thing in the middle of nowhere. By the size of this vessel I guessed that it was a small trader plying between Ecuador and the Galapagos. As it passed close by I gave a merry wave, which, when I considered this in retrospect struck me as the sort of wave that President Nixon gave from the helicopter on leaving the office of President of the United States. If the reader can recall this wave was distinctive, given by the lifting of the arm with open palm giving a circular motion, then turning to proffer the back of the hand. It struck me at the time that this turning of the hand seemed to be a gesture of contempt. Must remember to wave with a more distinctive courtesy. Obviously the people on the ship didn't take this as an offensive gesture for they gave two very nice toots on the ship's whistle and I gave a merry wave in return.

The next afternoon I sighted a boat approaching at speed from right ahead. My first thought was, 'bloody, hell! Pirates'. This thought was short-lived, however, as fine on the starboard bow a Dan buoy was clearly seen, no doubt marking the nets vis-à-vis the boat, and as we were one hundred and fifty miles from the nearest land it was extremely unlikely that pirates would operate this far from a land base. As the boat came nearer I saw it was an open boat about twenty feet in length propelled by a large outboard engine, and containing three men in oilskins all of whom were gesticulating towards the buoy. By this time I had altered course to give the buoy a wide berth and by hand signals I alleviated their concern. They appeared to be well pleased. They changed the arm motions to a dumb show which I took to be asking for cigarettes. As I don't smoke all I could do was to show by apologetic hand signals that I didn't have any. This was taken in good humour and off they went at a great rate of knots. As I watched them leave it occurred to me that they might have been asking for something to eat, but they had left now. Not that there was much to offer that didn't require cooking, a tin of sardines maybe, but that would have been inappropriate under the circumstances; after all they were fishermen. This meeting did raise the question: what on earth were they doing so far from land, fishing obviously but, in such a small boat? One can only assume that there was a mother ship in the vicinity. Later that evening when dark had settled in I sighted lights far to the south, which judging by their intensity would certainly be those of a fisherman. By this time there was considerable distance between me and the small boat and relating the two was now academic.

For several days since leaving Panama one of the tasks that I had to perform as soon as convenient after the morning ritual, was to climb out of the cockpit and throw flying fish back over the side the dead that had landed on board during the night. After all they couldn't be left to rot in the sun. The fish were quite a reasonable size, maybe four or five inches in length which on reflection could, with a number of them make an acceptable meal. Sod's Law now took over; only one flying fish on subsequent days came on board. Plenty of shoals were sighted skimming the waves having been disturbed by the boat but they were all heading away. The one I did have was very tasty if very scant in bulk. No matter. Maybe in the future they would grace me in abundance sufficient to make a meal. As the opportunity never arose again I could only surmise that the word was out in the flying fish population that there was a boating guy eager to have them in the frying pan, so beware.

On this return tack towards Ecuador I did make sufficient southing to get across the equator into the South East Trades then directed the course to the west passing south of the Galapagos. The band of latitude between the equator and ten degrees south on which Heva-Oa lay was now my bailiwick. The wind at twenty knots was now on the port quarter giving the boat a very satisfactory speed towards this destination. There was quite a high swell running, no doubt created by the constant direction of the wind, which apart from giving the boat a rolling and dipping motion was no problem at all, the boat lifting easily to allow the waves to pass under. At no time during the months of sailing did the boat take a wave on board, heavy spray in inclement weather conditions, but nothing green and solid. In that respect this was a good sea boat.

The days and nights passed pleasantly with the wind constant in direction varying slightly in intensity that only made for a more interesting passage. No ships or other traffic were sighted, making the solitude even more acute. In fact there was nothing to disturb this happy experience. The skies varied between cloudy some days and clear on others, the clear nights being particularly delightful with the stars appearing to be enormous. Orion was right over head with the disconcerting view of Sirius pointing in the opposite direction from what it does in the northern hemisphere. This took some getting used to. Viewing it from the south of the equator rather than the north latitude one can see what happens as Orion's belt travels along the celestial equator. However, the clear nights were not as frequent as one would wish so there wasn't too much time to worry about the configuration of the constellation of Orion. Most nights being overcast precluded star gazing, and at these times I sought contentment by standing in the hatch feeling the wind and the easy roll of the boat in the swell. After all the hiccups prior to my arrival in Panama this problem free passage was indeed a balm to the spirit.

Ah! Yes. Complacency has no place on a boat, like anywhere else it only leads to a feeling of false security. Something like three weeks out from the start of this idyllic cruise, with 2440 miles to go from noon to the Marquesas, while I was enjoying an evening concert with Shirley Bassey belting out a selection of songs, the fresh water pump started up with a high pitched whine. Something wrong there I said to myself and switched off the circuit at the panel. Suspecting that the pump was being starved of water and assuming that with the boat heeled over on the port tack I thought the port tank would be the most likely culprit. Sure enough it was bone dry; the starboard tank wasn't much better being about a third full, or should I say, two thirds empty. This was a pretty pickle. The tanks were filled in Panama and it was unreasonable to have used such a large amount in so short a time. A leak in the water line, or the tank, was the most obvious reason, but could not be investigated at this time of night. I resolved to take up the problem of water loss in the morning and both tanks were isolated. There was some comfort in this predicament of water loss, and here we were looking on the bright side: the starboard tank could be accessed from the main cabin, whereas with the port tank one had to clamber over the engine and under the settee. Judging by the amount of water left for general use, serious restrictions would have to be adopted. With an estimated eighteen days to go that would mean diluting cooking water with sea water. After all one normally puts salt into the cooking of potatoes, not that there were any on board as the supermarket in Balboa didn't seem to cater in bulk for this item. There was plenty of rice however so here was a possibility. Then it occurred to me there was an untapped source of noodles, both chicken and beef in large quantities, having been bought in bulk from the original storing. There would be no showers unless it rained. Not much hope there as it hadn't rained for a week and then not enough to make any difference. Tea was the one item that wouldn't be curtailed at the moment; after all, one had to get one's priorities right, and a little indulgence in the right direction could mean keeping one's sanity.

Searching for a possible leak would mean putting a pressure test on the line, a situation that would only reduce the amount of water in the remaining tank. Hobson's choice, which is no choice at all, so the test would have to wait until the tanks had been filled. The pump would remain shut down and the water accessed through the inspection port. Who knows, it might rain.

There was little to record during the following weeks but agreeable weather, clear skies for the most part, wind constant in velocity and direction, in fact perfect sailing weather. Record the noon position, calculate the day's run and write up the journal. Now and again the weather bow would bang into a wave to slop water on the foredeck. Taking water on board forward had created an annoying situation, annoying in as much as somehow puddles of water had formed in the forward berth under the cushions. How this water had entered the boat to settle as it did remained a mystery, at first I suspected that ingress was through the chain locker and along the wire trace to seep behind the lining fabric. I sealed off this suspected area but the puddles still formed. It is well known that where water comes in is no indication of where it will come out, so there was nothing to do at this stage but wait until I made a thorough inspection on the outside. As the forward berth was not in use the cushions were placed on edge and away from the accumulated water and the hatch that was accessed under the berth were removed to allow the water to be baled into the bilges.

With this poser on the back burner I turned my attention to the teak deck. Progress had been made where the main cabin deck had been completely laid and one tube of caulking applied. The overall effect was stunning to the point where I was eager to purchase more caulking to finish the remaining section. However, as this was somewhere in the future, it was now considered practical to apply a sealing coat of varnish, and then tackle the raised section of deck in the dining area, the engine box top and the step into the cockpit. After a few days, this project I completed, *sans* caulking, a most pleasing appearance that dispelled all the bad happenings of the voyage.

The guys from the Dynasty in Panama had explained how best to approach the matter of inserting the caulking and these instructions were followed to the letter as it made the most sense for a clean application and avoided messing up the teak surface. Masking tape was placed on the teak, leaving the space between the strips open to receive the caulking by the caulking gun which could then be pressed into the joints and any excess pushed into the next seam. When a skin had formed the masking tape could be removed, leaving a perfectly clean deck ready for sanding and varnishing once the sealant had hardened.

Contact with base by e-mail had failed early on in this leg of the passage from Panama in that it was only possible to write a message while connected on line, which with the cost per minute of air time was not an option I considered. It just didn't make sense to communicate this way; rather it was more economical to telephone what was happening and have the message distributed by e-mail from base. At least there was contact so all the recipients would know I was safe and sound. Still some days away from Heva-Oa I decided to phone a friend in England to invite her to join the boat in Tahiti. I know this was going against my resolve to sail single handed, but then about this time I was enjoying this experience so much that a sense of wanting to share had taken hold, and what better person than Judy who was at this time between jobs and feeling very much down. As sailing was a new experience for her, not having been on boat before, it could be argued that it was still, for my part, a single handed experience. Well there was some logic in this premise. To my delight the offer was accepted and she made plans to her advantage. She would go as far as New Zealand only a short two week run from Tahiti. Ah! Yes, here we go again. Will I never learn not to anticipate the future?

Joy upon joy, the rain came. This unexpected occasion had me scrabbling to set up the water catchments plastic sheet and bucket. The rain came down in torrents, unfortunately though for only a few minutes before passing away to the north. No matter, beggars cannot be choosers and at least there was three inches of water in the bucket. Sadly this amount had a brownish tint and contained specks of black dirt, a tantalising situation, not clean enough for consumption and not enough for a body bath. What to do? The answer soon materialised and I stripped off, fetched the soap and towel and washed the parts of my body with water in order of priority: face, under arms and the nether regions. Not having bathed for quite some time this limited cleaning of selected body parts created a most unusual sensation. The washed areas felt fresh and clean in counterpoint to the grotty unwashed parts. No matter, something in the manner of hygiene had been accomplished and I felt a new man. Well partly.

To add to the delight of this experience, for the first time on this leg a school of dolphins came to play around the boat. It is always a pleasure to watch these wonderful creatures streaming through the clear water with no visible effort, to leap and cavort around the boat, racing ahead and under the boat yet never in any danger of being hit. On this occasion, there must have a dozen or more, but sadly they only seemed to stay long enough for the watcher to anticipate a performance of some duration then head off to other locations. As compensation though, they left me with a profound feeling of pleasure and a further lifting of spirits.

Prior to starting out on this adventure a neighbour, a young lady of maybe thirty years, had given me advice that I found amusing at the time, and which now came to mind. Apparently she was worried that I might be attacked by a whale or some other large sea creature. It was difficult to suppress my amusement at this piece of information and for my lack of faith I was promptly chastised. She was concerned that a creature may have been hurt by someone else and believing it was me, would attack my boat. Although I didn't put much credibility to her fears the memory of it remained. So it was then that during the latter part of the run to the Marquesas I was kneeling on the stern lockers, in the failing light of day, taking a leak when from under the boat what I took to be a sheet of plywood appeared. Odd, I thought, a sheet of plywood way out here? Then it flapped proving it to be not a sheet of plywood but a rather large ray. The neighbour's advice came like a shock to my mind causing me to quickly gain the safety of the cockpit, somewhat shamefaced. Ah! The powers of suggestion can be quite a force on the mind.

For some days, what I had taken to be a length of seaweed, kelp by the nature of it, seemed to have caught up on the stem and was streaming along the starboard side. Numerous attempts I had made with the boathook from the cockpit to capture this offending article and release it, all to no avail as it kept slipping off. One day the wind and swell having calmed a little, and the boat being steadier, I clambered forward to have a better look at where the kelp had been caught up. Well, to my surprise it wasn't kelp at all but the tubular insert of the rub rail. There was no way to re-insert it, just coil it up and secure it to the rail. I shook my head in wonder at what else would go amiss. Later I contemplated the rub rail insert coming free and wondered if this could be related to the water coming in to the forward berth. I was clutching at straws maybe, but it was something else to check on when time and place allowed.

On the last evening of this passage I was relaxing in the cabin after the meal thinking how nice it would be to have a glass of wine or something similar to celebrate the near conclusion of the six week run from Panama. A drink of anything alcoholic would do. I was jolted out of this reverie by a loud thud above my head. This needed investigating of course, so I stirred my stumps and went on deck to find that the mainsail was lying in a heap on the coach roof. With a sigh of acceptance that things do happen on this boat I clambered onto the coach roof to find that the topping lift halyard had frayed through. This shouldn't happen I thought in wonderment; there are sheaves to prevent this happening. Well there was nothing I could do about this matter at this time, being disinclined to scrabble around in the dark connecting the spare halyard. A gathering up of the offending heap on to the boom and a light lashing around the sail would have to suffice. Sorting this out would have to wait until morning as we seemed to be making reasonable progress under the genoa. The Hydrovane seemed quite happy with the situation also, so I went below determined to fix the problem in the morning.

So it was that after six weeks of easy sailing I saw Heva-Oa in the Marquesas rise out of the horizon. Throughout the morning this island loomed larger until more detail began to emerge. As I closed with the island I took the mainsail off the boom and stowed it, furled the genoa, and then, fired the engine to cruise along the coast to find a safe haven. Unlike most islands in the south Pacific there was not the expected coral reef protecting the shore, just sheer cliffs rising several hundred feet out of the ocean at the base of which the swells broke relentlessly. These cliffs were interspersed with deep, lush valleys leaving one wondering if there was any means of travelling from one valley to the next. It just didn't seem possible there were any roads that could reasonably be constructed through the dense jungle and around these steep sided mountains, and there were definitely no signs of habitation.

CHAPTER SEVEN

HEVA-OA. MARQUESAS

After an hour motoring along the coast, the entrance to the harbour at the western end of the island came into view. Now a sense of dread possessed me at the likelihood of numerous boats being in the harbour. After all wasn't Heva-Oa the first stop on the way to the South Pacific. Not that boats crowding the harbour was a problem, it was the thought of the people on board wanting to socialise that bothered me. Time spent on my own was becoming an obsession. Not to worry though for on rounding the breakwater there was only one sailboat at anchor. With a feeling of relief that my fears where unfounded I came to anchor. My relief was brief, however, as a head appeared at the hatch of a boat shouting and gesticulating towards the shore. I must admit to a twinge of irritation, for it seemed that I was to be bothered by people after all. All I could do was to gesticulate in return, indicating that his signalling meant nothing. At this he jumped into his inflatable and came over, which indicated a matter of urgency to his signals.

"Parlez vous, français?" he asked, as his boat came to rest by my bow.

"No, English."

He proceeded to inform me in perfect English that I was anchored in a restricted area, and pointed out two markers on the shore which indicated the no-go zone. It appeared that the spot in which I was anchored was plumb in the middle of the approach to the quay for the trading steamers. Nothing for it then but to move. It was now came to light that the gremlins were still at work, for the electric windlass decided to go on strike requiring the anchor to be hauled in by Armstrong's patent.

During the shifting of anchorage the gentleman in the inflatable stayed close by to advise me of a good position, and because of his help my irritation was replaced by a feeling of goodwill and we soon fell into conversation. How fortuitous this was to my needs is beyond explanation, for a stranger who didn't speak French would have no idea of how to clear inwards or the best and only way to get to the police station to perform this function. There was no public transport so the only way to get into Atuona was by thumbing a ride, or shank's pony and the road, was long and tortuous, something to be avoided by the less energetic. Matters with this agent of goodwill were becoming more and more to my benefit and understanding my need for an alcoholic beverage he took me over to the store, to buy supplies. Bad luck though for the store didn't sell alcohol, so a drink less evening was looming. Pity as a little of what does one good would have helped me unwind.

This Good Samaritan it transpired was retired from the French Army, still a young man on a pension that allowed him to spend his future on his boat just cruising around the islands of the Marquesas and visit with his many friends and contacts accumulated over the years he had spent here. Something like a latter day Paul Gauguin. As he had a female companion on board, and in a part of the world where there was no fear of storms, his life must have been idyllic, just pottering around from island to island as the inclination took him. The French painter Paul Gauguin found these islands compelling, so why not modern man? The twelve islands that make up the Marquesas cover an area of 1000 square kilometres so there would be plenty of scope for an island hopper to fill one's days. Unfortunately, though there is a down side as supplies are very expensive, having to be brought over from Tahiti. Heva-Oa was also without any services for the boater either. The sail repairs would have to wait until Tahiti where I was informed by my new found enlightener there was everything the heart could desire.

In due course all the information that would be required to have a trouble free stay in Heva-Oa had been passed on and my French friend took his leave to leave me planning the adventures of tomorrow. This would incur inflating the dinghy to get ashore then hope for a ride into town to get inward clearance. These thoughts were distracted by a knocking on the hull, which on investigation proved to be the Frenchman again. On this occasion he was an angel of mercy as holding his inflatable steady alongside with one hand he waved a bottle of wine with the other.

"For your evening meal," he announced, handing the bottle over.

"Well, thank you kindly," said I, "you are a lifesaver. What do I owe you?" I asked, reaching for my wallet.

"Nothing, enjoy. Maybe one day you can return the favour." And with a Gallic wave he was zooming back to his boat.

The slight discomfort at having been the recipient of this fortuitous gift was short lived and I was soon tucking in to the evening meal and raising a glass of this wonderful libation towards the boat of this kind man. Is there anything more worthwhile than a glass of fine wine to excite the pallet?

*

After a good night's rest in the forward berth I was ready for the new day. After breakfast the dinghy was inflated and launched in readiness to go ashore. Viewing the harbour wall through the binoculars for a possible landing place didn't reveal anything that filled my heart with joy. There was but one set of steps to effect a landing on which the water surged with an incoming swell. To avoid getting my feet wet would need some nimble footwork.

While contemplating the best method of getting ashore my erstwhile friend from the previous evening had up-anchored and was motoring past, no doubt to yet one of the other islands. With a merry wave and a hearty 'Bon Voyage', he was gone.

The scramble up the steps wasn't all that difficult as it turned out. Being sockless it was just a matter of carrying my sandals to dry ground. In fact, there was nothing difficult to cause any concern. It was just a short walk to the road where a passing car gave me a lift into the town of Atuona. Having located the Gendarmerie only proved that nothing ever goes smoothly, as they were closed for the weekend, this being Saturday. This must be a crime free island for the police to close up shop for the weekend. Well, there was nothing for it but to return on Monday. First though I wanted to wander around the shops and see what they had to offer. Bread was high on my wish list and as I am partial to those long French loaves, what better place than a French island to satisfy this whim? Oops! Not to be. Bread baking was only carried out for Monday delivery to the shops. What I did find odd was the number of shops all selling general merchandise and three of these were on the same street. There wasn't anything to keep me in town, which was just a collection of shops. Post Office, a bank all spread out as though to give the impression of size I supposed. So it was back to thumbing a ride to the other side of the harbour and the boat. Before clambering into the dinghy though I wandered up to the store visited the previous evening. Might as well do some grocery shopping here where it isn't too far to carry the goods. What they had to offer in the way of food appeared to be only canned goods. If this was the situation on Heva-Oa life must be very dreary meal wise and no, no bread until Monday.

Water and fuel though, were available but, not without difficulty, or so I first thought. The procedure was to take up the anchor and approach the store, then turn to present the stern of the boat to the steps that led down from the store into the harbour, drop anchor and back up to within two feet of the steps. The store owner would then take the mooring line securing the boat in position. Surprisingly, this manoeuvre didn't present any difficulty even for little me on my own. I made a few adjustments to the anchor line which required a few trips to the foredeck, but apart from that everything went smoothly. Within the hour the boat was back in the anchorage where a pressure test was put on the water line. This proved nothing except to present a mystery as to where the fresh water had disappeared. Well if there was no evidence of a leak in the line there was nothing to fix; however, a close watch would have to be made on the water level in the tanks on the passage to Tahiti.

Having rigged a spare halyard for the main sail and the afternoon having progressed to what would have been time for sundowners and as there was nothing to drink anyway; I contented myself with watching what would appear to be the local sport. This involved an individual paddling an outrigger canoe at a furious pace. The design was more like a kayak of some fifteen feet in length with an outrigger, and like most things these days, of a fibreglass construction. Although there were several people involved, all paddling with impressive energy, there didn't seem to be any competition amongst them. Could it be they were in training for some event? What did interest me however was when the exercise was over the boats went around the end of the quay wall at the inner end of the harbour. Could there be a better landing place there? Something to be investigated on Monday when it was time to re-visit the Gendarmerie for the inward clearance and, now I had decided not to tarry here I would also acquire the outward clearance for Tahiti.

Early Sunday morning I observed a great deal of activity at the landing place, with people dressed in white tropical uniforms setting up an awning and tables. The reason soon came to light as a Cruise ship had anchored in the outer bay and was disembarking passengers into the ship's boats which soon came chugging around the breakwater to disgorge them at the landing there to board busses. More than likely to tour the delights of the island, this traffic went on all morning and into the afternoon bringing people ashore and taking them back to the ship. Well a sight such as this can only hold one's attention for so long and I had wonders to perform, so it was then that I attended to replacing broken slides on the mast. To

my surprise a voice addressed me by name and enquired what part
of Victoria I was from. Of course this grabbed my attention, and on
turning I noticed that one of the liberty boats was lying just off my
stern with a body leaning half way out of the hatch.

"What part of Victoria are you from?" he asked again,
volunteering that he was from the James Bay area.

It was obvious that he had read the boat's name and port of
registry on the stern. No prizes for reading 'Ron's Endeavour.
Victoria.'

"Pender Island, actually. The boat's registered in Victoria."

A short conversation followed with this fellow of goodwill,
along the lines of what he was doing on this floating hotel, and what
I was up to. Then it was back to ferrying passengers to base. I was
assured they never left anyone behind. Quite a feat I thought, all
these bodies wandering around and not losing one.

During the night a swell had built up running around the
breakwater which produced a discomforting rocking motion making
it difficult to get any sleep. This confirmed my decision and the plan
of action for the next day: clear inwards and outwards at the same
time, then get away for Tahiti. The run to this port would put me
well ahead of the arrival of my friend Judy, but at least I could be
doing something constructive in the way of bringing the boat up to
efficiency.

So, the following morning these plans were put into action.
The observed landing place proved to be ideal, a low sloping shingle
beach sheltered from the swell by the projecting end of the seawall. It
was only a matter of clambering out of the dinghy dry footed and
pulling it clear of the incoming tide and off to town.

By mid-morning, after availing myself of the bread delivery,
I was chugging out of the harbour into the Bordelais Channel
between Heva-Oa and Tahuata.

*

This archipelago was first discovered by the Spanish sailor
Alvaro de Mendana in 1595, landing at Tahuata. He named the
islands after the wife of the Viceroy of Peru, Marquesas de Mendoza,
soon to be shortened to the name that it now bears. Sadly, the
Islanders first meeting with a European was bloody as the Spaniards
massacred 200 locals causing a violent hostility to future visitors to
the island. Even as late as 1842 a Polynesian chief set up a fierce
resistance to the French, who tried to take control of Tahuata, France
having annexed the Marquesas in that year.

Captain James Cook rediscovered the islands in April 1774, fixing more accurately their latitude and longitude. As with most other islands in the Pacific Ocean, the Western sailors brought diseases that devastated the local population. French missionaries and colonial administrators nearly destroyed the ancient culture of these Polynesians by forcing European religion and mores into their way of life. According to Cook and his officers these people of the Marquesas were not merely the most beautiful people in the South Seas, but the finest race ever beheld, all tall and well proportioned, with good features.

The Marquesas comprise 12 islands spread over an area of 997 square kilometres with each of the islands being very similar in structure. They are high and volcanic in origin, dominated by peaks of lava, five of which are higher than 1000 metres. Apart from Tahuata there are no coral reefs to protect the islands from the pounding of the Pacific Ocean swells, which accounts for flat coastal surfaces being rare.

CHAPTER EIGHT

HEVA-OA to TAHITI

With winged heels, as English Mercuries,
For now sits expectation in the air.

Henry V. act 2

Once clear of the Bordelais Channel the sails went up, and what a sad sight they presented. The Genoa had suffered the most injury on the passage from Panama with the repairs made there having come apart. The leach or what was left of it was wrapped around the starboard spreader with a flapping remnant entangled with the shroud. An attempt to untangle this unsightly symbol of heavy sailing with the boat hook had come to naught with the spreader being tantalisingly just too high, or conversely my arms being too short, to be able to unwind this fluttering rag. A further encumbrance was having to hold on with one hand and stand on tiptoe taking swipes with an unwieldy boathook on a heaving deck. What was needed was for someone to be hauled up the mast to cut it free. However, as it was physically impossible to haul myself up the mast the offending article would have to remain in situ until Tahiti when the sail maker/rigger's services could be engaged. Renewing the broken slides on the mainsail I had attended to in Heva-Oa which solved the problem of losing the wind through the luff. Some satisfaction had been gained there; it was now only a matter of repairing the Panamanian repairs around the area of the reef points. Thankfully, the battens had prevented the sail from ripping down to the foot so, if not perfect, at least all was satisfactory with the main, for now anyway. This business of having to make do with sails that had seen better days had me thinking about new sails of sturdier construction. But when? As the South-East Trade winds still prevailed and the passage to Tahiti being just a week's sailing the decision could be put off until then.

There were four halyards on the mast, two leading forward and two leading aft. One of the forward halyards was used for hoisting the genoa, with the other as a spare. Of the two from aft one had parted, allowing the mainsail to come down with a thump the night before arriving at Heva-Oa, which left the spare. This halyard had shown admirable service by hauling the Radar reflector up the backstay. The situation now was that this halyard had been rigged to hoist the mainsail and the reflector switched to the forward spare halyard. To prevent a repeat of a breakage and lose the services of this now mainsail halyard on the trip to Tahiti was going to require regular checks for any sign of fraying. Lowering the sail, twice a day, to check for any sign of fraying was a bit of a nuisance but it would be foolish to ignore such a critical exercise. As it turned out this halyard remained in perfect condition, which in turn had me wondering what could have caused the initial halyard to fray. Some things it seems are destined to remain forever unanswered.

Leaving Heva-Oa earlier than expected I would arrive in Papeete with days to spare before my good friend Judy arrived. This early arrival would be needed to sort out the lay of the land so to speak. Being a stranger to this part of the world it would make sense to first get established, and then find out the best way to get to the Airport. The flight was due to arrive at one-thirty Saturday morning which added a problem of getting to the airport at such an ungodly hour. No doubt all would be revealed in the fullness of time and it was pointless worrying at this early stage. For the time being there was nothing to do but enjoy the cruise and ponder the problem.

The course I set was in a south-westerly direction to pass to the north of King George Island in the Taumotu Archipelago and the numerous reefs in the area, thence south to Tahiti. The first part of this plan went well and I made good progress as far as the course alteration to the south. This change of direction put the wind forward of the beam, and although the sails were flattened to sail to windward the boat still made considerable drift widening the distance to close Tahiti. Realising that before long yet another change of course would be necessary to reach Papeete, thus putting the wind right ahead, I decided to take down the sails, fire up the engine, then motor the rest of the way. While lowering the mainsail I noticed that the lower batten had disappeared which was yet another puzzlement to ponder, as this batten prevented the reef points ripping the sail to the foot when reefed. This problem would have to be addressed before any reefing could be carried out.

Originally, before leaving Panama my intention was to make for Fiji from the Marquesas so the appropriate charts were purchased. However, the best laid plans often change and during the previous weeks it had been decided to call in at Tahiti instead, this island being on a more direct line with New Zealand. Time was the guiding factor in this decision as I deemed it sensible to be out of the area before the onset of the storm season. After all making a decision to avoid the Atlantic Hurricanes only to find myself in a Pacific storm would not be a very clever situation to be in. The problem was there was no large scale chart on board as Heva-Oa, true to form, was destitute of a seaman's requirements. The only chart on board was of the general area showing Tahiti but not Papeete. All was not lost; however, as there was on board the Admiralty publication, Ocean Passages of the World, which gave the geographical position of Papeete. With this information it was possible to set a course from where I was to where I wanted to be.

The morning was bright and sunny, the wind brisk from right ahead bringing the occasional spray over the bow. Otherwise the cruise along the north coast of Moorea was most pleasantly relaxing. Within the hour Moorea had been left behind and I crossed the channel to Papeete. Next problem to address was to find out how to get into the harbour with the lack of chart information. Viewing the situation through the binoculars I saw a long whitish wall which seemed to be the outer limit of the port but, no break that would indicate the entrance. There was nothing for it but to observe and watch for any other vessels leaving the port, or failing that, proceed as close as possible to see if anything lent itself to an answer. As I closed the distance towards the breakwater to about two miles, a large vessel which turned out to be the Moorea ferry came steaming out of port. Although, due to the angle, a break in the seawall couldn't be located the general area could. Step one solved. Now to proceed until the opening could be located. During this period of trying to locate the entrance to Papeete harbour a person on a Skidoo was observed bouncing about in the waves, no doubt having a great deal of fun. As fate would have it when the entrance opened into view this Skidoo decided to put an end to his games and made for the opening in the seawall. Could one wish for a better pilot?

The island of Tahiti is nearly totally enclosed by coral reefs on the west side and the approaches to Papeete were no exception. However, there are passages well marked by beacons, and as the ferry had come through the reef there was no reason to think that my little boat could not do the same, not to mention the Skidoo operator. All that the situation required now was to navigate the darker blue water through the reef into the port of Papeete, which soon found me inside the breakwater wondering where to go. There was no indication of a marina; from what could be observed this port seemed to handle big ships only. While chugging slowly past various structures for the benefit of big vessels, a familiar sight of a Travelift I noticed situated on the inside of the seawall, so it was to that place I directed my course. My arrival produced a great deal of consternation with many people gesticulating in a Gallic manner, presumably indicating that my presence was not welcome. Eventually someone who spoke English arrived to whom I expressed a desire to book a haul-out, not that that was my intention at this moment but a possibility to be decided on at a later date, but then what else could I do to appease these gentlemen, and I might as well do just that while I was here. So Friday at ten-thirty was agreed on, and I got directions where to moor in the meantime.

Once more I was chugging around the port of Papeete, this time though with a better knowledge and confidence of where to go. To my delight when rounding the stern of an ocean going freighter, before me were a few sailboats of varying sizes moored stern to the quay wall. That was not the only delight for the moorage was right in town, something like the pictures one sees of places like Monte Carlo. Before long, the anchor was down and with the assistance of a lady and her two teenaged children from a boat with the unusual name of 'Fruity Fruit'; I was securely moored stern to the quay and lying with a pontoon on the port side.

CHAPTER NINE

TAHITI

Look stranger at this island now, the leaping light for your Delight discovers.
												Auden

The first Europeans to visit Tahiti were Captain Samuel Wallace and the crew of His Majesties Frigate, Dolphin on the 21st June 1767. They had been commissioned to search the Southern Ocean between Cape Horn and New Zealand to establish the possibility of a temperate land in these latitudes. After battling storms for four months to pass through the straight of Magellan they came upon Tahiti, the first land of any note that would provide the necessities for replenishment of provisions. Their arrival in Matavai Bay on the north coast was vigorously challenged by the natives, who were only subdued by the firing of the guns; a display of the white mans superiority. Henceforth trade was established, with nails being the unit of currency, for both the securing of provisions and the favours of the local women. Wallace named this island King George's Island after the young British monarch. Once friendly relations were established with the Tahitians and the easy favours of the women extended to the ships company this island soon earned the recognition of Paradise. The Dolphin was just five weeks at Tahiti when having replenished water and provisions she returned to England.

The second European leader to arrive at Tahiti was the French commander Bougainville in 1768, remaining for just over a week.

This discovery of Tahiti led to an expedition under the command of Lieutenant James Cook in 1769 to observe the transit of Venus across the face of the sun. This, with other observations around the world hoped to determine the distance between the earth and the sun. Cook had a fort built on the low lying land on the north side of Matavai Bay to protect the valuable instruments from the thieving which was prevalent among the natives at this time. This point of land is still known today as Point Venus.

William Bligh of HMS Bounty was also here to collect breadfruit plants which it was believed would provide food for the West Indies slaves. It is a well known fact of history what the results of that visit became.

After the sailors came the Missionaries to oversee the decline of this sailor's paradise. In 1816, however, two Roman Catholic Priests were expelled to the great annoyance of the French Government who demanded an apology and a most favoured nation treaty from the Tahitians. In 1843 the island became a French Protectorate, the British more than once refusing such an offer. 1880 saw Tahiti become a French Colony.

As a result of western influence the island soon became less than the Paradise that it was seen to be when first discovered. Paul Gauguin on his arrival soon realised that Tahiti was not the place he had expected and took himself off to the Marquesas, hoping for a better life.

*

By the time the boat was secured it was noon and time for lunch and a snooze. After these most important obligations I took myself ashore to report inwards to the Immigration. The location of these offices must have been designed with boaters in mind as they were only a matter of a few minutes walk along the quay wall and all departments were located together in the same low one story building. Indeed a better organisation could not be imagined for the benefit of the boating community, and bearing in mind the difficulties faced in the Cabo a blessing to be thankful for. Another piece of good fortune was the fact that the officials all spoke excellent English which eased the process of clearance. However, before the formalities could be entered into I was required to go to the bank and make a security deposit against overstaying my welcome then return with the proper documentation. The amount of the security deposit, paid by credit card, was quite considerable, but as it would be returned on departure the pain was bearable.

These formalities concluded I was free to explore the immediate locale. Having noticed a Tavern across the road from the berth I proceeded there for a beer and to watch the world go by while pondering a plan of action. My euphoria at being on land again with the prospect of having all my troubles with the boat put to rights was rudely shattered when it came to paying for the beer. To say it was expensive would be an understatement, the price was exorbitant. But then I came to realise in the following days that everything was. This apparently came about when France was carrying out nuclear tests in the Polynesian Islands. Highly paid French personnel competed with the locals for the basics of life; riots followed which resulted in the wages of the populace coming into line with the French. Not the best deal for tourists however.

The inner man being satisfied, if not my pocket I took time to take a wander and find out the lay of the land. In the immediate vicinity of the boat moorings parallel to the sea wall a wide pavement presented benches and planters, and discretely hidden by a low containing wall, garbage containers for use of the boating community, all very neatly kept and functional. Next to this was a wide road of two lanes, each way separated by a median. I later learned that this road encompassed the whole island. The traffic was heavy indeed but, thankfully disciplined, as all vehicles came to a stop when a pedestrian chose to use the designated crossing. On the far side of the road were shops, hotels, banks and the like, in fact quite a commercial section of Papeete. Supplying the needs of the boat began to look promising; however, these needs would have to wait until the morrow as it was too late in the day to conduct a search to track down the help that was required. My stomach was telling of a far greater need, and I decided that someone else's cooking was more desirable than mine, so a restaurant became the object of my search. Down one of the side streets and not too far from the boat a restaurant presented itself. The hour was still early for most diners so I had the place to myself with personalised service. The meal of a main course of the local fish, followed by a cheese plate with French bread and several glasses of excellent red wine was an absolute delight. So much so, that from my position in sight of the kitchen door, I could observe the waiter showing the cook the returned plates which held not a morsel of food, which they seemed to be view with a great deal of surprise. Must admit though that the bread served admirably for wiping up the juices and the small specks of the meal, and they weren't to know just how starved I was for such a well cooked meal. It had been a long day and as is the case in a strange place with its traffic noise and unfamiliar crowds, a tiring one mentally as much as physically. After a short constitutional stroll along the quay wall it was back to the boat to read for a while and an early night, happy and content with the thought that all would be right with the boat projects during the coming days.

*

The following morning as soon as reasonably possible in regard to the opening of business I took myself off on a search of the service agent for the gyro compass. The waiter of the previous evening had given me directions to a shop selling charts only a short distance away as the best place to start. This morning though I was better prepared and had taken the precaution of writing down the address of the agent from the service manual. The gentleman who attended me, much to my surprise, looked at the name and address on my piece of paper and with much confidence denounced my information and wrote out directions to an establishment called Nauti-Sport. This left me a little perplexed as to how he knew the right people to approach, but who was I to argue. As I searched for this place of business I soon came to understand that in Papeete it was a case of wheels within wheels so to speak. Each business operated with other businesses in the boating industry, hand in glove for their mutual benefit no doubt. It certainly was beneficial for the customer also not having to drag around town trying to find the services required.

It was a long hot trek, but soon I presented myself at Nauti-Sport to make my request for the particular service agent only to be told that this gentleman didn't do repairs only installations. The service agent had no ties with Nauti-Sport but, as mentioned everyone seemed to be aware of everyone else's movements I must point out at this stage that each person that I spoke to on this quest spoke excellent English, which posed the question, would a Frenchman meet with the same novel gratification in an English speaking country? However, that is by the by, although I was relieved at not having to make myself understood by signs. The help that was forthcoming I much appreciated as another person was recommended and contacted on the office telephone; the result of this was an arrangement for him to come to the boat the same afternoon. Feeling I was on a roll I also asked if a sail maker could be recommended. This prompted yet another telephone conversation and another arrangement for tomorrow, Friday morning, before moving over to the boatyard. As previously stated, ask one person and, like a domino effect all other needs are met. To a visiting boater, a stranger, could there be a better arrangement? The morning was not yet over and here we were with all requirements duly arranged. Conscious of all the agreeable help that had been forthcoming the least I could do was to purchase a few small but necessary items of a chandlery nature for the further prosecution of the voyage.

Heading back to the boat at a leisurely pace gave me the chance to look around a few unexplored areas of the back streets of

Papeete. A laundrette and also a car rental establishment were noted for future reference. Had I been thinking right and not just letting the mind dwell on future needs, or for that matter letting my mind wander with the sights and sounds, I would have enquired about renting a car. After all I had to be at the airport in the wee hours of Saturday and some mode of transport would be needed. Well there was always tomorrow. For the moment I was basking in the euphoria of having arranged so many tasks so easily to bring the boat back to an operational standard and didn't worry too much over the needs of two days hence.

The back streets of Papeete seemed to be of no consistent nature as one would expect from the orderly manner of what I'm pleased to call the Corniche encompassing the waterfront, rather they wandered off at different angles and directions all built up with shops and like establishments. Soon I realised that if I didn't get my bearings and make my way back to the Corniche I would probably end up in the outlying countryside. The morning was becoming quite warm, this coupled with the blood sugar telling me it would soon be time to eat, brought urgency to the situation. Abandoning the meandering I took the first right hand turn regardless of where it might bring me. All I was certain of was that the harbour lay in that direction, which proved to be correct although not much further towards the boat from where I originally turned off. No matter, at least I wasn't wandering any longer. A relaxing lunch and a beer at the open air restaurant across from the berth soon had my good feelings restored. This happy attitude had me accepting the high prices. It seemed there were no mental protestations, only a resolve that in these circumstances one beer was better than two or more, most certainly.

The family from the Fruity Fruit were heading in to the restaurant as I was leaving which gave occasion for a few pleasantries and an exchange of local information. The lady of the group dominated the conversation while the man, whom I took to be her husband, said not a word. Subdued came to mind, which could well be the case as the lady's opinions were most positive and brooked no argument. The two teenagers also remained silent, not looking too happy. It must have been an odd situation for them to be cooped up on a boat with their parents and not have any friends to do teenager things with. All that could be said about such a situation is that it would be an experience the memory of which would last a life time. To sail around the South Pacific was not an experience that everyone would have in their lifetime. I was given to understand that they would shortly be leaving for the Marquesas to wait out the storm season. I too would have to get my skates on also and make tracks for New Zealand before too long.

After I had a short snooze and pottered around on the boat the gentleman came to fix the gyro. However, nothing was done and after asking what the problem was he just looked at the offending object and announced that he would return on the morrow with a replacement gyro compass and make more tests. That was the last I saw him.

Nothing much seemed to go seamlessly on this boat and after breakfast on the Friday morning I attempted to start the engine prior to proceeding to the boatyard. This proved to be futile, nothing, nix, nada, the thing had died. This presented a bit of a quandary as without a telephone number I couldn't contact the yard, and for that matter I had no idea how to get there except by water. Quite a pickle it seemed. While pondering the problem for a period of time who should turn up but the sail-maker, deus ex machina one might say. On being acquainted with the engine problem he pulled out his mobile and made a call, conversing in French. He then advised me that the mechanic could not come to attend to the problem until Monday which helped matters not at all. Although I appreciated his input it still didn't get me over to the boatyard, so yet another call was made resulting in the information that the yard was sending a boat over to tow me there. All this strengthened my belief that all the people involved in matters boat worked hand in glove with each other, quite a bonus for one seeking help with no knowledge of Papeete. All these machinations had the effect of taking the matter out of my hands making me feel rather extra to requirement, but certainly appreciative. As the haul out wasn't all that critical and the appointment only made to calm the irate boatyard workers on my intrusion on their bailiwick on arrival when it was directions to an appropriate berth that was really wanted. The haul out could have waited until a more appropriate occasion in the future, and therefore I was quite prepared to wait where I was for the mechanic. As matters turned out the whole business proved to be an advantage for the gremlins hadn't finished with me just yet. The yard manager promptly arrived with his boat and an assistant, in a mood I took to be concern for the falling tide and whether there would be enough water at the boatyard over this delay. After several attempts to haul in the anchor it proved to be impossibly fouled on some underwater obstruction resulting the manager's behest to cut the rope rode at the chain, and be ignobly towed away, leaving a valuable anchor and forty feet of chain lying on the bottom of Papeete harbour. Had an appointment for the boatyard not been made, then on departure from Papeete I must have allowed for maybe the total loss of the anchor and chain, the worst scenario, or be left with trying to engage the diver which the yard would provide? That's how it goes sometimes, chance taking a helpful hand.

The lift out and positioning on the hard was soon accomplished. We had enough water to remain afloat regardless of the delay, which was fortuitous; otherwise a rescheduling for the following week would have been necessary as the yard closed at two-thirty on a Friday until seven-thirty on Monday morning. The boat had been placed by the fence bordering the road which proved to be a bit of a nuisance as this area on the far side of the road was used as a late night party spot for the younger generation. Fortunately, when disturbed, I could stand in the cockpit and bellow my displeasure, accompanied with arm gestures for the revellers to turn down the volume on the ghetto blasters and move further down the road. Another feature of this position on the hard was the close proximity of a stand pipe located immediately under the stern, handy for water both for the workers to clean up after their days labour and as a supply for the boat tanks. In the absence of a drain, puddles had formed around the boat, which proved that the convenience of an available water supply could be a less favourable benefit in the days ahead.

The first task after being settled and for getting down off the boat was to present myself at the office to do the paperwork. I must say that the manager of the yard was more than helpful over and above matters relating to a haul out. The first item on the agenda was the filling of the propane tanks to which he instructed his assistant to take me to the depot, which was only five minutes away but too far to walk carrying two ten pound canisters. It was a most welcome and generous gesture and much appreciated. Alas! As they only filled tanks during the mornings it was too late in the day to cater to my needs. But all was not lost for with yet another kindness from these Tahitians of French extraction I was instructed to write the name of the boat on the tanks and was assured they would be ready to be picked up on the Monday morning. I was really warming to these considerate people.

What work that I needed to do on the boat could be completed by the following Monday so it was arranged to go back in the water at noon on Tuesday. The anti-fouling that was applied in Panama was still in excellent condition with no evidence of breakdown or marine growth. This was indeed a bonus that gave me the resolve to use Glidden's paints in future maintenance work. While I was arranging the propane a diver had been organised for the Tuesday afternoon to retrieve the anchor and chain so everything was coming together again. The one problem that remained was how to get out to the airport at such an early hour. In consultation with the manager various options were bruited about. Renting a car? On phoning around I found this too expensive? Hiring a taxi? Could this be relied upon to turn up in the middle of the night? Close by the town berth there was a taxi rank to which I had made enquiries and I was assured that there were taxis there throughout the night. This revelation was comforting, but to get to the rank would require a walk of about two miles as the boatyard was located on the outer seawall of Papeete harbour. Out in the sticks one might say. This business of getting out to the airport in the wee hours of the morning had developed into somewhat of a quandary.

Both the manager and I fell into a silence no doubt pondering the options, certainly on my part with no small concern. I was more or less resolved to walk into town before the witching hour, get a taxi out to the airport and hang around until flight time, not an option particularly filling my soul with joy.

"You can take my car," The manager announced bringing me out of my reverie in a most abrupt manner, as though I didn't believe what I'd heard.

"Sorry?" I asked, in disbelief as to whether he was being serious.

"You can take my car," he repeated, showing amusement at my confusion.

"But what will you do? How will you get home?"

"I have my motorbike. Come, I'll show you."

We went down into the yard and across to a vehicle parked close to the boat. It wasn't a car as such but rather a small van, but who's complaining. It transpired that the van was for the yard usage, fetching supplies and errands of that nature. Having explained the workings he handed over the gate keys with the admonishment to make sure the yard was not left open and then took his leave. So this problem had been solved with a profound and much appreciated kindness.

Promptly at two-thirty the yard suddenly emptied, leaving me with silence and two or three cats that rolled around in the dust, no doubt aware that they would not be disturbed until Monday morning. Left to my own devices I took the opportunity to wander around the yard for the sake of familiarisation before tackling the boat jobs. Not only was this establishment not just for the haul-out and maintenance of small craft, it was also a boat building enterprise. Inside a large construction shed an aluminium fish boat was in the final stages of completion with yet another being fitted out in the yard. During this walkabout I came across a scrap bin of cast out aluminium bits which brought to mind my need for a strut to stabilise the rudder post. After mulling the idea around about the best way to construct this bracket, I realised that with funds running low and already spoken for regarding the sails it would serve my purpose best to wait until New Zealand where prices, I hoped, would be more reasonable.

With the working of the rudder post the bottom seal was showing signs of cracking in way of the hull again. Although it wasn't about to break away, for the sake of good order until the aforementioned bracket could be fabricated a strengthening with fibreglass cloth and epoxy would have to suffice, if for no other reason than to reduce the ingress of water into the boat in this area. This project was put to one side as there was another job that also required an epoxy application and it made sense to perform these tasks at the same time.

For some time now I had convinced myself that the only place water could be getting into the forward berth was via the rub rail, at least all other avenues had been explored and rejected, and let's face it where water comes out is no indication of where it comes in. In fact, it could remain a mystery forever given the right circumstances. It was to this task that I attended, by pulling out the insert that earlier had been assumed to be a length of kelp caught up on the anchor, and throwing it onto the scrap heap. Likewise, the actual rub-rail would also end up in the same place, extra to requirement, another example of something being a good idea at the time, but subsequently becoming useless. While removing the retaining screws my mind was working on a more suitable replacement rub-rail of teak to be installed when my odyssey was finally completed, another project to add to a growing list of things to do when I finally returned to my home port. By the time the rub-rail was consigned to the scrapheap it was too late to start mixing up an epoxy putty rather it made sense to get cleaned up, make something for dinner then have a lie down and snooze until midnight, the designated time to take off for the airport.

*

Over the years, out of interest rather than necessity, I had trained my metabolism to wake me up at any given time, thus doing away with the need of an alarm clock. On occasions of great need to be awake at a certain time this acquired gift often goes into overdrive which has me waking up several times before the appointed time. I check on the clock then drop off again. Fear of oversleeping is probably the reason for this. Well, what can I say? No-one is perfect and a purpose is served. This particular night proved to be of this nature, which gave me the opportunity to have a cup of tea before setting out.

The road out of the industrial section and the docks of Papeete where the boatyard is located joins up with the main highway that encircles the whole island, and from here it is a short run of ten minutes to the airport. At this time of night there was no traffic and the whole of Papeete was as quiet as the grave. This appeared to be peculiar to French Colonial life in the tropics. Having noticed this phenomenon on several other occasions in my younger days on returning to my ship after a night out, it came as no surprise to have the town to myself. With the roads empty I could concentrate on driving this strange vehicle and watch for the turn off for the Airport without being concerned with how other traffic would behave.

The terminal seemed strangely deserted too, with only one or two young people kipping on the floor. Wandering around looking for other signs of life I found a lady who by her uniform belonged to either the airport staff or an airline. I asked her when the Air New Zealand flight from the UK was due. Being very helpful she used her mobile and phoned for advice. Much to my dismay the flight had been delayed in Los Angeles and would not arrive until two o'clock in the afternoon. Well, there you go, nothing unusual in airline delays, so I thanked her for the information and set out to the boat to turn in again.

I was a little uncomfortable about driving out to the Airport again as the manager of the yard had given me the understanding, but not stressed, that the use of the van was for a middle of the night run only and not for general use. To my credit I did agonise over this unfortunate turn of events, whether to take the van on this necessary second run, or to walk the two miles into town and get a taxi. Did another trip to the Airport constitute general usage? With the yard empty of personnel this Saturday with no one to ask to solve this dilemma I suppressed the uncomfortable feelings and took the van, commonsense prevailing over a minor guilt being my logic.

Arriving in good time at the airport I went to the Cafeteria for refreshment. However, the only means of getting refreshment was from coin operated dispenser, not what one would expect where a coin is popped in the slot and voila, one's choice is produced, Oh, no! After depositing the required coins nothing happened. Puzzling over this hiccup for a while I then went over to the counter to complain and was directed to the instructions on the side of the machine. Now, I ask why put instructions around the side of a machine. Well there was no way I was going to get my choice of refreshment. Although the instructions were in English as well as French the machine would only work with a token purchased from the main counter, presumably after purchasing something to eat. All this nonsense became academic because by putting proper coins into the infernal thing it had become inoperative, with the coins jamming up the works. Time to make myself scarce.

Tahiti Airport is uncomplicated, comprising one low building on the level of the road outside with no stairs for the visitor to negotiate. At one end there is the cafeteria and washrooms, a few shops and lounges, and arrival and departure gates along the length of the concourse, all open to the pleasantly cooling air on the road side of the building. A mezzanine floor over the lower facilities contains what one would presume are offices relating to the operation of the Airport.

Quite a few people had started to gather around the arrival gate which suggested the flight had arrived. The 'meeters and greeters' in their bright and colourful dresses and holding the traditional garlands of flowers began to gather which strengthened the suggestion that the flight was discharging its passengers. Time to take up a watching position at the gate. Soon the passengers started to drift through in dribs and drabs at first, some avoiding making eye contact with the waiting people, no doubt not expecting to be met. Others were anxiously scanning the crowd and breaking into wreaths of smiles when contact with those known was made. After a little while a loose group came into view and, there in the middle a head above the others was Judy looking remarkably refreshed after such a long delayed flight. What always gave me pleasure when meeting with Judy was the way she walked, tall and self assured with a slight movement of the shoulders, something akin to a nautical roll. Indeed she was a pleasure to behold, a posture developed no doubt by her love of hiking, horse riding, cycling and other outdoor activities.

After I remarked how fresh she looked after such a disrupted flight, she told me that due to the pilot getting earache the flight was suspended at Los Angeles to await a new crew, all the passengers being put up in hotels for the night. We considered how much an earache could cost an airline.

There being little traffic on the road this Saturday afternoon we were shortly back at the boatyard. It must have been somewhat of a letdown for Judy to have to climb up a ladder to get into the boat; after all this doesn't suggest a cruising mode, a boat high and dry is not the same as a boat in the water. By the time Judy had been given a tour of the boat, shown where everything lived and her gear stowed it was time for pre-dinner drinks. A duty-free bottle of Famous Grouse was produced like magic from the depths of the dear lady's bag to celebrate this occasion. What a delightful thought and, so considerate to cater to my preferences. There was much to discuss with reference to the objections from a family member for her to come out to Tahiti for this adventure, quite unfounded in everyone else's opinion and although noted, the objections she ignored. Time passed quickly as it does in good company and in no time at all dinner had to be started, so out with the electric frying pan to cook some rice and diced tinned veggies. Not an auspicious fare to welcome the new crew but, needs must when the devil drives. Not having located a Supermarket to shop for provisions we would have to make do with what was on board. Tomorrow we could walk into town to that restaurant which provided such wonderful fare on my first night in Papeete. Judy never commented on my cooking but in subsequent days she took over these duties which I suppose could be considered as comment enough. As long as the cook was kept supplied with wine during the preparation of our evening meal my input was considered satisfactory.

As my duties didn't require me to keep a lookout for shipping or attend to the sailing of the boat I was able to do justice to the FG and relax in great company with an easy and wide ranging conversation.

*

The morning tea was my bailiwick and as I'm an early riser I was able to give my guest her tea in bed with the suggestion that she should relax and take her time before facing the first day in Tahiti. Judy was not a person who required constant attention so I could leave her to her own devices while I got on with the epoxy jobs on the rudder shaft seal and the area of the removed rub rail. These projects took most of the day and as the epoxy hardened in a reasonable time it could be sanded down in readiness for painting. The topside paint was showing signs of mange again with large areas coming away and exposing the filler coat. Much as this needed attention I was prepared to delay this until New Zealand where, I was hoping, materials would be less expensive. Not that I was averse to subscribing to the Tahitian economy but I would have upcoming expenses, new fore sail, wind generator and the like. Another haul out to fit a large through-hull valve for the holding tank was required so it made sense to carry out the painting of the hull topsides at such time.

The yard being deserted made it possible to carry out what maintenance was needed without any distractions, at least that is what should have been. During the lunch break Judy drew my attention to her exposed skin which to my horror, as well as hers, was covered in mosquito bites. Once over the initial shock and discussion about how this could happen, I realised that the creatures must have been breeding on the stagnant water under and around the boat. But why had Judy and not I been subjected to this attack? One possibility could have been I was tanned and Judy wasn't, but out of deference to Judy's situation I accepted her comment regarding my ancient meat being less preferable than the younger fresh quality. Nothing could be done about it until the shops opened on the morrow and a balm could be purchased. In the meantime all that she could do was keep covered up and deter another night attack from these bloodsuckers. A fine introduction to a sailing holiday, but at least it was understood and comforting to know that this species of mosquito didn't carry disease.

The walk into town for the evening meal was pleasant as the temperature cools, and the slight humidity clears at this time of day. For me the meal was a bit of a disappointment. The staff were less friendly than the first time I was there, and Judy disapproved of the cost. Sure it was expensive but this was Tahiti and that is what one must get used to if one wishes to eat out. From my point of view I was prepared to put up with the cost, at least until I'd got over my own cooking prior to arriving at Papeete, and could purchase provisions at the yet to be found Supermarket. With this walk into town at least the shops where mosquito repellent could be purchased were located, so it was not altogether a futile adventure.

*

Monday: First thing after the yard personnel had arrived was to buttonhole Henry the foreman for a ride to the propane depot. The securing of propane at such a fortuitous time in the scheme of things was most timely as the electric frying pan had finally given up the ghost. On its last outing the previous lunchtime it had expired without even giving out the usual puff of smoke from the thermostat. With a kind thought for the service it had given I committed it to the garbage heap. This act prompted me to think that during this voyage, I seemed to be staggering from one minor calamity to another. At least we were still mobile and hopefully all the necessary work to put the boat fully operational again would be finalised at New Zealand which seemed to be the most likely place. I was pinning this premise on the fact New Zealand has a viable sailing community. Cost too was a factor that was uppermost in my mind.

As the engine mechanic was expected that morning and my presence would be required, Judy took off for town by herself in search of a salve for the mosquito bites. Having been bitten myself in past years, although not to such a degree, I could sympathise with her situation. Even one bite is an aggravating experience never mind having both legs covered with the damn things. Her stoic manner in putting up with the torment had my whole-hearted admiration.

The mechanic arrived in due course, another Frenchman who spoke perfect English. His efficiency didn't end there as within a matter of a few minutes he had sussed out the problem, something in my ignorance of all things mechanical I would never have traced in a hundred years. Watching him work I thought whether it wouldn't be sensible to take a course in engine mechanics. When and how this opportunity would come about was also a subject for debate, and I realised that a long apprenticeship might be involved before proficiency would be gained. The idea was reluctantly shelved. Between the engine and the control panel is a harness of sixteen wires, some sixteen feet in length, supplying the power and information for the engine to be started. Apparently there was a broken wire somewhere in the bundle. To trace which wire was the offending one would have only been academic as it couldn't be repaired anyway. So, fortunately there was a replacement harness in the mechanic's shop, and off he went. Before noon he was back and had the engine in service again. Now this strengthened the premise that all trades, or businesses, were working hand in glove as he instructed me to settle his bill with the sail-maker.

After lunch and for the rest of the afternoon I worked on sanding and painting the area of the removed rub-rail. Arrangements also were made with the office to put the boat back in the water the following morning with the happy thought that in the next few days it would only be a matter of the sail-maker finishing his tasks, and then we could take off for Rarotonga. There I go again, anticipating the un-anticipatable.

*

The first casualty in the expected line-up of events for a smooth running progress towards departure was the fact that the boatyard would not take credit cards, cash only. This arrangement had Judy and me hoofing it into town to the bank. This unexpected turn of events, due to the launching time set for eleven-thirty left little time to do anything but hurry there and back. Hurrying in the Tahitian climate soon had both of us working up, in Judy's case, a glow and in mine a free flowing perspiration, but at least we made it back to the yard in sufficient time to pay the bill and make the tide.

The engine fired on the first attempt with a satisfying roar and with a merry wave to Henry of Propane fame, we were heading back to the original berth at the town quay to await the diver and the repaired sails. Happy in the knowledge that there were no mosquitoes there to create a bother, and once moored on the pontoon, we crossed the road for lunch and a celebratory beer.

During the following days the anchor and chain were rescued from the bottom of Papeete harbour. With the anchor having caught on the pontoon mooring chains the diver found it quite easy to lift the flukes off the obstruction and it was soon back on board, the rope rode spliced onto the chain and all stowed in the chain locker. The mainsail was repaired to a much better condition than the Panamanian effort, and securing the luff to the slides the sail maker had used was particularly satisfying with bindings sewn to the slide and the sail. This method, as long as the slide didn't break, was preferable to the old method which tended to rip the sail. So far matters seemed to be on the up and up, at least on these first few days. This illusion was soon shattered though as the genoa, in the sail maker's estimation, had become so worn that it was pointless trying to repair it. This put me on the horns of a financial dilemma as a new sail was beyond my current means. The sail-maker, however, thought he could locate a used foresail of better quality, and with a little adjustment have it fit the furling system. This was agreed to as a satisfactory alternative but we were not out of the woods yet. The sail-maker, having climbed the mast to reeve a new halyard, had noticed that several strands of the fore-stay were broken. I had a slight feeling of despair, with thoughts of staggering from one critical situation to another seeming to be never ending. There was nothing for it but to replace the forestay as it would be the height of folly to leave it partially broken and at some time in the future have it part completely with the subsequent bringing down of the mast, an option not to be considered. On recommendation from the sail-maker I agreed to a heavier wire which the furling system was capable of handling.

With all these projects in hand it left plenty of time for Judy and I to wander around town exploring the back streets, getting a little lost and finding our way back to the main road and the harbour. I don't think we ever really sorted out which direction to take without confusion of some sort, but that is Papeete. I was convinced that it would take quite some time to be absolutely sure of which direction to take for any given location. Frequenting the internet cafes, to keep in touch with the outside world became a daily routine. Once the Super-market which was within walking distance of the boat had been located shopping for groceries for the next leg of the voyage also became a regular feature for the remainder of our stay. An item that gave an immense feeling of pleasure in exciting the taste buds was the local pineapple, a like of which I had never experienced before; so sweet and juicy, one fairly drooled in anticipation while one was being cut open and prepared for eating.

On Saturday, as no work was in hand, we hired a car, which to my surprise was nowhere near as expensive as previously quoted when in the boatyard, and drove around the Island. This didn't raise any problems regarding navigation as there is only one road and one travels either right handed or left handed on this circumnavigation. Just follow the road to return to the starting point. This premise holds good for Tahiti-Nui which is the largest section of the island. Tahiti-Iti is the smaller section stuck like an appendix on the south-east side of Tahiti-Nui by a narrow strip of land. Here the road branches in the direction of the settlement of Teahupoo on the south side and its world famous surfing beaches, although no surf was up when we arrived. On the north side the road leads to Tautira. Both these roads are dead ends and one must turn around and go back to Tahiti-Nui to continue the circumnavigation. No need for route planning on Tahiti. There were one or two sights to visit which were taken advantage of, the Paul Gauguin museum to which Judy wished to visit, and particularly, for me, Venus Point on the north of the Island. It was easy to see why Captain Cook chose this place for the observation of the transit of Venus across the face of the Sun in 1769. Venus Point is low lying and encompasses to the north the natural harbour of Matavai Bay within the reef system, and must be about the only flat area of land suitable to build a fort and also have access to his ship and of course have Venus and the Sun on the right side of the island. Being a keen follower of all things Cook, and this was a highlight of his career, I started taking photos of the obelisk that presumably, although the descriptive plaque had fallen off, marked the spot of Cook's observations, and snaps of the surrounding Bay. Much to my chagrin, the gremlins were still at work as the film transporter lever had jammed, preventing any further records of this delightful and historic place. To really put an end to this photo-op Judy's camera had also failed. I think this was the most disappointing event of the whole trip so far. This was a place I had often read about and anticipated visiting for so many years, and to be denied a factual record was, well, what could one say? The memory of this historic site had been stored away in my brain and I had managed to get four shots of the place, so there was some satisfaction in that I suppose and, as beggars can't be choosers, I had to be content with what I had.

All in all it was a most enjoyable day out, even though it took only half a day. There is a road across the island through the mountainous interior but, being accessible to four wheel drive vehicles only, rental cars being excluded on the agreement, this section of discovery was denied us. Pity really as the scenery and views must have been spectacular from the high mountains of the interior, if the travel brochures are to be believed.

The remainder of the following week was spent waiting for the sail-maker to complete his tasks with side trips to his loft to check progress with the replacement sail which, although not full size was at least serviceable for our needs until a sail could be made in New Zealand. The replacement forestay and furling system also was proceeding satisfactorily, so all that remained was to obtain the clearance and retrieve the posted bond from the bank. Nothing seems to proceed in a satisfactory manner and having the bond returned proved to be no exception, for although the security had been paid by debit card I was offered local currency as repayment, with no option. Now, one can only wonder at the uselessness of a great wad of Pacific francs when departure was imminent? For whatever reason repayment by debit card reversal was not possible so it was a case of buying New Zealand dollars. At least the old adage of it being better to buy currency than to sell came in handy, so there was some remuneration gained in the exchange rate, and it would give me a ready supply of currency for Auckland and Rarotonga without having to seek out a bank.

On the Friday we went last minute grocery shopping, the water tanks were topped up from the shore supply, and the rigging of the replacement genoa, which had somewhat less sail area than the original but was acceptable for the run to New Zealand via Rarotonga, was also fitted. By early afternoon and, after a last lunch at the cantina across the road, all was ready to make our way to the refuelling depot further down the coast. As previously mentioned this side of the island was protected by coral reefs so, on leaving Papeete, we wended our way inside the reef following the numerous beacons. The airport runway extends into the lagoon and we required permission from the Control Tower to proceed past and around to the far end of the runway where we had to report the completion of the passage. No doubt this precaution was to ensure that any aircraft taking off doesn't take off a sailboat's mast.

There was an interesting cluster of thatched roof cabins between the airport and the fuelling station. These cabins were perched over the lagoon on stilts and connected each to the other and to the shore by walk ways and numbering twelve in all. These apparently were part of the hotel, providing interesting accommodation for guests. Quite an impressive display they made, although on reflection it would be interesting to find out how waste water and the like were disposed of; not into the lagoon one would hope.

Fuelling was completed in good order and we were soon heading through the gap in the reef to the open sea. This presented a disconcertingly strange spectacle as while we were passing through the narrow opening in the reef there was a young lad standing on the reef with the water only half way up his shins. A strange apparition it was while passing only a few feet from him. However we were soon clear and making a course for the south of Moorea, so up went the sails and off with the engine to ride easily on a low swell.

CHAPTER TEN

TAHITI to RAROTONGA

......in whose company I delight myself.
Pilgrim's Progress

It is always good to get away from civilisation out into the peaceful ocean, although it must be said I enjoyed Tahiti and the people we came in contact with, so helpful and pleasingly proficient in the English language, which dissipated any misunderstandings with my lack of French. It is not surprising the early sailors considered this beautiful island with its delightful climate to be Paradise.

Shortly after sunset while we were passing the reefs off Moorea the wind died, no doubt due to us being under the lee of the land. In the stillness of darkness the surf could be heard breaking on the reef which, although not presenting any immediate danger gave me cause to fire up the engine again until the wind picked up once more when we left the lee of the land. Judy, although under the effects of a bout of mal de mer, had produced the evening meal. Considering how the effects of seasickness had laid me low, during that period of my life when I had succumbed, I could only have admiration for Judy's fortitude on remaining on her feet, not to mention cooking a meal. Seasickness, if my memory served me right, can be a most debilitating experience so my admiration also had a hint of envy.

Prior to lying down to rest I went on deck to check the situation, and as circumstances would have it, was just in time to see the replacement sail rip vertically from top to bottom and across the seams too. As the wind was only twenty-five knots and not even strong enough for me to reef down the mainsail, the destruction of this new replacement caused considerable chagrin. There was nothing for it but to roll up the useless article, furl it completely and get along best we could with the mainsail. I pondered this new setback for a while then decided to phone the sail maker and advise him what had happened with the view to him taking the matter up with the person he had bought it from, and maybe securing some compensation. On making contact and exchanging pleasantries I had only just advised him of the situation when the phone went dead. Odd, I thought, and tried to make contact again only to eventually get an unanswered ringing. Rather impolite of him not to hear me out I thought, then I got to wondering if he had knowingly sold me a sail that was suspect. Well, as I would never know the answer to that one, all that could be done was to proceed on our way the best we could under the circumstances. To return to Papeete and demand retribution I briefly considered but soon rejected that as futile. No doubt if he saw me coming and he was guilty as charged he would make himself scarce. This late in the game with so many problems behind me I was becoming quite philosophical. Having one more problem didn't worry me too much. Soldier on was the order of the day. Maybe Rarotonga would produce some reconciliation.

Having fallen back into the old routine of getting up to make frequent checks on the surrounding ocean during the night I was ready for a cup of tea come daylight. I debated with myself whether to let Judy have a lie in, what with her being seasick the previous evening, but then resolved to take her a cup of tea instead. Might as well get her on her feet, as this was the best way to overcome the debilitating effects of the old Mal de Mary's. No sooner had I entered the forward berth and woke her up than we hit a milestone which caused a heavy spray to come over the bow and down the partially open hatch drenching the pair of us and overflowing the cup of tea. The humour of such a rude awakening tickled my sense of the ridiculous which produced a hearty, 'bloody hell' accompanied with a snort of mirth. Although Judy took it all in good humour she was suspicious of the cause of such a rude awakening and I was hard pressed denying that I had not planned it that way. From that time on Judy occupied the other end of the settee for her night time rest, probably reasoning that I wouldn't pull another stunt like that if I was in the firing line. What cruel thoughts some people harbour.

The following days were pleasantly balmy and in the warm sunshine with a cooling wind tanning sessions were enjoyed. During the evenings, once the meal was over, we passed the time listening to a selection of music, with Kiri Te Kanawa's 'Heart to Heart' being a firm favourite. Not all was decadence though as Judy expressed an interest in learning to sail. This request raised something of a dilemma as she had never been on a boat before and wasn't going to be long enough on the boat for any schooling in this subject to be of much use. However, such an interest could not in all honesty be denied and as pulling up sails was unnecessary as they were already up; the sailor's bible was produced with the intention of at least learning the sail parts and other nautical nomenclature. The difficulty of learning this new language and the totally alien practice of the tying of knots presented some interesting moments but her interest and perseverance brought some rewards. On the subject of crewing I had given some thought, should we keep watches being uppermost in this thinking. In all honesty this would have been the ideal way of ship keeping but then it would not have been very responsible of me to leave Judy on deck alone with no experience, and no doubt I would be checking on her more than I do with the normal run of things. As I had been following the routine of checking matters as a single-handed sailor and as Judy's tenure was going to be brief, there was no point in disturbing the rest of two people.

On the subject of rest, Judy reported hearing voices during one night of this passage. Odd that, as previously mentioned I, too, thought that I'd heard voices. As there was definitely no one else on board it can only be assumed that this weird occurrence was due to water swilling around in the bilges, or maybe the wind catching an obstruction at a certain angle and the sound being carried through the boat's structure. At least those assumptions gave us some comfort. As there had only been these two occasions it was better not to dwell too long on what else may have caused this phenomenon, unless of course one believes in bogeymen.

The passage to Rarotonga was an easy sail of ten days even with just the main, the trade wind still in the south-east, and the days passed pleasantly with no necessity to reef this one remaining sail. The movement of the boat in the seas however, caused some interesting moments attempting to get from the galley with plates of food or cups of tea. This required waiting for the boat to steady and then give an easy roll to port and then the one carrying the objects in question could launch oneself up the two steps from the galley and cross to the table where one would be relieved of the burden. This became quite an exercise of skill with the object of making the journey without spilling food or slopping the contents of the mugs. Because there were two people on board the load was double and did not give one the luxury of having one hand free for steadying one's progress.

On the evening before the day of arrival at Rarotonga the trade wind died and a westerly picked up. No doubt some low pressure disturbance had caused this change of direction in an otherwise reliable wind system. The wind was not very strong and as the boat didn't perform well into the wind I was decided to put the wind on the port beam and doodle along on a course to the north until daylight, hoping that the trade wind would pick up again. Come the dawn not much in the way of progress had resulted from this manoeuvre. The wind was still out of the west and being only forty miles from our destination I decided to motor the rest of the way. An excellent opportunity for Judy to get some serious steering practice and I was much impressed how quickly she picked this up. Just one explanation: when changing direction one should move the lubber line across the compass card and not the other way round, a common mistake with first trippers. She soon had the steering off like an old hand.

Rarotonga soon lifted over the horizon, just an indistinct blur at first but taking on a more detailed form the closer we came. By mid afternoon we entered the one harbour suitable for sea going vessels, the other being too shallow even for our boat. By the time we had moored up stern to the quay it was too late to report to the harbour authorities so we would have to wait until the next day. Meanwhile, as it was exceedingly difficult to get ashore over the stern without manipulating the anchor rode at the bow and the mooring lines from the stern, I busied myself inflating the dinghy and launching that for ferrying to a rather rickety set of steps for getting on land again. About twenty feet along the wall there was a boat moored which we had noticed in Papeete. It was particularly noticeable by having different company logos painted on the hull and, in large letters NSA, which caused a certain amount of conjecture as to what it meant. About this we were soon to become acquainted.

CHAPTER ELEVEN

RAROTONGA

The long arm of coincidence.

Chambers. 1860-1921

Raro, meaning down, Tonga, meaning south. Thus called by Iro, the famous Tahitian navigator when asked where he was going, at least that is a popular version of where the name originated. But then, so did the Samoan navigator, Karika, use the same terminology, calling it Rarotonga because to him Raro meant to leeward and Tonga also to the south. Both gentlemen being Polynesian, one can assume they spoke the same language and therefore we allow both meanings.

Rarotonga is the administrative capital of a group of fifteen islands named the Cook Islands which cover an area of the Pacific the size of India and centre on the town of Avarua on the north coast. Although James Cook sighted the islands and landed on many of the southern group, it is not recorded that he even sighted Rarotonga nor was he responsible for naming them after himself. The name Cook Islands was given to the group by the Russians in honour of Cook, the name first appearing on a Russian naval chart early in the nineteenth century.

The island of Rarotonga is the furthest south of the Cook Islands and is roughly round in shape and surrounded by protecting coral reefs. The centre of the island is extremely mountainous and rises to a height of 2140 feet which was originally formed by volcanic action. Now extinct the volcanoes are covered with tropical jungle. The principal road runs around the island close to the sea with the occasional side roads running to settlements and farms which produce, in the inland swamps, taro, the main crop of the island. To the west of Avarua and just a little way along from the harbour is a modern international airport that also serves the other islands in the group.

The weather is generally equitable with temperatures averaging highs of 28C with lots of sunshine. The wet season is from

January to early May, and the Cyclone season from December to
April.

*

    Due to the approaching cyclone season I was anxious to
have the sail repaired and to get on our way, but then as Robert
Burns said, 'the best laid schemes o' mice and men, gang aft a'gley,'
and my situation was no different. On reporting in to the Marine
Office for clearance and requesting information of a sail maker I was
informed that to the best of the Port Captain's knowledge he didn't
know of one. This information gave cause for concern as there was a
tear in the sail fifteen feet long and to sew a patch of that length,
even if I had that much material, would have taken some
considerable time. As it turned out two different good Samaritans
appeared, (Deus ex Machina again), to redress this problem. During
the first day while I mulled over this problem a gentleman appeared
on the quay, and seeing my boat's registry was Victoria and he being
from that city we fell into conversation. With the sail being
uppermost in my mind I broached the subject of how to have it
repaired and he advised that he had a friend who had a sailboat and
would ask him and report back. Well, I thought things were looking
up and if there are sailboats it follows there must be services.
    Also, while moored to the quay we got into conversation
with the young man on the boat with NSA emblazoned on the side
and he very generously offered to lend me one of his spare sails. As
we were both heading to New Zealand, it could be returned there.
Although reluctant to take him up on this offer as I was concerned
that for whatever reason I couldn't return the sail, this didn't seem to
bother him so; it was left in abeyance until the situation with the
injured sail was reconciled.
    This young man and I use this terminology from a distance
of my great age, had a stroke at the age of thirty-five and, on
recovery decided to collect sponsors and make a voyage of
awareness for the National Stroke Foundation. What a noble gesture
I thought, eyeing all the Company logos painted on the side of his
boat. Maybe I should have gone that route? It certainly would have
reduced the expenses, but no use being regretful in this matter, for
I'm far too independently minded to have thought about it anyway.
His boat was about thirty feet in length with a Heath Robinson repair
job to the self steering arrangement, which I was given to understand
had suffered grievously on passage. This apparently had caused little
concern as he had a girl even younger than himself as crew and

between them could take turns at steering. At least this arrangement had been useful for the time being as she was shortly to leave and go home to her boyfriend. I have to wonder how the younger generation view their lives; it seems they have an enviable independent spirit that was denied my generation. Roam the world? We were lucky if we could borrow a bike, never mind own one, to cycle to the next town a distance of eighteen miles and have the entrance fee of two shillings for the swimming pool. Now that was considered to be a real outing in those days.

The young man, Les Bissell by name didn't seem too perturbed about losing his little helper as with the self confidence of the young he had expectations of recruiting some other wanderer for the onward journey.

Tony McCulloch, the gentleman from Victoria, returned a little later with the news that there wasn't a sail maker on the island but at the Airport the upholsterer might help as he repaired airplane seating and the like, ergo, heavy sewing machine. Well this was good news so Judy and I took a walk to meet with this man who could help us out of our predicament. As it turned out he was just about to leave on a job on one of the other islands and, should we wish to bring the offending article to his shop he would have a look at it on his return in two days time. Things seemed to be definitely picking up with hope, the flavour of the month, boosting my confidence of yet once again being fully operational.

During the interim yet another sailboat arrived and with a bit of a squeeze moored on the other side of Les's boat. The interesting aspect of this boat was that it was the same design as mine, something that I had never seen before. The drawings for the design called for either aluminium or steel, and this new arrival had taken the steel option and had numerous rust runs tracking down the sides I was pleased to have requested from the designers drawings for a foam core hull laminated with fibreglass inner and outer skins. It was not a pretty sight having a boat streaked with brown unsightly runs. Not a pristine yacht with white paintwork glistening in the sunlight as one would expect of a boat. A great pity, as the design is very attractive.

Sunday, having taken Tony up on his invitation, Judy and I were given a tour of the island and introduced to the local history. Legend has it that the great Polynesian voyages started from Rarotonga, crossing the vast Pacific in their double hulled canoes to populate places as far away as New Zealand and the Hawaiian Islands. Indeed, we were shown a replica of one of these canoes and close up they looked truly large, large enough to carry several families and their provisions for immense distances. Having two hulls with a connecting platform between, one can imagine them capable of impressive speeds. A forerunner of the modern day Catamaran with the exception of the rig, the Polynesian canoe was rigged with two masts and mutton chop sails which, being wider at the top, gave lift as well as forward drive.

The main part of the town of Avarua stretches along the main road to the east of the harbour and comprises modern shops, restaurants, an open air market and all the modern amenities of business. The Law Courts and Police Headquarters were built with Chinese funds, thus developing close ties with China. A cyclone proof highway and an enclosed sports stadium have also been built with Chinese largesse. Hotels and holiday accommodation are for the most part right on the water's edge and, it was one of these holiday homes that Tony and his partner Nancy, our hosts for the afternoon, rented for their stay on Rarotonga. It was a most delightful low bank location right on the edge of the Lagoon, protected from the ocean waves by the reef some hundreds of yards away, cooled by the prevailing southeast trade winds, and shaded amongst the Palm trees. The Lagoon is safe for swimming if one stays well away from the Channels that cut through to the ocean; it is at these points that swift currents often run strong, strong enough to carry the unwary swimmer to a watery grave. However, the Lagoon is large and safe and Judy, Tony and I made good use of it well away from these channels. However, the effort of keeping afloat made me realise how the lack of exercise on a boat can put one out of condition. No longer the water dog (and I use the term informally), of my youth, I begged off on the second dip and the suggestion of going snorkelling. Judy, however, delighted in searching the seabed under Tony's guidance for the myriad marine life. I was content to sit and watch and socialise with Nancy and her other guests.

All too soon, as is always the case when enjoying oneself, the time came to return to the boat and dwell on what a wonderful time we had.

*

During the coming week there were interesting developments, and the sail was repaired and returned. This repair it turned out was a helpful attempt to get us mobile again as the upholsterer at the airport could only run a straight seam whereas sails require zigzag stitching for strength on the seams. But what could one do? The man didn't have a sail maker's sewing machine.

Although he understood the need for sail repairs on the island, his company just wasn't going to invest in such an item. Well, beggars can't be choosers and one could only hope that the repair would hold. It was not a happy state of affairs so I took Les up on his offer of one of his spare sails. Its return didn't present a problem as we were now going to Whangarei rather than Auckland which was much nearer to Les's destination of Opua. The reason for the change of plan came about purely by chance, as it often does in this life. While having my haircut by a New Zealand lady it came out in the conversation that we would be leaving for Auckland in a day or two. The lady hairdresser pooh-poohed the idea as being not very clever as the place was inconvenient for boaters. The moorage was vast and most problematic for taking on stores and access to the amenities that I would require and it was most difficult to find a place to park, anyway. Rather, she said, Whangarei marina was right in the centre of town and the Supermarket a short walk away and just across the road. She knew the place well having lived there before moving to Rarotonga. The sail maker, the marine stores and everything a boater would require was within easy walking distance. Who was I to ignore such advice? Besides on consulting the chart I found Whangarei was much further north than Auckland, and Opua would be on my way to pass north of the North Island on the way to Melbourne. Once again matters were falling into their convenient places.

One other incident that was purely coincidental happened while Judy and I were sitting in the cockpit relaxing with a coffee. A couple had ridden up on a motor bike and stopped to look at the boats in the harbour. Noticing the Port of Registry on the transom I was asked if we were from Victoria. They received the stock answer, "No, Pender Island. Victoria is the Port of Registry." "Oh!" The man said, "We are from Pender." Now Pender isn't all that big, maybe two thousand souls but there was no way I recognised them. This surprised me a little as having lived there for twenty years one generally runs into nearly everyone who lives there. Ah! Well, we live and learn. The point of this anecdote, however, lies in the fact that within a matter of days there was an e-mail demanding to know who that woman was who was with me. As I am foot loose and fancy free it never occurred to me to report my every action to the outside world. Funny though, even being so far away from base one is never safe from prying eyes.

It was getting late in the year and the cyclone season was in the offing which made me anxious to get away. I know I keep harping on that subject but, it was a real concern. Being caught in a storm anywhere, never mind at sea, would be sheer folly, not to mention having the added responsibility of an extra person.

The south east trades had returned which gave favourable conditions for the run to Whangarei. Water and fuel had been taken on, food also, for the anticipated relatively short run, so there was no point in hanging around any longer. The harbour dues were quite hefty I thought for the lack of amenities available, particularly the water supply which could not be accessed at the edge of the quay due to someone having cut off the hose connection. Les and I had to join both our hoses together to be able to connect to the tap at the hotdog stand on the far side of the quay. The complaint was passed on to the Port Captain who gave the impression that it had been reported and maybe something might be done about it one day. Not very reassuring but not everything in this life is perfect and this didn't detract from the overall pleasure of this beautiful island and the good people we had met.

So it was then that we made our goodbyes, with promises to keep in touch. Up with the anchor, and with Judy steering we passed through the harbour entrance into the ocean again.

CHAPTER TWELVE

RAROTONGA to WHANGAREI

Expect nothing. Live frugally on surprise.

Alice Walker

At the risk of repeating myself, as always is the case, it was good to get away from civilisation, to be out on the solitude of the ocean again. It had been touch and go whether I would have been on my own for this leg of the trip as Judy had been seriously considering jumping ship to fly to New Zealand. I couldn't fault her for this as she had always wanted to visit the country and do a bit of touring. She had friends there too, whom she hadn't seen for a very long time so it was quite in the cards for an early visit. Needless to say my thoughts on this need not be described, only to say that I didn't wish for such a good companion to leave. As it turned out she did decide to stay on the understanding that it was only a sixteen day run to Whangarei. Oh, Dear! Here we go again.

Judy hadn't slept too well during the past few nights so took to the forward berth in the afternoon for a snooze and to admire the upholsterer's handy work through the hatch and on the thorough job he had made. I kept my counsel on this matter not wanting to tempt fate over the lack of zigzag stitching, but appreciative of the effort he had put into this with the limited facilities he had.

For the first week the trades held with wind velocities of no more than twenty-five knots and we made comfortable progress towards our destination. Alas! The repair on the foresail didn't hold though and ripped again to a two part piece of rag flapping uselessly in the breeze. So down it came to be replaced by Les' contribution, which being of a laminated construction with the laminates separating, presented something less than a joy to behold. However, one doesn't look a gift horse in the mouth and no matter what the condition of the sail as long as it held together and was serviceable as far as Whangarei the object of the lesson would have been achieved.

Then the wind came around to the west again. Les had been sending us daily weather reports so it was obvious that the change in the wind direction was the result of a low pressure system to the southeast of our position, some distance away, which meant that we would not be bothered by it apart from the disruption of the trades. Well there was nothing we could do about the situation but wait for the trades to pick up again and sail at a tangent to the wind, heading north for half a day then change tack to head south again, as the boat would not make any headway in any point of sail but with the wind on the beam. I suppose one should be thankful that it was only leeway that was affected and not lost distance by being pushed back. Had this been the case it would have meant heaving to; at least as we were moving we did have the psychological effect of going somewhere.

After three days of this the wind shifted again back to the trades so we made progress once more at a satisfactory pace. The latest news from Les announced that high winds had hit Rarotonga which was good news for us if not for Raro. It seems the wind was strong enough for him to warrant streaming another anchor and running extra mooring lines to the quay. It had been his intention to leave a day or two after we had departed, but with one thing and another he was delayed. That's how it goes in the sailing world, very little goes according to plan. We were pleased to hear, however, that his crew had decided to stay on until New Zealand, saving him the unlikely possibility of finding a replacement.

In the fullness of time we reached 170 West Longitude the psychological position where the trades are expected to die away. As luck or whatever motivates these things the wind held for a few more days with our anticipation of moving into the Eastern Hemisphere. Whoops! The wind came around to right ahead again just half a degree short of the International Date Line and increased to 30knts. The swell too became heavier causing the boat to labour uncomfortably, with the result that getting food and or mugs of tea to the table became very much a matter of gymnastics. The warm sunny days departed to be replaced by grey, overcast dreary skies. Time to reef the mainsail before the darkness made the exercise risky. As the wind might increase it was deemed sensible to double reef the main and take in some of Les's sail which was already beginning to tear upwards from the foot. Dreams of a new Genoa were now almost constantly on my mind. Les's sail would also have to be repaired before being returned, which is par for the course it seems as no matter what I borrow it ends up having to be mended. Not, I might add, that things get rough usage by my hands, but rather that they are somewhat suspect to start with. Still, 'needs must when the Devil drives', as they say, and be happy for small mercies.

We were now twenty-three days out of Rarotonga and still three hundred miles to go with no progress being made in that direction. Another matter of concern was that the food was getting low and the water for some reason tasted salty maybe salt water in the bilges was somehow being picked up. This was one of life's mysteries as having put pressure on the line previously I found that no hole or split in the waterline. There wasn't anything for it but to shut off the tanks and resort to drawing water by dipping via the access ports again. At least the fact that the system was drawing salt water into the line would reduce the area to investigate as there wasn't much of the fresh water line that passed through the bilges. So it seems that life does have its compensations after all.

It was about this time that the bilge float switch gave up the ghost, the second one this trip. So much for the salesman's comment that this particular type of switch would last ten years, but he was a salesman and some will say anything to make the customer happy and clinch a sale. So it was a case of emptying the bilges with the manual switch; this worked for a day or two until one of the connections broke off. No problem as we still had power to the switch so it was a case of touching the bare wire to the broken connection to activate the pump. Strange though, regardless of the inconvenience of having to operate the pump in this way, I felt blessed and thankful that we still had power and didn't have to resort to Armstrong's Patent and bale the bilges with a saucepan. Be thankful for small mercies as they say. This voyage seems to have developed a tolerance in my spirit that had never been there previously.

The latest report from Les had him catching up with us; even though he had left Rarotonga a week after us he had managed to keep favourable winds and was now only a matter of two days behind. Not for long though as he would soon be experiencing the weather that we were putting up with, unless his boat sailed better into the wind than did ours.

After a week of the head winds they once again turned in our favour and we crossed the International Date Line thus gaining an extra day on the calendar. For two days we made good and hopeful progress towards Whangarei, and then what do you know the wind came around out of the west again. Back to the same old same old, up and down parallel with the New Zealand coast and only ninety miles to go. So much for the promise to Judy of only taking sixteen days for the passage. The loss of time was eating into her plans to see something of New Zealand and still be home for Christmas. But what could I say? Although I felt bad about it all there was nothing I could do, or say. We were at the mercy of the vagaries of the winds. She was very good about the whole business though and never complained.

On the dawning of the 18th December the wind having died away during the night came up again out of the north-west with a most favourable velocity thus creating a handsome speed towards our haven. The ETA off Bream Head would be at noon and put us under the lee of the land. It was my intention then to take down the mainsail and motor in after lunch. This meal was timely as the food supply had become exhausted. An Old Mother Hubbard situation and just as well we didn't have a dog. During the interim the VHF had been switched on in preparation to report our arrival when the weather report came on for Bream Head, 'winds southwest imminent 60 knots'. This alarming news had the engine fired up, Judy at the wheel, and me on deck taking in the sail like a man possessed. None to soon as before the sail was properly stowed the wind came howling down the Bay right on the nose again, the sea was whipped up in no time at all to a steep low swell with breaking tops and spray driving the full length of the boat. As luck would have it I'd had the foresight to don oilskin leggings and jacket and with the canvas wheel cover for extra protection managed to endure the cold and stinging spray while battering into this maelstrom, hoping against hope that the engine would keep going. It would have been too much for the engine to conk out and drive us out to sea again. While all this was going on dodging the spray, steering with one hand and a leg and trying to keep the wheel cover in a protective position, the legging part of the weather gear started to slide down around my ankles. At least it was heading that way before I arrested them in mid slide and made vain attempts to pull them up again. Some consideration was given to becoming a contortionist at some time in my life. My prayers regarding the engine were answered though and within the hour we were into the river and getting some shelter if not from the wind certainly from the breaking seas. This is where Judy came to be appreciated again, for had I been on my own, tired and cold as I was from the battering, I would not have been relieved at the wheel to dry off and warm up in the survival suit. Although the waterproofs were bought in Panama the leggings had not been used before, only the jacket. So it was with some dismay that on inspecting the reason for the leggings to behave in such a strange manner I found that both buttons on the bib had come off with a sizable piece of cloth, allowing the whole lot to make a downward progress. As the saying goes, buy cheap, pay dear.

Whangarei is some twenty miles up the Hatea River and deep water as far as the port for seagoing ships which was a little under half way there. It was to there we were directed to the Customs and Immigration Station for clearance. The wind was still strong as we came alongside the Customs barge and off the berth but, with a little clever manoeuvring and with willing hands to take the lines, we were soon safely moored. Twenty-eight days from Rarotonga.

Boarding with the Immigration Officer also came the Food Inspector clutching a large garbage bag to remove all imported food stuffs. This gave cause for some amusement as we were completely out of fresh food apart from a piece of ginger which Judy had bought to make a curry but never used. This item with all good will and humour was ceremoniously dropped into the garbage bag. The formalities I found to be rather tedious as all equipment had to be entered onto the proper form complete with product numbers, and expiry dates where applicable, which had me running back and forward to each item calling out the required data, all this with the added distractions of answering questions from the Port Health.

The formalities over with, permission was granted by the Port Captain's office to stay on this berth until morning when we would proceed to the marina. Judy had expressed the wish to stay over night at a hotel where we could have hot showers and a decent meal and a dry bed, a request I acceded to with alacrity. Nothing could be more desirable after the trials and tribulations of getting into port than a hot shower, and a meal that was not dominated by rice. It was then that we were introduced to New Zealand hospitality for, 'Bruce the Immigration' offered to drive us into town, some distance away, to a hotel, saving us the difficulty of securing transport from this lonely place out in the sticks. So kind of him and much appreciated.

CHAPTER THIRTEEN

WHANGAREI

Life has no greater pleasure than the joy of anticipation.

Meron

Whangarei is Maori for bountiful land, for which I can only accept their word as I have no contest with the accolade.

The immediate vicinity of Town Basin where the Marina was situated was all the lady hairdresser in Rarotonga had claimed it to be, with the close proximity of shops, restaurants and marine hardware stores for the delight of the visiting boater. We were fortunate to secure a berth here because with the strong winds that had been experienced during the past several days no boats had ventured out. However, the Marina manager had us rafted up in the river to a boat from Montreal. This port is truly an international gathering place with boats from just about every seafaring country moored in this crowded Marina.

Once secured in our berth we launched the dinghy and rowed over to the Office to make ourselves known and make the request for a sail maker, this being the first priority. The two boatyards which we had passed coming up river were also contacted for a haul out date which, due to the fact that Christmas was almost on us and no one worked over the holidays, was left in abeyance, it making no sense to pay for being on the hard with no services. Other matters concerning bringing the boat back to efficiency would be attended to in due course as and when convenient. For the present it was a case of finding an internet café and a visit to the Supermarket. The exposed film from Tahiti was also left to be developed and the address of a camera repairer acquired.

Over the next couple of days things started to happen. Judy, being disappointed in her efforts to secure a touring holiday, decided to return home to England for Christmas. It would appear that at this time of year the population of New Zealand decide to travel and every possibility for Judy to do just that had resulted in all accommodations and bus tours being fully booked. A shame really, as she had set her heart on seeing at least something of the country. While in town making arrangements at the travel agents she also went to pick up my film, which could not be developed as it had been spoiled by salt water, a great disappointment but no surprise. After all most things had suffered from the elements. The sail-maker came down to the boat and took away the sails that needed repairing and advised us that due to a heavy workload a new sail could not be made until the end of January. This news was something of a let down as I was anxious to proceed with the itinerary and set out for Melbourne where my sister lived. All other needs would have to be shelved too, as all other businesses whose services were required would also be closed for the holidays. So what to do? I didn't like the idea of hanging around the marina until the population returned to work in the New Year, so, I decided to fly to Melbourne and spend Christmas and see in the New Year with my sister's family. As a precaution a float switch for the bilge pump, this time of a different manufacture than the unreliable kind that had let me down so often, and a panel control were purchased and installed. These items were considered essential if my peace of mind was to be guaranteed while away. I had no wish to return to a flooded boat or for that matter one lying at the bottom of the harbour. It seems that I had developed a sense of paranoia over the past months with regard to the ingress of water into my home.

So Judy and I parted and went our separate ways, sad in many respects as she had been excellent company. I could only be thankful for the time she was on the boat and accept that it had been longer than originally planned, having taken so long over the original estimated passage time to get here. The parting wasn't without anxiety though for while waiting at the appointed place for the taxi the arranged time came and went, resulting in a frantic phone call to the taxi office. Shortly it appeared, having been waiting at a different location. Then we said our goodbyes with Judy waving from the taxi, and me standing on the pavement with a sense of loss wondering what to do with myself. Well, what does one do in these circumstances? With only a slight hesitation, instinctively I went over to the Supermarket, in a sense for comfort food and, practicing the premise of purchasing provisions when the opportunity arose. With a Supermarket so close it made sense to ease the loads by carrying small amounts.

*

On investigating alternatives regarding travel to Melbourne I decided to take the bus to Auckland and fly from there. Apart from any consideration of cost, the travelling by road gave a rare chance to see the countryside in this part of New Zealand, also to appreciate how fortunate it was to have had my hair cut in Rarotonga. The road into Auckland gave a good view across Waitemata Harbour to the crowded Marinas which, from my view point gave no indication of having any easy or obvious facilities for boat repairs, or for that matter easy access to storing for the next leg of the voyage. It was just a mass of boats moored fore and aft between mooring piles. How comforting it was to think, thanks to the lady hairdresser, that not all aspects of this saga were hapless happenings. Fate had certainly been kind on this occasion.

The inter-city bus terminal was conveniently located for the shuttle bus out to the airport, so after just a short wait and a tour around the city we arrived in plenty of time for the flight.

My nephew Stephen met me at the Airport as it was more convenient for him to come directly from work than anyone to take the long drive from the suburbs to the airport. The time spent with my sister and her family was a delight. Although I had been with them for a visit the previous year it was still a pleasure to see how close a family they all were. In fact I cannot remember ever seeing a family so lovingly close to each other.

With Christmas over I got to wondering if the boat was making any water, or maybe the bilge pump was misbehaving again. This morbid train of thought brought me to the point that I should return to Whangarei to put my mind at rest. And so I made arrangements to change the flight and take an earlier departure than otherwise planned. These arrangements caused something of a disappointment for my brother-in-law and nephew as a night out with the boys had been planned. Still what could one do? It would have been no fun to have a drink or two with visions of my boat lying at the bottom of the Hatea River.

As it turned out my fears were not totally unwarranted because although the bilges were dry, the house batteries had gone flat. Once again my thoughts turned to the need for a wind generator, which, as a promise to myself would be put in hand as soon as Whangarei became operational again in the coming week. In the meantime the batteries were charged with the engine. This early return had another bonus as on New Years Day who should appear on the scene but the owner of the sail maker's business. This was somewhat of a surprise as he wasn't expected until later in January, but much to my pleasure another customer had cancelled his order allowing mine to be put forward. However, I was advised not to get too many hopes up as he was only on board to take measurements. The finished article was still some days in the future. Incidentally the sail-loft was in Opua, north of Whangarei which is where Les was moored, thus making matters easier for the borrowed sail to be returned to the rightful owner directly from the repair shop, saving either Les a journey here, or for me to go to Opua. Seems as though the decision to come to Whangarei was bearing a veritable harvest of good fortune.

Having said that, there was an incident that if not of good fortune certainly could carry some humour. During the course of this voyage, I only wore underpants so my underwear through lack of laundry facilities had become decidedly grey. Planning ahead I took all I had with me to Melbourne with the intention of getting a proper laundering at my sister's. The results were definitely satisfactory being pristine in their whiteness again; however, when I returned to Auckland and put on clean underwear at the hotel and then ventured out to book the bus to Whangarei there was a definite discomfort in the nether regions with the sensation that my winkie was continually popping out, a most disconcerting state of affairs. On returning to the hotel the reason came to light; due to an excess of Nappy-San my sister had used to bring back the whiteness, the crotch had rotted out. Fortunately only one pair had succumbed to this treatment.

There wasn't much for me to do while waiting for the coming week except potter around on the boat and make frequent pilgrimages to the Supermarket to build up on sea stores for the next leg of the voyage and beyond. Although the run to Melbourne wasn't anticipated to be very long it made sense to make sure to be well supplied in case of emergencies, also it was anticipated that with family visiting the boat, there would not be any opportunity to store in Melbourne. As I had taken a particular liking to New Zealand beer this item received special attention on the basis of one beer a day to last as far as, if not beyond, Fremantle. Make hay while the sun shines as they say, and a satisfying stack of this beverage now resided in the forward berth.

During this waiting period the retaining battens for the windows were removed and the glass properly sealed around the edges, to prevent ingress of water in these areas. Before resetting the battens they were sanded to remove the old varnish, and provoked an irate marina Manager to express his displeasure at the dust drifting about. I did point out that the dust wasn't settling on any boats but drifting and falling on the river, but point taken. No more work that could cause displeasure to others would be carried out.

On Monday, now that the town was operational once more, I crossed the bridge to the other side of the river and made my way first to the camera repairer leaving the camera there then proceeding along the river side to the sail maker's Whangarei establishment where small jobs were handled, to make a deposit on my new sail. Much to my delight, immediately next door was a well stocked marine hardware store and here I ordered the wind generator so dearly desired over the past few months. As this was to be ordered in I would have the intervening period to plan and anticipate a world with fully charged batteries. I enquired about of a sheet metal worker and much to my delight this artisan was just behind the sail maker's loft. Things really were looking up and starting to go my way.

The sheet metal worker I was to learn within minutes of explaining my needs, was a most outgoing person, and had recently bought the business from his former boss and was just starting out on his own. Hamish, as that was his name, Hamish Mead, had a most disconcerting manner when being spoken to of holding his head to one side and peering intently at my mouth. I soon realised that he was deaf and this was the way he supplemented the hearing aid out of immediate sight deep in the ear canal. Watch my lips as they say. They do say that if a person loses one of his senses then another sense is increased, and this certainly applied to Hamish because he was a most loquacious young man, intelligent, efficient and most helpful and friendly. Over the few days of our acquaintance I really got to like him. On explaining the need for bracing to stiffen up the rudder post he immediately grasped the situation and had my rudimentary sketch amended to a more practical arrangement. Impressed by this young man I made my way back to the boat confident that this job was in hand and taking priority. This young man could add integrity to his resume. Although I would have liked to add consideration to this impression of him by an offer of a lift back to the boat, that would have been nice, but then he was about to finish an outstanding job and then tackle mine so the chance of a ride was neither offered nor asked for. Rather this quality would surface at a later date.

On returning to the marina I was called into the marina office to take a call from the camera repair man. He had deduced that the reason the transport lever was jammed, was because the inside of the camera was seized solid with rust and beyond repair. The elation of the morning's events softened somewhat at this bad news, and glumly I resigned myself to this setback, adding it to the list of ill-starred events. The loss of the camera was sad but the loss of the photos taken at Venus Point was felt somewhat more strongly. After all it wasn't every day that memorable sight could be visited.

In the interim, while I had been ashore, the owner of the boat next door returned with his wife from touring the North Island over the recent weeks since my arrival. Like most boaters he was helpful and friendly, the people in the boating world being kindred spirits I suppose. However, this meeting proved to be fortuitous as the down haul for the radar reflector had for some time come adrift leaving the reflector stuck at the top of the mast. To retrieve this object required the efforts of two people, one to ascend the mast, and the other to winch him up there. Much to my secret delight, Roger, volunteered to go aloft. The offer was received with alacrity and I soon had him in the bosun's chair and making the ascent. There are a few reasons why I stand back when an offer is volunteered for mast climbing; principally, I like to be in control of an operation as I know my equipment the best and how it operates. Secondly, on a previous occasion I was at the top of a mast when the boat was hit by a series of swells from a passing ferry causing a situation were the mast swung violently through a wide arc with me hanging on for dear life. Alarming though this experience was I have ascended masts since then, although not without a feeling of trepidation. Once Roger was back on deck with the operation successfully completed, the beer was brought out and a closer acquaintance established.

His wife, he told me, would only come on his boat when it was in port with not having any interest in being out on the ocean, so Roger had sailed from Montreal around Cape Horn, crossing the Pacific and, eventually ended up here in Whangarei. This truly impressed me as most people would transit the Panama Canal, but having done that on a previous adventure Roger decided on a different route. This particular day was Tuesday when beer was two for the price of one at the local watering hole and, with Roger's wife being in town, we repaired there for further discussions and to take advantage of a free beer.

After this pleasant interlude I only saw Roger at a distance as the following day I dropped down river to the boat yard for haul out and the fitting of a bigger through hull for the holding tank, the unreliable macerator pump having seized up once again. As there was no law against discharging effluence outside of territorial waters this pump had proved to be surplus to requirement anyway, and one of those unnecessary luxuries one acquires in ones enthusiasm when fitting out a boat. The discharge pump on the toilet was doing an excellent job of breaking up the solids so a macerator pump could be dispensed with. Also I did not have to siphon off the contents of the holding tank, a most disagreeable job, to remove the pump for maintenance. The topside paintwork also needed attention as due to the wave action over the past months the paint had come away in sheets again.

The yard had positioned my boat next to a boat that held a youngish couple. Much to my chagrin I was to listen to an almost continuous tirade of high pitched whining complaints of the female of the species against her male counterpart, whom I might add won my praise and admiration at not saying a word or for that matter not causing her demise and helping her out of this unsatisfactory world. To say she was a screeching harpy would be the understatement of the year. As Judy would have said they were having a domestic. But doesn't that take two? However, I was in mortal dread that she might try to strike up an acquaintance and involve me in her complaints. Still, as it happened I had my own problems to deal with and kept my own counsel.

The fitting of the through hull and the subsequent application of a coat of paint went well, although I attempted to connect the hose to the tank it proved to be impossible, no matter what I tried. Even after softening the hose with boiling water it still would not go onto the tank connection. Obviously, the North American hose size is slightly, just slightly, larger than the local size. Now what? Although the holding tank was empty it would need to be washed out before drilling for another tank connection, and there was no way that could be carried out in the boatyard. This matter, (no pun intended), would have to be transferred to a bucket and disposed of at sea. Once again I was wondering what else could go wrong. For this there was no long wait.

The topside paintwork was proceeding nicely with the white sheer nearly completed. With the ladder placed against the pulpit rail, I was applying the last of the sheer painting to the forward port side. When suddenly I felt the ladder starting to slip and I immediately grabbed the rail to stop further movement towards disaster. Considering the predicament for a moment, I decided, as I was only about four feet above the ground it would be safe to jump. I let go of the rail and made the leap. Even the best laid plans can be fraught with anomalies and this was no exception. When the ladder and I parted company my right sandal came free leaving my foot naked, and I came down heavily with my right heel on a stone. Obviously this ruined my well thought out plan of landing safely. The ladder came down with a clatter and I rolled on the ground which brought people running. Commiserations all round didn't allay the agonising pain in the heel or for that matter my embarrassment. All I could say was only my dignity was hurt, to calm their concerns. As it transpired the lady that had rushed over from a boat across the yard was the wife of a doctor. As enough fuss had been generated by this unfortunate happening I was pleased that the good doctor had not become involved. There had been quite enough attention for the moment. Gritting my teeth against the pain I assured all these good people that I was fine, and that I didn't need to go to the hospital. Eventually they left to let me get back to my labours. Later though, Anne, the doctor's wife, came over and invited me for dinner aboard their boat that evening and it was then that I met Graham her husband the good doctor. He deduced the heel bone had been bruised and dispensed a pain killer. So I was reduced to hobbling around on my duties in the comfort of knowing that time heals (once again no pun intended) all wounds. In retrospect I was immensely pleased that the shrew next door hadn't been around when this happened. I cringed at the thought what might have transpired.

The following afternoon Hamish came to offer up the rudder stock brace, and found me sitting on the settee resting my gammy leg. With hobbling around on my duties the ankle had swollen and caused even more pain. On learning the circumstances of my incapacitation he very kindly went back into town for a bag of ice. The result of this kind gesture managed to reduce the swelling and also eased the pain a little and, added consideration to his overflowing resume of good qualities.

Over the next few days the blue topside painting was completed, bringing the boat up to its normal pristine loveliness. Graham and Anne's boat had already left and it was my turn to go back in the water. While I settled the account, Charlie the yard manager wanted to know why I had told him the boat was forty feet in length. This had me puzzled for a moment. "Because that is the length," I said, bringing to mind the building plans. "No, it's not," he said. "It's thirty-seven," and produced a conversion table pointing at eleven point one eight meters. "Thirty-seven feet." he repeated. There was no denying the fact; I had never taken to this metric thing, being comfortable with imperial measurements, obviously to my detriment. "Bloody, hell," I said. "To think that all these years, I have been going to marinas paying for an extra three feet." Much chagrined at the thought, but most grateful to have been put on the right track, I thanked Charlie for pointing this out. Although the boat was forty feet on the plans, when it came to the survey for registration the measurement is from a vertical down from the top of the stem to the rudder post. Even at this late date one can learn something.

So it was then that I found myself back at the marina albeit tied up alongside another boat away from Roger's, waiting for the sail and making frequent peregrinations to the Supermarket and other establishments for the necessities of making the boat operationally efficient. As matters on the money front were healthy I indulged in a few extras; the rain gear that had let me down (literally) was replaced with a more robust set. The tea caddy had succumbing to the elements rust wise, was replaced with a set of porcelain containers complete with clamped rubber sealed tops to hold coffee, sugar, as well as tea. A particular treat was a small compass that was placed on the rack in the saloon section, this to facilitate easy reading during the hours of darkness of the course being steered, the gyro compass still being out of commission. An early warning system, one might say, of whether the boat had caught me unawares while resting and decided to head on a reciprocal course. This would save a journey into the cockpit to check the main compass. This would be particularly useful should it be raining as I would not have to don the rain gear. It was a wonderful feeling of joy to finally, after all these months, get the boat back to a comfortable efficient unit again. The feeling of being able to carry on and complete the dream was becoming palpable. The high point of this elation was the long desired wind generator; the mast being fabricated and fitted with the good services of Hamish, with myself doing the wiring and the assembly of the unit. No longer would it be a worry whether the batteries were fully charged. There was just one anomaly to all this; there was no way could I get service for the autopilot as the service agent was just not interested. The electrician who made the tests on the batteries and checked for any leaks should they be discharging to sea, even he when contacting his sources could get no joy. A rather disappointing result I thought as it is not unreasonable to expect a manufacturer to back up his products through his appointed agents. The magnetic compass, in conjunction with the Hydrovane steering system, was doing justice to the problem of steering a course so the fact that the gyro compass was malfunctioning became academic and thus was considered to be a luxury item.

During these days of waiting for the new genoa I ran into Roger, of mast climbing fame, who told me he had overstayed his immigration six month visa and was returning to Montreal. This announcement had me perplexed for a moment; after-all I had an unrealistic picture of him sailing his boat, and one doesn't just sail a boat from New Zealand to Montreal just like that. Surely the statement should have been, 'I'll be leaving soon.' As it transpired he was leaving his boat here in Whangarei and flying out, to then return for another six months or so. What a wonderful approach I thought; why rush around when one can take a leisurely nomadic progress through life taking the time to smell the roses as they say. But then I had a mind set about these things, and it was fixed in my mind to do a circumnavigation and I was too rigid in my thinking to change at this stage of the game. Maybe next trip. Apart from that I was only just keeping ahead of the weather, the next concern being the cyclone season in the Indian Ocean.

Les Bissell, the sailing representative for NSA, turned up on my doorstep so to speak. He was in Whangarei for an interview with the local radio station in regard to his promotion of the National Stroke Foundation. Of course these also involved a get together at the local watering hole for a beer or two and talk about our experiences of our respective passages from Rarotonga. He also had been delayed by the adverse weather even though he had taken less time than Judy and I had, not that his boat was a faster sailer it was just that with leaving later he had missed the weather patterns that had delayed us in the early part of our passage and therefore made good time as a result. However, his experience of the sixty knot winds was somewhat different from ours. While we managed to motor the last few miles to sheltered waters, he was caught out in the open and while heading for the Bay of Islands only managed, after a rough night to get under the lee of one of them and shelter there until the wind abated and he could make the run into Opua. There had been another boat, incidentally of the same design as mine as previously mentioned, which left Rarotonga with Les but sailing single handed. Their different courses had left them out of sight of each other after a few days but still in touch by radio for a while. Then the silence came. One cannot but wonder what had been the cause of that silence and hope for the best. He was heading for Opua also but hadn't turned up by the time Les came down to Whangarei. Having met someone under these circumstances only brings home a greater awareness of the possible dangers he might have experienced, and make the desire for his safety that much stronger. Those sixty knot winds had come so suddenly. Well, what can one say?

Anne and Graham Evans and I crossed paths again; they had been having dinner at the same place as Les and I and on the way out invited us to visit their boat for a nightcap. They were due to leave the next day, heading south for the Bay of Plenty to lie there for a while. Graham had accepted a medical position at Whangarei Hospital and they were filling in time cruising New Zealand until the appointment fell due. Anne, who was a radiologist by profession, hoped to secure a position also. Failing that, it was my opinion that she should become an interviewer as she was a delight to talk to and had with the utmost ease extracted opinions and circumstances of my life from me, something that with strangers I don't easily divulge. The new genoa had arrived earlier in the day and Anne had very kindly offered to help bend the sail. As I was expecting Hamish to return in the next day or two to finish up with the bracing of the rudder post, I had thought to prevail on his good services for this project while he was available. Still, the offer was much appreciated and I was once again made aware of how supportive the boating community is.

*

Shortly after breakfast the next day the Evans's passed by, heading down river with much in the way of shouted well wishes and jolly banter, to disappear forever from my acquaintance. A great pity as they were good people but, that's how it is; ships that pass in the night one might say. Les, having stayed onboard for the night, was the next one to leave, and remaining only long enough for a coffee then he took himself off for his interview and in the afternoon headed back to Opua.

Hamish came after lunch and finalised the rudder post bracing, a fine job he had made too, which left me well pleased. Thankfully no more worries with the post flapping about, creating a leak through the seal. The boat was now fully returned to operational efficiency, and what a joy that was. My elation was great that now I could progress through the remainder of the voyage with the boat shipshape and Bristol fashion. Now I could finally leave Whangarei, broke, but happy in the thought that there would be time for the pension to accumulate before funds would be required again.

CHAPTER FOURTEEN

WHANGAREI to MELBOURNE

And the gates of Hell are opened and riven, and the winds of Hell are loosened and driven………..

The Himalayan

The next day it was my turn to leave and first thing after breakfast I went over to the Office and settled the moorage bill, and then back to the boat to haul the dinghy on board, deflate and stow, and generally prepare for sea. While at the marina office the manager had arranged for me to meet 'Bruce the Immigration' at their Station at two-thirty for outward clearance, this appointment fell in nicely with my dropping down river to take on fuel prior to the rendezvous. The weather report for the Tasman Sea was excellent with two High Pressure Systems dominating the whole area, which promised a quick and easy passage to Melbourne. The situation really was on the up and up.

The arrangement for fuelling appeared to be based on an honesty system as there wasn't anyone to attend to the pump just a matter of getting self service, noting the amount taken then finding someone to take payment. Nice to be trusted, but no doubt there must have been some sort of check against thieving.

Well, what do you know; when I returned on board the engine wouldn't start. Here we go again, I thought, still staggering from one crisis to another. All was not lost though as there was a mechanic at this establishment and sporting the logo of just the type of engine that I had. After a short delay while the mechanic changed one of the battery clamps, the engine was operational again. So simple when you know how. Maybe one day I should take a course in small engine mechanics; the way piddling little things have gone wrong an achievement in that field would be an absolute boon.

Even with the hold up at the refuelling station I arrived at the Immigration dock on time, Bruce waiting to do the honours and with him a junior who was to take over Bruce's duties as he was about to retire. Nice helpful fellow was Bruce, but then with my limited experience of New Zealanders he was no exception. On our arrival at Whangarei at this dock, I had expressed to Bruce my intention of proceeding to Opua after leaving this port but, as the arrangement with Les and his sail had altered matters there would be no need to divert. Bruce needed reassurance that this was not now my intention as this would be highly illegal. Having being at sea all my life I was well aware of these procedures and assured him that should I have to divert to another New Zealand port I would clear inwards again. This understanding cleared the situation and I was allowed to proceed down river on my way to sea. The nearer I got to open water the stronger the wind became, finally blowing at about thirty knots from the south and right on the nose, driving spray the full length of the boat as I left the protective lee of the land. Well, I had my newly acquired rain gear on and when rounding Bream Head the wind would be on the port quarter so seeking shelter would not be necessary. Just chug along and dodge the spray. When I passed the oil refinery a ship was in the process of unmooring so that was something else to watch out for. When it came thundering past and so close the side of this ship seemed to be enormous but, thankfully with no concern, even the wash made no impact as the wind whipped-seas almost eliminated the effect.

Soon I was able to leave the channel and round Bream Head to set a course to the north. The wind was far too strong to attempt to hoist the mainsail so it was a case of bogeying along nicely with just the new genoa, a sail gazed at with much pleasure and admiration, a strongly constructed sail that would last for quite some time. This had me thinking this enterprise certainly had taken an upward turn. Couldn't help wondering though how Graham and Anne were making out with this wind as they would be heading into it, probably sheltering somewhere I would think. So here we were getting along very nicely on the next leg of this pilgrimage, and time for a cup of tea.

Keeping a reasonable distance off the coast, as is my wont, to avoid any coastwise traffic, I made good time, passing the Bay of Islands at first light the following day and rounding North Cape at midnight meeting the one and only ship on this leg of the trip. As we were on reciprocal courses it was quite easy to keep out of his way and out of danger. It wouldn't do after all that had gone in the past months to be run down at this stage of the game.

The days passed easily in glorious weather crossing the Tasman Sea with the High Pressure Systems remaining steady over the whole area, truly a fabulous sail with all units functioning nicely. The wind generator was performing wonderfully, allaying any fears of the batteries quitting again, always a niggling worry now placed firmly to the back of my memory bank. All was not a picnic though, as during the night prior to entering the Bass Strait the boat decided to turn around and go back the way we had come. This had me scrambling on deck to sort out the problem; once again the boat head wouldn't come across the wind to come back to the correct course so it was case of starting the engine to assist this manoeuvre. Fine, it fired immediately but when it came to putting it into gear the gear lever wouldn't budge, immovable, seized solid it was. Well I wasn't about to try and sort out this problem in the middle of the night so I turned the engine off and I resorted to jibing the boat, bringing the wind around the stern. Not a preferred practice but needs must when the Devil drives as they say. However, I was back on course and I was left to lie down again and ponder the mysteries of why the engine didn't go into gear.

After breakfast I tackled the problem and found no logical answer, which proved to be academic anyway as the engine came out in sympathy and refused to start. Now this was a pretty pickle I found myself in as the engine was necessary to get through Port Phillip Heads into the bay, which would be the ideal method. The alternative was to sail through should the wind become favourable, which at the moment didn't look too promising. Failing this, I suppose I could call for a tow. Due to my pride this would not be the option that I would approach with alacrity. But, then again, after the number of tows I had this trip maybe, I could accept the indignity this time. All conjecture at this moment in time though, as there were still three more days to go.

The following night yet another matter had brought me out on deck; this was in the way of a bump. Not the running-into-something-type bump but coming from the deck above. What passed through my mind was that maybe a fish had landed there, rather a wild guess I know, but then what else could it be? On investigation there was nothing lying around; maybe it had gone over the side again. All these thoughts and the probable answers could well be the product of a tired mind, and the matter of being engineless was still uppermost. I had hove to the previous evening not wanting to get too far into the strait and too close to the many islands there during the hours of darkness, so the bump could not be a result of hard sailing, or any sailing for that matter. Somewhat puzzled, I lay down again with the resolve to investigate the matter in daylight. Strange how things happen during the hours of darkness on this boat. Well, they do say that things go bump in the night.

What with setting the sails before daylight and setting a course into the Strait when daylight did break, the matter had left my mind until I happened to look up the mast to find that the Radar dome had disappeared. Taking a deep breath and letting it out in forceful exasperation, with a muttered, 'Bloody hell', I wondered what else could go wrong on this trip. I found it hard to believe that an item bolted to a mast bracket could just fall off; after all it had been there for six years. Then I got to wondering if the mast rigger had used steel bolts as this would guarantee an electrolytic action with the aluminium which would eventually rot out. At the moment this could only be wondered at until the matter could be investigated, and left me wondering how much new Radar would cost.

At least the day was proving to be absolutely gorgeous with a clear blue sky and a steady southerly breeze, which was something to be thankful for and progress was being made at a handsome rate of knots and as there was nothing that could be done about the recent problems, I resorted to enjoying the sunshine and the best way to navigate Port Phillip Heads *sans* engine. There were other chores to attend to, particularly finalising the caulking of the cabin deck. This job had been hanging on for long enough and it was only at Whangarei that caulking compound had come to hand. So just one more session, then once the compound had hardened it could be sanded and varnished. I must admit to feeling highly satisfied with the results so far and not a little smug at being so fortunate at acquiring the teak decking. The galley area had still to be done but that would have to wait until there was a possibility of the deck remaining dry long enough for the epoxy glue to take, which with the bilges taking water again didn't promise for the near future. Still, should I want to feel smug over teak decking I could always gaze at the cabin deck.

Lunch over and after a ten minute snooze, I went on deck again to enjoy a little more of the sunshine. The Hogan group of islands would be the next waypoint and these were expected to be cleared late evening. It was while pondering this event that I saw a white cloud on the horizon to the south. In a short while this cloud had spread the full width of the horizon and was making a steady progress north. The unusual aspect of this was that it was perfectly white and fluffy, quite spectacular with the blue sky both before and behind. Having seen this type of cloud before of the coast off New South Wales I was well aware that it presented a Southerly Buster that would bring strong winds in its wake. With alacrity, therefore, I had the mainsail down again and lashed, with the genoa rolled up to just a small 'v', in other words hove to again. Sure enough, within minutes of getting back to the cockpit the wind hit, building up in no time to forty knots. Indeed, fortunate was I to have had a previous experience with this type of phenomenon. On that occasion it was on a steam ship of five thousand tons which was somewhat different to my fourteen ton boat, a difference that wasn't long in presenting itself.

I hadn't been in the cabin very long, not even long enough to put the kettle on for a cup of tea even, when there was an almighty bang from out on deck. Of course this had me out on deck in no time to find with amazement that the genoa had unfurled to its full extent and was flapping wildly in the gale. It wasn't long before the reason presented itself: the haul-in line that controlled the amount of genoa to be let out had parted. Tying the two parts together as a temporary repair and then attempting to reduce the sail area once more proved impossible in such a wind and there was absolutely no movement at all that indicated the furling gear would take in the sail, so I suspected that the gearing could have jammed. There I was bouncing around on the plunging foredeck trying to control the sail, this thing possessed, with the sheets whipping and twisting themselves into a hopeless tangle. It dawned on me that in my haste to control this impossible situation I wasn't wearing a harness. Not a sensible situation under the circumstances and as the only possibility was to let the sail down and hope it wouldn't be lost, I went below to put on the harness and get the pliers to undo the shackle holding the lower end of the sail.

While engaged in this exercise the boat took on a violent shuddering. This shuddering didn't last more than a couple of seconds after which there was a terrific crashing sound. Expecting the worst, I was out on deck again to view a scene of absolute chaos. The mast had come down and was in the water over the starboard side, held on to the boat by the stays and shrouds. On its descent it had taken out all the starboard side stanchions. The rigging had decapitated the Hydrovane steering casting, and taken away the top half, complete with the wind vane, leaving a useless lower section. My beloved wind generator of just a few days had been knocked over, taking out most of the vanes. On viewing all the damage I must admit to a profound feeling of hopelessness at the way fortune had dealt all the wrong cards. I just plonked myself down on the cockpit seat and slumped. "Bloody hell! What next?" I asked myself. Matters had evolved far too quickly during the previous ten minutes for any great emotion to take over; I just sat staring at the latest misfortune until my brain dispelled the shock of it all and started functioning again.

"What's the next move?" I asked, always a good question under the circumstances. One reads about intrepid seafarers in similar circumstances rigging a jury mast and limping in to the nearest safe haven. Now that I was in the same circumstance, my mind of course mulled over the possibilities. First of all, something that would serve as a mast would be required, which apart from a boathook I didn't have. Not that a boathook would be suitable under the circumstances as it was too short to support a sail, which was over the side under the water, and could not provide sufficient propulsion to move a forty foot boat of fourteen tons. I have to admit at this moment I entertained doubts about the veracity of the stories one reads of man's determination to overcome misfortune.

While pondering, the question it came to mind that had I not been in the cabin when the mast came down, what would have been the consequences? It was not beyond the realms of possibility that with the wire shrouds and stays whizzing about causing such mayhem; I could have been seriously injured, decapitated even. At least I still had a head on my shoulders and the means to think of the next move so I could be grateful for that. Fate, it seems, still had some kindness.

Obviously, with not even an engine I wasn't going anywhere, just wallowing in a heavy swell with a gale whistling around my ears. At least the mast was acting as a steadying influence of sorts. The best thing to do would be to advise the Coast Guard of my situation and maybe get some advice from them. At least they would know I was out here and should the worst come to the worst, my family would know what had happened. These thoughts were not morbid considerations, rather a logical train of thought; after all wouldn't people like to know what happened? As I didn't have the wherewithal to access the telephone number of the Coast Guard I phoned my sister in Melbourne and asked her to get it for me and I would phone back in an hour. Big mistake telling her that I was in a spot of bother as this upset her sufficiently for me to ask her to put my brother-in-law on instead. After the hour I phoned back, and in the interim my nephew had turned up and took over the enquiries, a situation that needed his clear thinking and firm hand.

By the time I had managed to call the Water Police, or to give them their full title the Victoria Police Air Wing, as the Coast Guard is called in Australia, it was evening. They gave me three alternatives: wait for the availability of a boat big enough to come out and tow me in; have them redirect a ship to enact a rescue; or be lifted off by helicopter. With the lateness of the hour, and needing time to think before making a decision I agreed that I would give my position each hour during the night and let them know in the morning what had been decided. Believe me it was a tough one. The thought of giving up didn't fill my heart with joy but, after a night of agonising over the alternatives between the hourly reporting in, common sense won the day on the basis of cost. Should I opt to be towed in how much would a tow of forty miles to the nearest safe haven cost? Not to mention replacement of a Hydrovane, (I knew the cost of that and it wasn't cheap). Would a new mast be on the agenda?   The wind generator I felt might be salvaged with replacement vanes and straightening of the post. Totalling up the possible cost and realising that my funds were limited, not to mention that from day one things had gone wrong as though there was a curse on the boat, who was to say that this would be the end of forever throwing money into this particular hole in the ocean? Although these thoughts where going round and round in my head throughout the night I think at the back of my mind it was a case of facing reality and be taken off by helicopter. There was no consideration given to be taken off by a passing ship. In this weather it would be a difficult and dangerous operation trying to get me up the side of a ship. Besides, who knows where I would end up? Back in Panama maybe, or some, God forbid a place so far from anywhere that it would be well nigh impossible to return home? Morbid thoughts indeed. The only remaining option was to be taken off by helicopter. Being taken to Melbourne at least I would be with family. It was then that I began planning what to take with me. With wry humour I rejected the kitchen sink, and all other bulky objects. There were many items that would have been desirable but, considering the circumstances the only practical pieces were passports, credit and debit cards and most inconsequently a photograph of my dog. On reflection, I could only account for this oddity as subconsciously wanting to at least have something personal from my home of ten months. Whatever? Strangely the items that gave a twinge of regret were the cases of beer; all those lovely one-a-day treats I had planned for, going to the bottom of Bass Strait gave cause for heartache. Here I was planning to send my boat to the bottom and all the regret I had was losing a couple of cases of beer. Maybe it was time to get off while there was still some sanity left.

The wind hadn't decreased in volume during the night and it was still blowing a full gale. The mast which lay alongside had been acting as a steadying influence, lessening the violence of the waves, although the boat wallowed heavily, lurching from one side to the other. At full daylight I called the Water Police to inform them of my decision to be lifted off and suggested that when I saw the helicopter I would open the sea valves to sink the boat. This was met with a most vehement negative and told I was told in no uncertain terms to wait for the crewman to board and he would give instructions as to what procedures to follow. Well, I was aware of the rescue procedures. Only one authority should direct operations so as not to cause confusion, so it was then that I agreed, not without doubts though. It was imperative that the boat would have to be sunk, otherwise it would only be a danger to shipping, and with the boat bouncing around the way it was it didn't seem wise to hang around while any instructions were being issued. I was in the cockpit while this conversation was going on, and on conclusion of this the boat took a violent roll, jerk almost, which threw me off balance with enough force to smash the entry door with my elbow. Now the door was teak and although the door suffered so did my elbow, which bled profusely until a wood splinter was removed and the wound dressed with a tissue and I had applied pressure to stop the bleeding. The wind generator was bravely operating with the three remaining blades, bless it. However, as this might cause problems with the crewman I felt it wise to tie the blades to stop them spinning and prevent possible injury.

There was nothing left to do now but to get dressed in my go ashore gear, pull on the survival suit, and collect the relevant papers and documents in zip lock bags and place them in the pockets. On the off chance that it would be allowed, I collected my Journals and Notes of the voyage so far and placed them in a holdall. These were a record of my adventures and would be essential should I decide to write about the saga. As a sop to my regrets over the beer, I decided to open a can and have at least a taste of what was to be committed to the deep.

In due course the helicopter arrived and after doing a circuit, hovered to lower the crewman square into the cockpit, a manoeuvre that had my admiration for the professionalism of the pilot and his team. Immediately I was offered the harness but first I suggested that first the sea valves had to be opened. To this he acquiesced with I took to be a hint of annoyance, although this had me puzzled. The moment wasn't for questioning, but it was a bit odd, though, that having been instructed to wait until the crewman boarded, everything seemed to be going pear shaped.

Everything was ready for flooding the boat and it took no time at all for me to go below, open the ball valve and return to the cockpit. To my amazement the crewman had disappeared from the cockpit to be observed in the water some twenty feet away from the boat beckoning for me to join him. Much as this situation was displeasing to me and as it would mean the Journals getting soaked, it was not a situation to argue over. So over the rail I went and lowered myself into the waves to swim the short distance to my erstwhile saviour. A bit of a struggle as it turned out with the down draft from the helicopter blowing spray all over the place, not to mention twelve foot waves breaking over us both. However, the harness was quickly placed over my head and under my arms and the lift commenced. With the wave action the harness had slipped down around my waist and I found myself coming out of the water upside down with my legs around the crewman's neck, soon to be dropped down again, and fighting to get my head above water. In quick time, at least before I drowned, they had a very subdued survivor being winched up to the helicopter, wondering if it was possible to have any more indignities thrust upon him. I wasn't kept in the waiting too long as with the slow turn of our bodies in the ascent the last sight of the boat as it came up on a wave showed a considerable expanse of the bottom before our turning took us out of the view. I really thought that the bloody thing was mooning me. Not a comforting last sight to store in my memory of our shared time together.

<u>EPILOGUE</u>

I never saw the boat again. After the double dunking and being half drowned it was enough for me, after being hauled into the helicopter, to sit on the floor very subdued dripping water, with dejected thoughts over the loss and drained emotionally. The door had been pulled to so the view was shut off. Had I been inclined to lean over for a last look at my home of the previous ten months, I would have felt no better.

I reflected on the events that led to me having to abandon my adventure, beginning with the parting of the control line for the genoa when only a small area of sail was exposed to the elements. It seemed very unfair, as I felt I could ride out the storm had the failure not occurred. That saying we had when kids about, 'for the want of a nail the shoe was lost,' and so on, with the progression of events failing until the battle was lost, came to mind. Well it had happened, and there was nothing to be gained by playing "what if?"

The flight to the Air Wing Station took only a few minutes at least that is how it seemed at the time. It could have been fifteen, twenty. Clambering out of the helicopter I released a flood of sea water from down the legs of the survival suit to form puddles on the tarmac. Even in my dejected state I could find some humour in this. The crew member and I plodded over to the building to be met by a person of authority, no doubt, as he was reluctant to allow us inside. By this time I was shivering uncontrollably, wind and water producing a good combination for this effect. Maybe it was this or maybe the crewman's persuasiveness softened this person's heart for he finally allowed us in. The staff, however, proved to be most considerate and helpful as I was directed to the shower and given dry clothes. The underpants were not my usual choice having no fly and of a vivid red bikini style, but beggars can't be choosers and I was thankful for the consideration. A plastic garbage bag had also been supplied into which went my wet clothes, now all the possessions I had in the world. Well as they say, when at the bottom there is only one way to go and that is up.

The pleasant guys continued to be friendly after my welcome shower and had a cup of coffee ready on hand. He that had met us at the door continued to be off-hand, however, which had me wondering what his problem was. After all in this situation I could hardly be considered to be a bum asking for a handout. Even when I thanked him for the shower he only grunted. No matter, as after a short while we were back in the helicopter on our way to Essendon Airport, the main Air Wing Station to wait for the Immigration clearance and a taxi to take me to my sister's.

The train of events from the rescuer's side had been explained to me during the interim and it had transpired that they had tried to contact me via VHF to open the sea valves and be ready to be lifted off immediately the crewman had landed in the cockpit. Obviously with the radio antennae being at the top of the mast and the mast in the water, there was no way such a message could be received. Because of this, once again a sequence of events was brought into play; with me having to go below to open the sea valve. Even though it was such a short space of time it was sufficient for the boat to be hit by a wave and for the wind to catch the helicopter in a gust strong enough to push it off station, thus catapulting the crewman overboard into the sea to land some twenty feet away, thankfully unharmed. While in the water with the strop in place we were both forced under by wave action, causing the strop to slip down, with the result that I left the water upside down with the crewman frantically holding onto my leg. The winch man seeing this lowered us into the water again and this I was given to understand from a height of twenty to thirty feet. No wonder I felt subdued when I finally got into the helicopter.

The newspapers the following day reported how bad the weather had been; apart from many small craft dragged ashore from their moorings and suffering damage, the Melbourne to Tasmania ferry had suffered heavy structural damage, and passengers were injured making it necessary to put back into port. There was a little bit about my adventures, too, tucked away in the main article. Seems it had been quite a storm.

I didn't stay with my sister and family for more than a couple of days as they, with my brother-in-law's sister and her friend, were taking off for a tour of Tasmania. There was time, however, to purchase a limited wardrobe, limited in the sense that with having nothing and the realisation that one doesn't need very much, enough is enough. It was a just buy what is needed to live policy. Up to the time of writing I have followed that principle, realising that to accumulate goods and chattels for the sake of having them is only a drag on living. At least something came out of the adventure.

From Melbourne I went to Fremantle to stay with my good friend Debbie for a couple of weeks, then to Kalbarri to stay with another good friend Norman, Both, with me are keen Endeavour Replica aficionados and we have joined up in different places in the world to be volunteer guides. I have to say how much I appreciated their generosity and understanding of my situation by not raising the questions that must have been at the forefront regarding my recent exploits. They gave me the time to sort myself out and adjust to the loss of my boat and the abrupt termination of a dream.

From there it was a leisurely progress by way of England and then home to Canada bringing to mind and making notes of the adventure along the way. The loss of the journals I regretted as the picture would have been much fuller. However, on reflection might have made for a story bogged down in detail to the point of being tedious. It only remains for me to say that what has been related actually happened without resorting to flannel or too much detail.

I often think of the adventure and ask myself: Will I go again? Well, that would have to depend on resolving many, many logistical questions, which seem at this moment in time to be insurmountable. But, who knows?

The people I met in the boating community remain a fond memory as they seem unique in their outgoing friendly and kindly manner towards others in the same situation. Although, ship's that pass in the night, never to be seen again probably, I still hold their memory in high regard.

On a personal level I feel I have gained by the adventure. I left Pender with only my boat and my pension, and came back with only my pension. I'm happy and content in this situation, as now I don't have to worry about being tied down with the responsibility of material things. I'm free! To lose is to win.

While writing this account I have been advised that the helicopter crew have been given awards for bravery from both the Australian and Canadian Governments for their part in the rescue. Well, there is nothing like a couple of awards under the belt to enhance a career. Glad to have been of help, fellas.

As for myself; my rewards were in the experiences of the whole adventure warts and all, and would I go again?

"Bloody Hell! Yes."

Pender Island, BC.
14th June. 2006

CPSIA information can be obtained
at www.ICGtesting.com
Printed in the USA
LVHW091649020323
740195LV00011B/22